I WON'T DATE THE WOLF PRINCE

WOLF ISLAND: SEASON 1

WOLF ISLAND

LUNA M. ROSE

CHAPTER

ONE

I stepped off the boat, my leather sandals scraping over loose sand on the dock. I sucked in a deep breath, letting the salty sea air fill my lungs. The island landscape was nothing short of stunning. Even after staring at it for the thirty-minute shuttle ride from Turks and Caicos, it still felt brand new. Turquoise waters lapped at the white sandy beaches. Palm trees swayed in the wind. Thatched-roofed huts peeked out through underbrush so green, it looked over-saturated.

I pulled on a sunhat and glanced around for my luggage. When the other guests walked straight toward the beach without a second thought, I followed suit. *Guests.* I almost scoffed at the word. More like inmates. Though maybe that was only me.

But the idea that any of these shifters would want to be relegated to the equivalent of a reality dating show for a month, regardless of the location, made me cringe. The older generations needed to accept that finding a fated mate was a tradition of the past. Sure, some people still felt the bond, but it was rare. The argument that this decline was evolutionary hadn't gone over well with my alpha father, though.

Hence my current predicament.

I strode along the path past two she-wolves in bikinis and a half-naked shifter giving off major dominant energy playing beach volleyball. I snorted. Most of the men here were likely alphas. We lowly female omegas were being offered up like side dishes.

This place existed for one reason: for my parent's generation to feel like they were doing something to stem the tide of unmated single adults. But I wasn't there to find a mate. I was there to get my law school tuition paid. That was the deal I'd made with my father. Follow the rules, go through the camp for a month, and he'd pay for everything.

Watching Sandman over there helping one of the girls tie up her bikini string made me wonder if it was worth it.

My muscles ached from the journey. My mind was beyond weary. I looked over my shoulder to see a team of impeccably dressed men and women moving our luggage. Five-star service on a deserted matchmaking island.

Of course.

I followed the others up a narrow path through what could only be called tropical jungle, to a reception area. It was stunning. I stepped onto the smooth, polished wood of the deck, my eyes widening as I took in the surroundings. Elegant lanterns cast a soft, golden glow over the space, and delicate flowers were arranged in crystal vases on each table. The scent of the ocean mingled with the faint aroma of tropical blooms, creating an intoxicating blend.

Inside, the venue was grand, with high ceilings and large windows that showcased the island's natural beauty. It was the kind of place I would've loved to visit under different circumstances. With my sisters or friends. But this wasn't a vacation. It was the Wolf Council's version of *Love Island*. But maybe there was a way for me to enjoy this. At least partially. If I didn't talk to anyone and just read a book on the beach?

I scanned the room, my discomfort growing by the second. It was like I was back in high school, being dragged to a party I didn't want to attend. The only difference was that now I had to play nice with strangers instead of trying to make small talk with girls I'd known since kindergarten.

My eyes darted to the other attendees, who were already mingling with each other. They seemed at ease, laughing and chatting as if they were all best friends. I slid along the wall to hopefully meld with the leaves of a plant that looked like it was from the Mesozoic.

This was good. From here, I could watch. Catalog. I was good at assimilating information and drawing conclusions, hence law school. I just needed to find an ally . . .

My gaze instantly snagged on a man standing near the bar. He was tall and well dressed, his hair neatly combed back. He leaned back on the polished wood surface like he owned the place. Maybe he did. His face split into a wide grin, and though I couldn't hear his laugh over the music and conversation, I could almost feel it.

Okay, so there were handsome shifters here. Of course there were. It wasn't like I'd expected a swanky dating getaway to be filled with runts. Still, a wave of nervousness washed over me. I needed a drink, preferably on the opposite end of the bar from *that guy.*

I made my way to the bar and ordered something tropical and fruity. I didn't even care, as long as it had alcohol in it. It arrived a few moments later with a slice of pineapple and a paper umbrella. I took a sip and sighed.

Hell, yes. At least the bartenders here knew how to serve shifters. We needed at least triple the alcohol that humans did to get a buzz. I took another long drink and scanned the room. Everything about the venue was breathtaking and perfect.

"You look like you're having as much fun as I am." A woman with long, beachy blond hair and a sun-kissed glow stood next to me, holding a tropical drink garnished with an orange slice and a cherry.

I swallowed. "Mmm. Except you don't seem to be avoiding all human contact."

"Well, when you see someone with an expression as inviting as yours." The woman grinned and put out a hand. "Willow. You?"

"Kate." I shook it. "Where are you from?"

"California." She twisted her fruit spear in her drink. Her lips were glossy, pale pink. I wondered if she'd applied lip gloss or if they naturally looked that perfect. "What about you?"

"Minneapolis."

Her eyes lit up. "I stayed there once. We went to the Mall of America."

"Did it live up to the hype?"

Willow shrugged. "I'm not really a huge shopper."

"Let me guess. You prefer beach days and second-hand vintage shops." I winced, realizing the alcohol was wreaking havoc on my social filter, but Willow only laughed.

"Ugh. I'm such a cliche."

I liked her instantly. Before I could say anything else, another woman joined our table. "Mind if I butt in?" She didn't wait for an answer before setting down her drink. "I'm KB. I'm from Canada. Yes, we have electricity, no, I don't know your uncle who lived for three years in Saskatchewan, and yes, I freeze my ass off most of the year."

I laughed. "Sounds like you've already made the rounds."

KB gave me a knowing look. "I hate small talk. This right

here?" She motioned to the bar. "Is exactly why I haven't found a mate."

"Right?" Willow slumped over the table. "If we could skip this awkward stage, maybe we wouldn't have to come to adult summer camp to find a mate."

I looked between the two of them. "Are you both here by choice?"

KB shook her head. "My alpha nominates two pack members between the ages of twenty and twenty-six each year. I pulled the short straw."

Willow took a long sip of her drink before lifting her eyes. "Why do I feel like you'll judge me for my answer?"

I blew out a breath. "Because I've already blown my cover as a sweet, naive Omega from the Midwest?"

KB laughed. "If that was your cover, you probably shouldn't have gone with a collared satin shirt."

"It's a tank top," I scoffed.

"It's shiny. With buttons and a collar." KB looked at me like every law professor I had first semester. *Really, Kate? You forgot to format your sources.*

I looked around at the other shifters in their beach garb. Yeah. Okay. She had a point. They all looked like they were here to break the "no shoes, no shirt, no service" rule while I looked prepared to inspect this bar's liquor license.

"My alpha is paying my tuition for the next three years of law school if I stay the month," I blurted.

Willow's eyes widened. "You're in law school?" she asked, just as KB said, "Your alpha would do that?"

I groaned. "My alpha is my father."

KB turned into a seagull that had just spotted something shiny. "Oh, Kate. Your daddy bribed you into coming here to find a strong alpha?"

Willow's grin widened. "That's great, isn't it? If someone

offered to pay my tuition in exchange for a month-long beach vacation, I'd do it in a heartbeat."

I nodded. "I know. Not the worst. But I have to 'fully participate.'" I did the air quotes.

Willow nudged my shoulder. "How bad could the activities be?"

As if on cue, a woman with a radiant smile and a bubbly personality approached our table. She had deep bronze skin with her black hair braided with colorful beads. "Hello, lovely ladies! I hope you're enjoying your first evening here at Wolf Island. I'm your entertainment director, Trinity, and we have a little icebreaker planned to help everyone get to know each other."

I tightened my grip around my glass. There was no way I was going to play some humiliating party game.

"Tonight, we're going to play musical tables!" Trinity raised her voice, her enthusiasm palpable. "When the music starts, you'll move to a different table and when it stops, you'll introduce yourself to your new table mates. Ready, set, go!"

I groaned inwardly. Willow and KB were my safe place. Sure, we'd only known each other for three point five minutes, but they didn't have alpha testosterone swirling through their veins. Well, maybe KB had a little.

Willow squeezed my shoulder before the three of us drifted through the crowd. The entertainment director walked through the room, making sure none of us ended up together at the next stop.

When the music stopped, I ended up at a table with three men, my stomach clenching with nerves. I hadn't been around a group of shifters this large since the last council meeting I'd attended with my father. I had to remind myself that none of them were going to bite. At least not here in the lounge.

"Well, this is interesting." A man with sandy blond hair

and playful green eyes grinned at me. He had a slow southern drawl that was oddly comforting. "I'm Patrick. And you are?"

This? *I was a this?* "Kate." I barely got the word out before the second man cleared his throat. He was tall and muscular, with a sharp jawline and piercing gray eyes.

"Max." He didn't bother with pleasantries, just took a sip of his drink and looked around the room like he was assessing his competition.

I shook the ice in my glass, wishing I'd gotten a second drink before walking from the bar. "So, what do you two think of this place?"

Patrick leaned in. "Honestly? It feels a bit like a meat market."

A bit? Granted, it could have been worse. I'd read up on the Luna Bay Resort. There were twelve private beach huts, though "hut" was a misleading term. They were modern, gorgeous private homes set around a spacious pool area with a swim-up bar. It looked as if there were twenty plus shifters there, evenly split between male and female. If the rest of the women were as down-to-earth as Willow and KB, I might have a shot of surviving until the end of July.

Max scoffed. "I'm here because I have to be. My alpha thinks I need to settle down." If Patrick's voice was smooth, Max's was the opposite. He was abrupt. Brash.

I raised an eyebrow. "And you don't want to settle?"

Max shrugged. "I don't need help finding a mate. If I wanted one, I'd have one."

Patrick chuckled. "A bit full of ourselves, huh?"

Max twisted his glass. "Insecure people often misunderstand confidence."

Patrick's jaw tightened just as the music started a second time. I gave a small wave and moved to the next table. I met three other men and two women while carefully avoiding the table where the man I'd seen at the bar still stood. He didn't move when the music turned on, which made orbiting him a simple task. I didn't know anything about him besides the impact he had on my pulse when I looked at him. That was enough of a reason to steer clear.

I was pretending to be interested in a story about water treatment in the Ozark's when another well-dressed man, this one with salt and pepper hair, stepped up on the small stage next to Trinity at the front of the room. He clapped his hands, and the chatter in the room ebbed.

"Good evening, everyone," he began, his British accent smooth as glass. "I'm Mac, your managing director, and I'm thrilled to welcome you to Wolf Island and the Luna Bay Resort. I'm sure you're all curious about what the next month will look like, so let's get right to it, shall we?" He paused, scanning the room to ensure he had our full attention.

My heart pounded in my chest, the sound almost drowning Mac's words. While they had plenty published online about the resort's amenities, there was nothing about the shifter mating program. For obvious reasons.

"Here at Wolf Island, we believe in efficiency," Mac continued. "Our goal is to help you connect with your inner wolf and find your perfect match. We don't waste any time. Starting tonight, you'll be paired with one of our other guests to share a hut. Possibly a bed if you choose." He winked. "This gives you the opportunity to get to know one another on a deeper level. We aren't looking for superficial connection, as you're all experts in that already. For the first week, you'll switch partners every night. After that. . . well, it will depend on how you place in the challenges and who you choose."

There were a few hoots and hollers. My palms began to sweat. *Share a hut?* As in sleep in the same room? I glanced around the room, noting the varied reactions. Some of the attendees looked intrigued, even excited. Others, like me, seemed more reserved, their expressions guarded. I searched the crowd for Willow and KB.

Had anyone else heard the first part of that statement? Connect with your inner wolf? There I was at twenty-one, and the last time I'd felt even a twinge from my wolf was at least five years ago. I felt that same stab of guilt every time someone brought up our wolves. Thankfully, it didn't happen often these days. Most of my friends growing up experienced the same thing I did. A flicker of that voice and then a fizzling out. The elders couldn't explain it. My parents certainly couldn't. It was a worldwide phenomenon that I doubted Luna Bay Resort could solve in a month, though their clientele was obviously more than happy to throw money at the issue.

"Next week, there will be challenges every other day," Mac explained. "These will test your compatibility and teamwork. Winning teams will receive rewards, including the ability to choose their companion for the next couple of nights."

My mind raced. Challenges? Rewards? This was absolutely some twisted reality show. Without cameras. *Please, for the love, they wouldn't have cameras, would they?* I spotted KB at the back of the room. She downed a shot and set her glass on the table.

Mac's smile was almost fatherly. "I encourage you to embrace this experience. Step outside your comfort zones and open yourselves up to the possibility of finding your mate."

My heart became a war drum. My plan had been to avoid everyone. To sit on the beach, eat good food, and participate when I had to, but this? If I had to spend the night alone with an alpha male? Do challenges together?

The resort wasn't pulling any punches, I had to give them that. Fated mate bonds were snapping into place less frequently, but the elders didn't believe it was due to a lack of bonds. During the council meeting I'd attended with my father, the elders had made it very clear that it was my generation that was the problem. We were wrapped up in our devices. We weren't spending time together in person anymore. The mating bonds only solidified after shifters had intense emotional experiences together and plenty of physical contact.

Which was why I generally holed up in my apartment and spent my time with online textbooks and case studies.

I wanted to find all the data on this place. How high was their success rate? What made the difference for those who didn't find a mate? Given the situation, I was going to have to find a different strategy to avoid a bond, and numbers always helped. My hands clenched at my sides as Mac's eyes glinted with anticipation.

"But let's not get ahead of ourselves. We have our two most highly anticipated days ahead of us. There are twelve huts here on the island, which means there are twelve potential fated mate pairs sitting here among us. Tomorrow, you'll enjoy Luna Bay's Instinct Day. You'll start with our famed 'Trust Trials' and then move on to the fast-paced 'Heart to Hearts' after lunch."

Mac winked, drawing a few grins from the crowd. "Day Two, you'll have time to relax by the pool in the morning, then we'll start our party games and 'Moonlight Confessions.' And yes, it's exactly as it sounds."

Mac smiled, pausing for dramatic effect. "We hope that will give you an opportunity to get to know each of our incredible guests. You were all selected for a reason. And with that, we'll move on to our first pairings for the evening. Please remain seated as we call you up one by one."

The room buzzed with nervous energy as the staff moved into position. My pulse quickened, my breath coming in shallow gasps. This was happening. I was about to be paired with a stranger and expected to sleep in the same room with him. I clutched my empty glass tighter, my knuckles turning white.

Mac stepped up to the microphone and pulled a small box from the podium. He reached inside, and my heart raced, my palms slick with sweat.

Distraction. I needed a distraction. I glanced around the room, taking in the dimming lights. Everything about this place was luxurious and intimidating. From the soft glow of the chandeliers to the velvet drapes framing the windows, it felt like I was in a different world.

Mac pulled out the first slip of paper. "First up, we have Lukas and Emma."

Cheers lifted from the table next to the bar. The one I'd been avoiding all night. The tall, muscular man with dark hair and piercing blue eyes waved to a woman across the room with auburn curls and a confident smile.

Lukas. His name was Lukas.

I tipped my glass and sucked an ice cube into my mouth. At least he was off the table. The managing director called another pair, names I didn't recognize, and I focused hard on the wood grain beneath my glass.

"Mateo and Willow."

I turned my head, and there she was, standing a few feet away. Her cheeks were flushed, and she shot me a grin as she passed to one of the tables near the front.

Mac pulled out another slip of paper. "Next, we have—" He paused, his brow furrowing as he read the name. "Paul."

I swiveled in time to see the man who must've been Paul adjust his glasses and raise his hand like he was in elementary school.

"And Kate." Mac looked up, peering into the crowd, and my whole world dropped into slow motion.

Paul's lips twitched as he turned to look at me. He stood

and walked over to our table, then wiped his palms on his jeans. As soon as he met my eyes, a crooked smile spread across his lips. "Kate."

I only knew he said my name because I was capable of reading lips. No sound could make it through the ringing in my ears. He strode closer, and my cheeks felt like I'd spent four hours in the sun without sunscreen.

Patrick's hand touched my elbow, and the lounge tumbled back into full speed. "You look like you just got sentenced to a night in prison."

I looked over at him, and he gave me an apologetic grimace. "It's just one night, right? How bad can it be?"

TWO

After two more rounds of musical tables and a light dinner, Paul and I walked down the path to our hut with the keys Mac handed us. I wasn't sure what to say, so I didn't say anything. How was I supposed to have a conversation with someone I barely knew, especially given the circumstances? It was like we were jumping into a middle school sleepover, and I was the girl who'd never been to one.

I glanced at Paul and caught him staring at the ground. He was muttering to himself, which seemed to be his go-to move when things got weird. I was a little jealous that he had a coping skill for this.

We reached the hut, and I scanned my key, then pushed open the door. Inside, soft lighting bathed the small space in a golden glow. A small living space. A kitchenette. Then a wide open door to the bedroom.

I pulled my indoor flip flops from my bag and swapped footwear, then walked forward. Two beds sat on either side of the room, separated by a nightstand with a lamp and a little vase of flowers. The walls were adorned with beach-themed artwork, and the sound of waves crashing through the open screened windows was the cherry on top.

I suddenly wished I had someone. Anyone to share this with who wasn't a random stranger. But that thought was laughable. Since I put in less than zero effort on the dating front and had no desire to change that pattern, a random stranger was going to be my forever option.

Paul scanned the room, his eyes darting from the beds to the nightstand to the artwork. "Two beds, as promised." He walked over to the nightstand and picked up the vase, inspecting the flowers. "These are hibiscus. They're native to tropical regions."

"Paul," I tried to hide my smile. "I appreciate the info, but you don't have to narrate everything."

He set the vase down and nodded. "Right. Sorry. I just— most people don't like dead air."

I sat on the edge of the bed on the right side of the room. "It's okay. How was your day?"

Paul's eyes lit up. "Good. The food was nice, besides the salad. They used a balsamic vinaigrette, which isn't my favorite, but it was still enjoyable."

I grinned, surprised at how much I enjoyed his brutal honesty. "That's good to hear. I had the bisque and stuffed mushrooms." I pulled my suitcase closer to the bed and unzipped it.

Paul nodded thoughtfully. "Both good choices."

I stood and grabbed my toiletry bag, then walked over to my suitcase and pulled out a pair of pajamas. "I'm going to change and brush my teeth. I won't be long."

Paul nodded and started unbuttoning his shirt. I turned away quickly and slipped into the bathroom.

I took my time, savoring the brief moment of solitude. I changed into my pajamas, then washed my face and brushed my teeth. There was a fully open glass shower and a huge window that looked out into verdant green jungle. The whole hut had a classy island feel, decorated with dark wood and smooth stone accents.

When I couldn't think of any other reason to prolong my bathroom stay, I opened the door and stepped back into the room. Paul had stripped down to his boxers and stood folding his clothes, placing them in neat piles on top of his suitcase.

"It's better to fold your clothes before bed. It reduces morning stress by twenty-three percent," he said.

I did a double-take as I passed. Paul was more athletic than his clothing let on. "Is that so?"

He nodded. "There was a study conducted by the University of California that found..."

I sat on the bed and listened to him while I plugged in my phone charger. Not that it was any use. There appeared to be zero data on the island, and I couldn't find one single, crappy WiFi network.

Paul finished folding the last piece of clothing and glanced at me. "Do you want to hear about the optimal sleep position for spinal health?"

I shook my head and set my phone on the nightstand. "So, what do you do for work?"

Paul straightened his pillow and pulled back his sheets. "I worked as an engineer for a while, but I recently had a career change. I've worked for my mother in her accounting firm for the past two months."

"Accounting? Do you like it?"

Paul nodded. "I enjoy the numbers. They're predictable and make sense if you follow the rules."

I smiled. "I get that. I'm studying law right now. Numbers aren't my thing, but I love rules. There's something satisfying about seeing order in the world and understanding how it works."

Paul's eyes lit up. "Do you believe the American legal system is fundamentally flawed?"

I blinked. "Well, that's a loaded question."

He shrugged. "I'm just curious. I've read a lot of critiques, but I don't have any practical experience. I like to get firsthand accounts when I can."

I pulled back my sheets and slid into bed. "I think it's like any system. It has its issues, but it's also done a lot of good. There's always room for improvement."

Paul nodded thoughtfully. "That makes sense. I've read about the benefits of incremental progress versus radical change. There's a balance."

I turned off my lamp and lay back against the pillow. "Exactly." Was I enjoying this conversation with my random stranger for the night? I couldn't quite tell. It was pleasant. I felt oddly comfortable, like Paul wasn't a threat. Or I didn't have to impress him? One of the two, or possibly both.

"This was nice," I said.

Paul turned off his lamp, and for a moment, the only sound was the gentle crashing of waves outside. "I agree." Paul was silent for a moment, then said, "I've never done this before."

My heart skipped a beat. "You've never slept in the same room with someone?"

"Not with someone I didn't know."

"Right." I cleared my throat. "Me neither."

Paul chuckled. "I assumed that was a given."

"What's that supposed to mean?"

Paul turned over in bed, and I could barely make out his profile in the shadows. "I mean, you don't seem like someone who's had a lot of experience."

"Oh, really?" I pushed up on my elbows. "And why is that?"

Paul hesitated. "I didn't mean that as an insult. I just meant that you seem focused."

I lay back against my pillow. "That's fair."

Paul took a deep breath. "I've never been in a relationship before."

I frowned. "A serious relationship?"

"No, a relationship. At all. My mother says I'm 'an acquired taste.' I think she meant it kindly." Paul fell quiet again, and I wondered if he'd fallen asleep. I rolled onto my side and tried to think of something other than the fact that I was lying in bed a few feet from a man I'd just met. A man who had a really nice torso.

I had no interest in Paul, but that didn't mean I was blind. He was attractive, even if he was a little awkward. I liked that he didn't try to be someone he wasn't. Maybe he wasn't capable of being anything other than himself. He probably didn't see it as a gift, but I was again a bit envious.

I sighed and turned onto my other side, trying to get comfortable. A few moments later, Paul's voice broke the silence. "Is it okay if I hum?"

I exhaled, my eyes closed. "Hum?"

"It helps me fall asleep faster."

The corner of my mouth lifted. "Sure, Paul."

Paul didn't waste any time. He started humming, his voice low and soft. It was oddly soothing, like a lullaby. I exhaled and let the melody wash over me.

I woke up with the sun. It took me a moment to remember where I was and why. When I did, a wave of relief washed over me as I realized Paul was still asleep. He lay across from me. His hair flopping over his forehead, his face boyish. I had the strangest urge to pull his comforter up to his shoulders and plant a kiss on his cheek.

I had no idea what time it was, but the light filtering through the thin curtains was enough to tell me it was still early. I didn't want a repeat of last night's awkwardness, so I quietly slipped out of bed and gathered my things.

My thoughts raced as I tiptoed to the bathroom. The night had been uneventful. Surprisingly. I didn't normally sleep well in my own bedroom at home, so the fact that I hadn't woken up once? It had to be my body at sea level.

I brushed my teeth, washed my face, and pulled my hair into a ponytail. I changed into a fresh pair of clothes I'd grabbed from my suitcase, then shoved my dirty clothes into the plastic bag they'd provided for laundry service. I took one last look at Paul, who was still sound asleep, and slipped out into the living area where I found an announcement on a digital board next to the door.

High tech.

My eyes immediately snagged on the word "WiFi" and I read the line below it.

The WiFi lounge is located in the main reception building. Meet with Zara for details.

I EXHALED WITH RELIEF, then checked to make sure I had my key and my phone and exited the hut. The cool morning air hit my skin, and I took a deep breath.

The path to the WiFi center was deserted, the only sounds the rustle of leaves and the bird calls that made me feel like I was at an exotic zoo. My heart swelled at the floral scents and cheerful sounds, and when I smelled bacon cooking, I cursed under my breath. *Why did this place have to be so damn wonderful?*

I reached the main building and walked up the steps, my sandals slapping against the wood. The front desk was empty, but there was a sign pointing to the talk-backs. I followed it down a hallway and turned a corner, my eyes landing on a door with a small plaque that read "WiFi Lounge."

I pushed it open and stepped inside, then stopped short. The room was already occupied.

"Good morning," a woman said, her voice smooth like honey. I blinked. She looked like she'd just stepped off a catwalk. She wore a wide-brimmed hat that cast a shadow over her perfectly sculpted features, and her outfit looked like it was tailored to fit her curves specifically.

"Hi, I'm Kate. I wondered—"

"I know who you are." The woman extended a hand. "Zara Maretti. I run the media and entertainment department here at the resort."

Media and entertainment. I started to hyperventilate. They were filming. Shit. How had I missed the cameras?

Zara eyed me up and down, then sighed. "You look like you've been through the wringer. Not a morning person?"

Okay, ouch. "Not really, no." I pulled out my phone and pointed to the plaque.

She smiled. "Ten minutes with me, and then you can have thirty minutes of internet."

I nodded once. "Sounds like a fair trade."

Zara beamed at me. "Let's get started then."

THREE

TALKBACKS

K ATE

Zara: Your first night on the island. How was it?

Kate: Hmm. Nice.

Zara: You seem surprised.

Kate: Yeah. I guess I didn't expect to feel so comfortable.

Zara: Do you think you and Paul are a good match?

Kate: Probably not. As a couple, I mean. But I think we're friends.

Zara: Why do you say that?

Kate: I don't think we're looking for the same things.

Zara: . . .

Kate: I'm a bit skeptical about this whole process to be honest.

Zara: Which process? Staying at the resort or finding a mate?

Kate: Straight to the point. Both, I guess.

Zara: That's fair. And Paul?

Kate: He's a gentle soul. I don't know much about mates, but I'm sure he'd make the right person happy.

Zara: Hmm. What do you think of the island?

Kate: It's stunning.

Zara: You haven't seen the best parts yet.

Kate: Looking forward to it.

Zara: Did you have any specific goals or expectations going into this?

Kate: . . .

Zara: No?

Kate: If you count making my father happy and getting school paid for, then yes.

Zara: Do you think finding a fated mate is possible?

Kate: Maybe, but it's probably rare. Relationships are built on common values, mutual respect, and shared goals. The idea that there's one person out there who's perfect for you is romantic but not necessarily practical. I mean, look at the statistics. There are millions of people in the world, and the odds that your perfect match is going to be in the same place at the same time as you? Slim to none.

Zara: So you're not a romantic?

Kate: What gave me away?

Zara: And what about your wolf?

Kate: . . .

Zara: Most people here haven't felt much from theirs. I wondered if you—

Kate: No. I haven't.

PATRICK

. . .

ZARA: Morning Patrick. How was night number one?

Patrick: Well, I didn't get laid, so there's that.

Zara: You were trying to get laid?

Patrick: No, I—no. I'm not an asshole.

Zara: Did I say you were an asshole?

Patrick: . . .

Zara: . . .

Patrick: I was kidding.

Zara: Do you often deflect questions with humor?

Patrick: Damn. Is this a therapy appointment? Did I accidentally sign up for the mental health retreat?

Zara: Another joke?

Patrick: If you have to ask, it's not funny.

~

PAUL

ZARA: Hey, Paul.

Paul: Hello.

Zara: Did you have a good night?

Paul: It was enjoyable. Yes. The mattress was stiff.

Zara: That's . . . a bad thing?

Paul: No. Did it sound like it was a bad thing?

~

WILLOW

. . .

Zara: Your first night on the island. How was it?

Willow: Magical. I mean, the whole idea of finding a mate is exciting, right? It's what we've been dreaming of our whole lives.

Zara: I'm glad to hear you're optimistic. How was your night with Mateo?

Willow: Mateo was interesting. He's not exactly what I pictured, but that's the point of this, isn't it? Pushing ourselves out of our comfort zones?

Zara: What do you think of the island?

Willow: Gorgeous, obviously.

Zara: What about the other men?

Willow: I know we're supposed to focus on our date, but I couldn't help noticing a couple of them. Lukas—he's got a smile that could melt ice. And Orion, he's got that brooding, mysterious thing going on. Definitely intrigued.

KB

Zara: How was your first night on the island?

KB: A bit overwhelming.

Zara: I get that. How did your night with Orion go?

KB: Do I have to answer that?

Zara: No. It seemed you already made some friends.

KB: Yes. Can I spend the night with them?

Zara: *laughing*

KB: I'll take that as a no.

Zara: You're not the first one to ask. But you felt comfortable with Orion? There isn't something I should be—

KB: No, nothing like that.

Zara: Good. Trust Trials today.

KB: Hmm. Fantastic.

Zara: Are you looking forward to getting to know anyone better?

KB: . . .

Zara: Not Kate. Or Willow.

KB: Probably Paul then. He seems quiet.

~

LUKAS

LUKAS: You're really making me do this?

Zara: No special privileges. Even for you.

Lukas: But you already know what I'm going to say.

Zara: Surprise me.

Lukas: Fine. Let's get this over with.

Zara: Lukas, how was your first night on the island?

Lukas: Well, Zara, it was exactly like I thought. Everyone loves me.

Zara: You say that like it's a problem.

Lukas: They love the idea of me, Zar. Not the actual me.

Zara: Did you show them the actual you?

Lukas: . . .

Zara: Lukas—

Lukas: I didn't want to come.

Zara: Do you like the island?

Lukas: It's beautiful like you said.

Zara: So maybe you could keep an open mind. Especially since—

Lukas: I'm completely open. Can't you tell?

Zara: . . . They'd like you, you know. The real you.

Lukas: For how long? I give it a week before someone finds out.

Zara: Perhaps. But that's a week of—

Lukas: Not worth it.

CHAPTER

FOUR

I sat in the WiFi lounge on one of two plush chairs after making a small cup of mint tea. The windows along the far wall were floor-to-ceiling, and for a moment, I forgot all about my phone. The sun sparkled off the gentle waves, and the sand shimmered gold. I settled in and scrolled to my email first. I only had thirty minutes, and then I could lust after the gorgeous beach view as much as I wanted to.

Two messages from the University of Minnesota needed my attention. I read through them, my brow furrowing as I considered the implications. More opportunities for the fall, and internship applications for next summer. *More deadlines.* I entered them into my calendar and exhaled, then moved on to my texts.

Several messages from my friends waited, and I quickly scrolled through. Sam, my roommate back home, sent a picture of the sunrise with the message "Miss you!" My younger brother Aaron found a meme about law school that made me laugh out loud. It was a picture of a man in a white T-shirt and aviators holding up his hand with the text: *"Sprinkling my law school essays with Latin legal terminology like—"*

I grinned, my finger hovering over the keyboard to type a response when the door opened. A man walked in, and the air in the lounge seemed to thicken. It was Lukas. His dark hair framed his face, slightly disheveled from sleep, and his barely stubbled jawline was sharp enough to cut glass. He wore a white shirt that clung to his broad shoulders and jeans that hung low on his hips.

Lukas scanned the room, and when his eyes landed on me, his lips twitched. He didn't say anything as he turned toward the coffee bar along the side wall. The room was too small for me to not notice him. I couldn't help but glance up from my screen as he filled a cup. He didn't add cream or sugar, just blew on the surface and took a sip, then lazily walked to the couch across from me and sat down, pulling out his own phone.

My mind raced. We were the only two people there. Should I say something? But what? Ask him how he slept? Probably fantastic since every girl at the pool last night was ready to hop into bed with him. Definitely not something you bring up with a perfect stranger at seven-thirty in the morning.

Seven-thirty. He was up early, too. Or had he never gone to bed in the first place?

Okay. I was judging him hard. But he kind of deserved it. You know, based on his looks which he definitely was in control of.

I turned to the text messages from the group chat with my parents.

DAD:

How was your night? Anything noteworthy?

Mom:

Ignore him. He was supposed to make small talk until at least Wednesday.

Dad:

how is that not small talk?

Mom:

this is small talk.

I clicked on the linked article and read the headline. "Rumors of Rheinhardt: High Alpha in Hospital."

I groaned, then froze when Lukas looked up. *Not alone.* "Sorry."

He glanced at my phone, then back to my face. "Bad news?"

I pursed my lips. *He was talking to me?* I didn't know if I'd even heard him speak before. I hadn't noticed any accent, but the way he formed that last word. . .

"No. My mom is obsessed with the Royal Rheinhardts."

Lukas' brows knit together. Maybe he didn't know what it

was? "It's a shifter publication in the US. Dedicated to the High Alpha and his family."

Lukas grunted and reached for his coffee.

"I know. Americans, right? I don't know how people are still reading about them. Its not like they care about any shifters beyond their ritzy little borders."

No answer. *So glad I said something.*

I swiped out of the article and went back to my texts to write back.

> I slept well. That's noteworthy, I think.

> Don't get mad if I'm not texting, though. You sent me to a technological dead zone.

THEN I TAPPED on my brother Lee's number. There were three recent texts. All from me with zero response. I exhaled and typed.

> Hey. On the island and it does't suck as much as I hoped it would. Which is annoying.
> Love you.

I PRESSED SEND, then reached for my tea. But just as my fingers curled around the handle of the mug, my foot bumped the table, and it wobbled. Hot tea sloshed over my hand and puddled on the table.

I hissed air through my teeth and set my phone on the

chair, about to get up and retrieve some napkins, but before I could move, Lukas was on his feet. "I've got it." He grabbed a handful of napkins from the counter and handed them to me.

"Thanks." My cheeks burned. I mopped up the mess as best I could, then noticed Lukas still standing there. He reached out a hand for the soiled napkins, then tossed them in the trash and sat back down without a word.

Well. That was embarrassing.

Lukas was already fixed on his phone screen. There was definitely something off with him. Gone was the charm and charisma of the night before, and that only made my cheeks burn hotter. Was I not worthy of the smiles he was flashing on a whim to all the other women in the bar the night before?

I blew out a breath. I shouldn't care. I didn't care. Then Lukas took another drink of black coffee, and I realized he may just be hungover. Wolves didn't usually get hangovers like humans did, but Lukas had been partying hard. "They may have some pickle juice in the restaurant. If you need some."

Lukas looked up from his phone. "What?"

"My favorite hangover cure."

He drew a breath, his brow furrowing. "I'm not hungover."

"Hmm." I nodded and went back to my phone. Perfect. At least now, he'd definitely want to avoid me.

"Do I seem hungover?"

I kept my eyes glued to my screen. "Not exactly."

"Then what?" His eyes were on me, and I couldn't help but glance up.

I shrugged. "I don't know. You don't seem as energetic as you were last night."

Lukas' brow arched. "You noticed me last night?"

Definitely an accent. It was soft. European? His mouth was narrow when he formed his vowels. I wet my lips. "I think everyone here noticed you last night."

The corner of Lukas' mouth lifted. "Good to know." He set his mug back on the table. "Last night *you* didn't seem very energetic."

My heart rate sped, and I was immediately annoyed. One comment, and the idea of him noticing me was suddenly cardio? Yes, he was stupidly attractive, but it didn't matter. After this month, he'd go back to whatever European country he was from—that made a lot more sense of his perfectly fitted jeans, by the way—and I would go back to school. There was no point to this interaction.

I looked up from my phone and met his eyes. "I'm only here to get free tuition."

Lukas' expression shifted slightly. "Noted."

My WiFi cut off, and I stood, holding up my phone. "That's my thirty minutes. Thanks again for the napkins." I walked out the door, trying to calculate how many more days I had to endure this awkwardness. Right. Thirty. It was only day two.

I stepped into the breakfast area and found only a few other guests scattered throughout the room. Early morning light streamed through the open windows, casting a warm, golden hue on the white tablecloths and wicker chairs. I grabbed a plate and walked up to the buffet, my stomach growling in anticipation as I took in the platters of fresh tropical fruits, buttery pastries, and an array of jams that looked like they were made from every fruit imaginable. My fingers itched to reach for a croissant, but I held back. I needed protein. Something filling.

I was in the middle of scooping a heaping serving of scrambled eggs onto my plate when a petite woman with short, curly hair and a friendly smile stepped up to the buffet. Her name tag read, "Sophie."

"Good morning! How's your breakfast so far?" Sophie

asked, her eyes twinkling with enthusiasm. *Was her accent French?*

I returned the smile. "I haven't tried anything yet. Are those croissant waffles?" I pointed at the golden, flaky pastries next to the jams.

She nodded. "They're to die for." She pointed at the jams. "My personal favorite is the passion fruit and guava blend. Or the mango chili if you're feeling adventurous."

I raised a brow. "Mango chili? I'll have to try it."

Sophie grinned, and with a wave, she moved on to the next station, leaving me to finish building my plate. With two waffles.

I walked to an empty table and sat down. I was halfway through my eggs when the door from the WiFi lounge opened. I didn't look up since I was 99% sure I knew who it was.

Lukas walked past me without a glance, heading straight for the buffet. I tried to focus on my food, but it was impossible not to be aware of him. He was like a magnet, drawing my attention whether I wanted to give it or not. *There just weren't enough places to look.*

As he reached for a fork, something twinged at my center. Just below my ribs, back against my spine. Was that—?

I didn't have time to think about it because someone was calling my name. It was Willow coming through the door to the lounge, her long, beachy waves cascading over her shoulders. *Had she been in there with Lukas?* She wore a pair of white linen pants and a cropped tank top, and her smile lit up the room.

"Hey, you!" Willow called, her voice smooth and melodic. She grabbed an empty plate.

"You have to try the croissant waffles." I pointed to the end cap.

Willow grinned. "I feel like I'm in a food commercial."

I laughed. A few moments later, Willow finished loading her plate and walked over to my table. "Mind if I join you?"

"Of course not." I motioned to the empty chair across from me.

"Tell me all the things." She took a drink of her tropical juice blend.

"Nothing much to tell."

Willow eyed me suspiciously. "Nothing?"

I shook my head. "Seriously. We talked for maybe ten minutes total and then went to sleep." I took another bite of my croiffle. "What about you?"

She grinned. "He kissed me."

My eyes widened. "Did you want him to?"

"Shh!" She laughed, motioning for me to lower my voice. "Yes. I think if I were to list my favorite hobbies in order, they would be first, making out. Second, going to the beach. Better if I can do both at the same time."

I wanted to judge her, but I couldn't. She was just too full of bouncy energy. Plus the fact that I was a teensy bit jealous of her laissez-faire attitude with men. Maybe if I could treat things more casually, I'd be willing to spend more time with them.

The restaurant was humming now, filled with the clatter of silverware and the murmur of conversation. The staff threw open the windows, letting in a breeze that smelled of salt and tropical flowers.

"Kate!"

My head snapped up. Patrick stood next to Paul at the end of the buffet line, his sandy blonde hair tousled as if he'd just come in from a run. He winked at me. *Okaaaay.*

I gave a small wave, not realizing he'd take it as an invitation.

"Did you sleep well?" he asked, walking over.

I was about to respond when the speakers overhead blared to life. "Attention, Luna Bay Resort guests! Your attendance is requested at the beach. Please report to your entertainment director within the next ten minutes."

My stomach somersaulted, and I glanced down at the time on my phone. It was almost nine. I had no idea what to expect, but the air in the room shifted from laid-back to electric. Everyone stood, abandoning their plates and cups of coffee like they were late for a flight.

Paul stared at the buffet, then down at his plate, then back to the buffet. I stood and walked over to him. "You've got a few minutes, I'm sure. Just sit and eat. I'll wait with you."

Paul nodded, then turned and took a seat at our table next to Patrick.

"You ready for this?" Patrick was already shoveling scrambled eggs in his mouth.

I took a deep breath. *Free tuition. Free tuition.* "As I'll ever be."

FIVE

I stood with the group in the jungle, eyeing the setup for the Trust Trials. A mix of determination and amusement bubbled up inside me. I was ready to put my best foot forward, but I was also acutely aware of how ridiculous this whole situation was.

Not for the others, necessarily. But the last time I did anything athletic that didn't involve a treadmill or a yoga mat was probably in middle school. At least they'd allowed us to change into swimsuits and athletic wear.

The obstacle course stretched out in front of us, complete with ropes, logs, and what looked like a balance beam. Beyond that, there was a floating dock that was definitely an occupational hazard.

Trust Trials. More like *Trust Issues Waiting to Happen*. It was a good thing I already had plenty cued up and waiting for company.

I took a deep breath, steeling myself as Trinity revealed the board with our first partnership assignments.

"So exciting, right?" Willow bounced up next to me and

threw an arm around my stiff shoulders. "Ooh, tense. Did you have a weird night of sleep?"

"Surprisingly, no."

Willow grinned. "Paul looks like a perfect gentleman."

I glanced over to see Paul adjust his glasses. He gave me a small wave. "He's kind of adorable," I said.

"Like a puppy." Willow sighed.

I searched the board and found my name across from Alec. Did I know an Alec?

I was about to. A man with bronzed skin and jet-black hair that fell in a gentle swoop across his forehead strode over to us, exuding confidence as if he'd designed the damn course himself. "Alright, Kate. Me and you. Let's do this."

I nodded, my throat acting like I had a sunshine allergy. "Sure."

"Good luck," Willow whispered. She squeezed my arm and skipped off to find her partner.

I followed Alec to the beginning of the course. "Do you want to go, or—"

"I think the she-wolves are supposed to go first."

I grimaced. "Don't call me that, please."

His eyebrow quirked. "What should I call you then?"

"Kate. Just Kate." One of the staff handed Alec a blindfold, and he tied it over my eyes.

Immediately, my world shrank to the sound of Alec's voice. "Okay, first step forward. There's a log about a foot in front of you. Lift your leg high like you're stepping over a toddler."

I snorted. "Is that something you do regularly?"

"Hey, it's a good visual. Now, there's a rope on your right. Grab it, but don't pull too hard. It's not a swing."

Not using my sight made me hyper-aware of all my other senses. The breeze on my cheeks. The rough texture of my sandals. Thankfully, I'd worn my Chaco's. I reached out and found the rope, gripping it for balance. "Got it. What's next?"

"Step forward again, then take a small hop. There's a low hurdle." Alec's voice was smooth. Just the hint of an accent I couldn't place, though I'd never been good at that. Last semester, I met a guy in my Civil Procedures class and asked where in the UK he was from.

He had a speech impediment.

I followed Alec's instructions, feeling a rush of accomplishment every thirty seconds when I still hadn't face-planted.

Alec narrated every move with the precision of a play-by-play sports announcer. "Alright, now you're coming up on the balance beam. It's about six inches wide, so think tightrope walker without the pole."

I put one foot in front of the other, wobbling slightly. "This is harder than it looks."

"You're doing great. Now, just a few more steps, and—oh, shit!"

I stumbled, reaching out instinctively for something to grab onto. My hands grazed the air, desperate for a hold, and then they collided with warmth—solid and unyielding beneath my fingers. My palms pressed against the ridges of a toned torso, muscles tensing under my touch. My breath caught as an unexpected heat surged through my body, leaving my skin tingling and my pulse skittering in my veins. The sensation was overwhelming, every nerve in my body suddenly aware of the closeness, the strength beneath my hands.

"Easy there," a familiar voice murmured, low and steady, and the sound vibrated through me like an electric current. Where had I heard that before? His hands came up to cover mine, guiding them gently as he steadied me, the warmth of his skin seeping through my fingers.

My mind spun, the blindfold still covering my eyes but doing little to dampen the intensity of the moment. My skin burned. Then, from somewhere nearby, I heard Alec's voice, breaking through the haze. "Thanks, Lukas."

And just like that, everything clicked into place. The realization hit me like a jolt, my hands still pressed against his chest, his breath brushing against my cheek as he stood close enough for me to feel the heat radiating from his body.

Lukas stepped back.

Alec grunted. "Sorry, I didn't see that there."

I turned, hands on my hips. "You didn't see the tree?" Lukas was gone. I couldn't feel him in front of me anymore. "Also, didn't you say only the 'she-wolves' were supposed to be on the course?"

"I was focused on the balance beam, and yeah. I guess Lukas broke the rules. Surprise, surprise," Alec muttered.

Interesting.

I was a bit shaky, but we successfully completed the course, and then I was paired with Grayson for trust falls. *What was this, a contact lens sales rep company retreat?*

It took my eyes a minute to adjust, but that was fine because Grayson had launched into a detailed explanation of the physics involved. "So, the key is to keep your body straight, like a plank. If you bend at the waist, it throws off your center of gravity and makes it harder for the person catching you."

Mansplaining. A perfect addition to my morning. "Got it. Plank, not noodle."

Grayson smiled. "Exactly." I had half a mind to ask him if he was a lawyer. He had that look about him. Clean cut. Winning smile. Like wearing shorts and a T-shirt wasn't his natural habitat.

He demonstrated first, falling backward with the precision of a gymnast. He had at least five inches and sixty pounds on me, so I caught him high enough that he didn't flatten me to the ground. I celebrated not allowing my intrusive thoughts to win. Because there was definitely a split second where I considered stepping back completely.

"How many of these do we have to do?" I asked.

Grayson shrugged. "Until we get a feel for each other?"

I snorted. I'm sure that was exactly the point of this exercise.

After our hands had been sufficiently introduced to each other's bodies, we were waved on to the last challenge. The balance and catch on the floating dock.

"Matteo." A man who was the traditional tall, dark, and handsome joined me, stretching his arms. He was already shirtless, and it was obvious he did more than treadmills and yoga mats. "Alright, let's see who can last the longest."

I raised an eyebrow. "Isn't the point to fall and catch?"

Matteo grinned. "Sure, but where's the fun in that?"

I stripped off my shirt and shorts revealing my plain black bikini and stepped onto the dock. I immediately regretted my life choice. The thing wobbled like a drunk on roller skates. Matteo held out his hand, and I grabbed it, trying to steady myself.

"Ready?" he asked, his eyes gleaming with mischief.

"Ready." I was such a liar.

We both leaned back, trying to throw each other off balance. I wobbled, and Matteo laughed. "Come on, Kate, you can do better than that."

I gritted my teeth and leaned in, trying to push him off. Instead, I lost my footing and windmilled forward, gripping onto Matteo and dragging him with me. We both splashed into the water, coming up sputtering and laughing.

The ocean was warmer than I expected, and though my

eyes were stinging when I broke the surface and grabbed onto the dock, it was refreshing.

"Nice job," Matteo said, wiping water from his eyes.

I swiped my hair from my forehead. "I blame you for that."

"Hey, you were the one who lost your balance."

I splashed him, and he retaliated, sending waves crashing over my head. I laughed in spite of my commitment to not enjoy these activities. As we climbed onto the dock, I glanced up and found Lukas leaning against the dock with a petite blonde, waiting his turn. His eyes met mine for the briefest second, and then he turned to the woman in front of him and said something I couldn't make out. She tipped her head back and laughed.

I grabbed a towel and dried off, taking longer than necessary as Lukas and his partner wobbled on the dock, then strode back to watch the others on the course. Patrick and Lindsey were doing great, Patrick guiding her through the obstacle course with ease. Paul was over-explaining every action to Elise, who was starting to get snippy. And Max, well, he was flexing his muscles during the trust falls with Sevina, who was eating all of it up.

By the time we made it to the beach for lunch, the sun was high, and a row of large umbrellas provided a swath of shade over a long picnic-style setup. The ocean sparkled in the distance, and I already felt my muscles relaxing at the sight of food and the rolling waves.

We plopped down on the sand, settling onto the blankets and cushions that had been set up for us. Willow, a girl I hadn't met, and KB joined me. Willow introduced us to Chariya, and we all laid back and sighed in unison.

"Well, that was a morning." I reached for a piece of pineapple from the platter in front of us.

Chariya nodded, rubbing her arms. "I used muscles I didn't know I had."

KB laughed, but didn't even try to pretend she hadn't done CrossFit as recently as the week prior.

Willow stretched her legs out in front of her and leaned back on her hands. "At least we didn't have to do them in the water."

I scoffed. "Some of us had Matteo as partners." The ocean sparkled in the distance, a liquid blue horizon that seemed to stretch forever. *This wasn't the worst.*

Chariya raised an eyebrow. "Oh, do tell."

I rolled my eyes. "He may have insisted on playing King of the Hill. At least I accidentally took him with me."

"Uh-huh, 'accidentally.'" Willow winked.

I threw a piece of pineapple at her, and she ducked. "Hey, no wasting food!"

KB laughed. "I'm just glad I didn't get partnered with Paul on the course. That looked like an experience."

I exhaled. "Yeah. Poor guy. He's trying so hard."

Two guys ambled over, dropping onto the sand next to us and introducing themselves as David and Ethan.

"You ladies have fun this morning?" David groaned, stretching his arms above his head.

Nice. Subtle.

Ethan grinned. "I think I nailed the balance game." He grinned, his Canadian accent making everything he said sound a little more laid-back.

I raised an eyebrow. "Oh? You nailed it?"

He nodded. "Absolutely. Didn't you see? I was like a freakin' tightrope walker out there."

"We should cool off," Chariya suggested, pushing herself up onto her elbows. I took another bite of pineapple, then tossed my clothes next to hers and strode down the beach toward the waves.

David and Ethan didn't take the hint and immediately stripped off their shirts to fall into step next to us. At least there were others already bobbing in the surf.

Patrick and Elise floated, their eyes closed and faces tipped to the sun. Paul stood up to his waist a few feet to their right.

"Hey Paul, what was that thing you were saying about the buoyancy of water?" Patrick called.

Paul pushed his wet hair from his eyes. "I was just explaining how—"

Patrick held up a hand. "I'm kidding, man. Don't explain it again."

Paul nodded, then turned just in time to be swallowed by a wave. He coughed and sputtered, then righted himself. "I guess that was my cue to shut up, huh?"

I dragged my legs through the water to stand next to him, curling my toes in the soft sand. Paul was nice. I wanted him to know that at least someone here wasn't annoyed with his neurodivergence. "Have you ever surfed?" I asked.

Paul shook his head. "I don't. Water is unpredictable."

"Yeah. I've never done it either."

Another wave crested, and Paul valiantly tried to jump with it, but he was too late. He was sent tumbling again, this time going full ass over teakettle. He came up, his hair plastered to his forehead and his eyes wide with panic. Somehow his glasses were still on his face.

I hurried over and offered my hand. "You good?"

Paul stood, a smile splitting his face. "Fine. It's surprisingly exhilarating. The raw power of it."

For a brief second, I considered spending all my time with Paul. He was safe, and he wasn't making much headway with the others. But he wanted to, didn't he? It wouldn't be fair for me to choose him as my comfort person when I felt no attraction to him.

Then an idea struck. I strode closer, and Paul's smile slipped a little as he tried to figure out what my intentions were.

"Paul, I was thinking. What if I introduce you to some of the other women?" I turned and waved to my friends. "I think they'll really like you."

His smile completely evaporated. "I don't think so, Kate."

I put a hand on my hip. "Trust me, Paul. Sometimes it takes a little time for people to see what's beneath first impressions. Women like men like you. Just maybe not right at first."

It was a little harsh, but I could tell my honesty made Paul more comfortable, not less.

He nodded once. "Okay."

"And if you have any questions, you can ask me."

"About what?"

I shrugged. "I don't know. What women like."

Paul's cheeks flushed, and I had to turn to hide my grin.

Trinity's voice lifted over the waves from a loudspeaker on the beach. "Ten minutes to Heart to Hearts!"

Patrick popped out of the water next to me, throwing his head back and wiping the water from his face. "You ready for my questions?"

I shot him a look. "I think they're on the cards. I saw them setting up the tables."

He grinned. "Doesn't mean we have to follow them."

CHAPTER
SIX

The shaded area of the beach where the heart to heart cards were set up was like something out of a tropical romance novel. Tiny tables with chairs were arranged in a circle, each pair with just enough space to feel intimate but not isolated. The waves lapped against the shore. The sun warmed the sand beneath our feet.

I settled into my first chair, my gaze flitting around the circle. Sevina was already leaning forward, her eyes locked on Lukas as if he held the secrets of the universe. My ribs cinched at the memory of his hands on my arms. The way I honed in on his grip and his cool scent since my eyes were covered with the blindfold.

I turned to look in the opposite direction. Willow was fidgeting with her hair, shooting nervous glances in Ethan's direction, and Patrick took the seat next to me, his eyes twinkling with amusement. "Do I get dibs?"

"On me or the chair?"

Patrick laughed. He had an easy, boyish quality about him.

He didn't make me feel as comfortable as Paul, but he didn't set off any warning bells. Except for the one.

"Wait, are you wearing actual shoes?" Patrick glanced under the table.

"Yeah. Why?"

He pointed at his bare feet. "Because we're on the beach."

"I hate going barefoot."

Patrick gave me a quizzical look. "Even on sand?"

"It's all gritty between my toes."

He laughed, then looked at me like I was a rare bird. He was maybe, possibly, a little bit interested in me. Whenever we were in a group setting, he somehow wound up next to me. Though, I had been the one to wander into the ocean earlier. Maybe he was getting the wrong impression.

"You're welcome to sit here, Patrick, but I'm probably not your best option." I didn't want to come right out and say it. I shouldn't have been so blunt in the lounge with Lukas or with Zara in my talk balk. If the coordinators got word that I wasn't taking this seriously, would they allow me to stay the entire month?

I had to stay the entire month. About two hundred thousand dollars was riding on it.

Patrick raised an eyebrow. "How so?"

I exhaled. "I'm not romantic." I smiled.

Patrick blew out a breath and reached for the first card as Trinity rang the bell for us to start. He glanced down at it with a small, uncertain smile. He cleared his throat and read aloud, "Okay, here's a classic: 'What's your biggest fear in a relationship?'" He shifted in his chair, looking almost apologetic. "Not exactly easing into things, huh?"

I forced a laugh, trying to hide the unease creeping up my spine. "Yeah, not messing around." I paused, buying time as I tapped my fingers on the edge of the table.

My thoughts immediately turned to Lee, my oldest brother, and a familiar ache settled in my chest. He'd found his fated mate when he was barely twenty-one. Sarah had been everything to him—his anchor, his other half, the piece of him he didn't even know was missing until he met her. They had five years together. Five beautiful, perfect years.

And then she died. A car crash—just an ordinary accident on an ordinary day. Normally, something like that wouldn't be a big deal. Our bodies heal so fast. But her heart had stopped. Nobody knew why.

One moment she was there, and the next, she was gone. Lee never recovered. He'd gone from the kind of man who laughed easily, who could light up a room just by walking into it, to someone hollow. Empty. He'd lost not just Sarah, but himself, too. He stopped showing up to family dinners, started drinking too much, sleeping too little. The man who'd once been so full of life, so grounded by his love for her, was now lost in a fog of grief that had no end.

He wouldn't even return my text messages.

So. Biggest fear? *That.* Not a fated mate dying in a car crash. I knew that wasn't likely. But having someone I loved so much that losing them would destroy me? Hell, no.

"Hmm. I guess my biggest fear is being with someone who expects me to change who I am. You know, like being with someone who thinks I should be different to fit their idea of 'perfect.'" I tried to make it sound intense. Like this was definitely the worst thing that could happen.

Patrick nodded thoughtfully, his expression softening. "Yeah, I get that. I think mine would be, well, being left behind. I mean, like, not keeping up with what the other person needs or wants, and then suddenly they're gone. Like they outgrow you, you know?"

I hadn't expected that. His answer took me off guard. I

studied him for a moment, seeing past the easygoing smile he usually wore. "Has that happened before?"

He shrugged, his gaze dropping to the cards in his hands. "Something like that. But hey, this isn't about me wallowing, right?" He picked up another card and forced a smile, the shadows lingering behind his eyes. "Let's see what else we've got. 'What's the most important quality you're looking for in a partner?'"

I bit my lip, mulling it over. "Honestly? Respect. For what I do, who I am, my space. I've got plans. And I need someone who's okay with me not being around all the time. Who isn't intimidated." I thought of the endless case briefs and late nights at the library that awaited me back at law school.

"Has that happened before?"

I shot Patrick a look. "Perhaps."

He leaned back in his chair. "You are kind of intimidating."

I scoffed. "Or just a jerk?" Most people would say stuck up, but it felt better to pretend it was purposeful instead of something outside of my control. "When it comes to dating, I'm not really the type to drop everything for a guy. Not a romantic, remember?"

Patrick's lips quirked up. "Law school, right? What's that like, balancing all that?"

I shrugged, a small smile tugging at the corners of my mouth. "It's not a balance. It's more like all or nothing. But I'm used to it, I guess. You don't get through torts and contracts without sacrificing Netflix time."

He chuckled, the sound warm and surprisingly genuine. "So you're focused. Determined. It's kind of impressive, actually."

I waved him off, heat creeping up my neck. "Thanks, but it's just what I have to do, you know? It's not some noble sacrifice or anything."

Patrick studied me for a moment, and I searched for something to break the silence.

"You're not the playboy I thought you'd be. Based on your face." Based on your face? What the hell?

Patrick threw back his head and laughed. "Don't spread it around. I've got a reputation to maintain."

Trinity's bell rang, signaling the end of our time, and Patrick stood, giving me a lopsided grin. "It was good talking to you, Kate. Thanks for. . . you know."

I nodded, and glanced up to see Lukas standing across from me. He looked as if he was about to move my direction when Matteo slid into the seat across from me.

"Hey, Matteo."

He clasped and unclasped his hands. "Hey."

"You recovered from your fall, I see."

Matteo laughed. "Yeah." He ran a hand through his hair. He was clearly less confident here talking than he had been goofing off on the dock. He took a deep breath, then reached for the stack of truth cards, shuffling through them. "Mind if I just dive in?"

"Be my guest." I motioned for him to continue, wondering if he'd pick one of the easier cards, like favorite ice cream flavors or ideal vacations.

He finally settled on one. "Okay, here we go. 'What is your happiest childhood memory?'"

I pondered that. The word "happiest" made me search for a pinnacle experience, not just any old happy memory. I smiled, wishing Paul was there so we could parse out the logistics of the question together.

I leaned forward on the table. "Alright, happiest childhood memory. That would probably be the summer my family took a trip to Italy. I was ten, and we stayed in this tiny village on the coast. I remember the smell of the sea, the taste of fresh pasta, and my parents laughing together. It was perfect."

Matteo nodded, his eyes softening like I'd just given him a beautiful gift. "That sounds amazing. I've always wanted to visit Europe. Did you get to see any famous landmarks?"

"Not really," I admitted. "We mostly stuck to the small towns. My dad insisted that the real Italy wasn't in the tourist spots but in the places where the locals went. I think he just didn't want to deal with crowds."

Matteo seemed to take this to heart. "That sounds really meaningful, actually. Like, you got to experience the real culture instead of just. . .I don't know, taking selfies in front of famous statues."

"Hmm. Alright. Your turn. What's your happiest childhood memory?"

He didn't hesitate. "My grandparents had a cabin on a lake in Ontario. Every summer, we'd spend a week there. Fishing, swimming, roasting marshmallows. It was the one time of year where everything felt simple. Like there wasn't all this noise, you know?"

There wasn't all this noise.

Yes. I did know.

The bell rang before we could dig deeper, and Matteo stood quickly, giving me a small wave before moving to the next table.

Damn you, Luna Bay. Upon arrival, I'd been dead set on not liking any of the guys on this island, but now? I already cared about at least three of them.

I scanned the tables in front of me, but Lukas wasn't there, and before I could turn, Max took Matteo's place with a swagger that made me roll my eyes almost on instinct. He flashed his cocky grin. It had been one day. And I already knew it was his signature.

"Well, well, look who it is. The lawyer and the lover, together again."

"A self-proclaimed nickname. Nice." I settled back in my chair.

Max leaned in, his voice dropping to a low rumble. "I call myself a lot of things, Kate. But you can call me whatever you want."

I snorted, shaking my head. "I'll think on it."

He winked, then reached for the cards, holding them up like he was about to do a magic trick. "Shall we?" Max flipped through the cards, then dropped them. "Favorite sexual position."

"Reverse cowgirl," I answered without hesitation. Because I got to be in charge and they couldn't see my face. I kept that part to myself. Max stared at me. "What, you didn't think I was going to answer?"

"No, I just didn't—you don't seem like a girl who would do anything but missionary."

"You mean she doesn't seem like a girl who would do you?" A deep voice sounded next to me, and I turned. Lukas stood from the table on our right and motioned at Max. "Switch me."

Max scoffed. "The bell hasn't rung yet."

"Does it look like I give a shit?" Lukas walked forward, and Max, surprisingly, got out of his chair and retreated.

"Asshole," he muttered as he stalked across the sand to the table where Lindsey, a redhead with a pixie cut and a nose ring, was sitting.

"Sorry," I mouthed, but she only rolled her eyes. Understandable.

"What the hell?" I hissed as Lukas took a seat next to me. My heart jack-hammered against my ribs.

Lukas lowered his voice. "You don't want to be here."

"Obviously. I already told you—"

"Neither do I, so I think it makes the most sense for us to stick together."

I blinked at him. "I don't think we have a choice." What was he proposing? Lukas was like a modern-day Casanova. He flitted through the women like a hummingbird through flowers. Now he was talking about creating, what, an alliance?

"We'll have a choice starting Monday."

I frowned. "Yeah, if we win, but—"

"Good talk." Lukas patted the table, then rose from the chair and walked back to his table with Lindsey. He shooed at Max like he was a fly on his burger.

"What the hell, man?" Max threw up his hands, and I turned away from them. Hoping that would prove I had nothing to do with whatever happened next.

One of the staff interceded, and we all made it through three more rounds of card picking and bell ringing. Then, on Trinity's cue, we gathered in a semicircle on the beach, staring at the board where the partner assignments for the night were about to be revealed. It felt like we were waiting for the results of a high school class election.

Lukas stood a few feet away from me, his hands shoved into his pockets as he gazed out at the ocean. Next to him, Sevina's shoulders were tense, her lips pursed in a thin line. Willow was shifting from one foot to the other, her eyes darting between the board and Ethan. I couldn't help but smirk. Apparently, I wasn't the only one with a favorite.

"Alright, everyone," Trinity called out. "Here are your partner assignments for tonight."

She pulled the cover off the giant board, and I scanned the list, my heart pounding.

Kate. Kate. Look for the K, and—

Kate & Barnes. Who was Barnes? I glanced down the rest of

the list noting Sevina & David, Willow & Enzo, Elise & Max—good luck with that—and—

KB & Lukas.

My skin suddenly felt too tight. KB was great. And she didn't want to be on the island either, so they'd be a great pair.

I should've been happy for them, but their names together made my stomach sour. *What if he chose her as his partner or non-love ally or whatever?*

I groaned internally. One comment from him, and now I was invested in his little deal? Ugh. Gross.

I exhaled and spun in a circle, taking in the rest of the group. Sevina's shoulders slumped. She was paired with David, who seemed nice enough but wasn't her first choice. Willow stared daggers at the board. Max was smirking, his arms crossed over his chest. And then there was KB. She looked like she'd just been slapped with a fish. I followed her gaze to Lukas, who already had a perfect smile plastered to his face. Was his jaw tight? It seemed a little tight.

"Heya, Kate?"

Heya. Who said, "heya?" I turned to find a guy in a backward baseball cap, a T-shirt, and jeans. *Where did they find these guys? From a fireman's catalog?*

He put out an arm, and with a *"what the hell,"* I took it.

CHAPTER

SEVEN

The resort pool was a slice of paradise the next morning, a shimmering oasis that looked like it had leaped out of a travel brochure. The water was so clear it could've been glass, reflecting the sun with a dazzling sparkle that danced on the surface. Palm trees ringed the pool, their fronds rustling gently in the breeze and casting dappled shadows over the clusters of lounge chairs.

I'd survived the night with Barnes. Really, all I had to do was get him talking. He was a Texas boy, and Texas boys loved to talk. I knew because my brother had been friends with one in high school. So far, Barnes and Patrick had lived up to the legacy.

We'd slept in late and shared breakfast at the restaurant while I learned more than I ever wanted to know about fence maintenance. Now I floated on my back, letting the water buoy me up as I took it all in. The peace and quiet. Soon, we'd be shuffled into party mode and forced to play whatever games our entertainment director had dreamed up, but for now, there was this.

When I got too close to the edge, I flipped over and glanced over to where KB and Willow were chatting near the pool's edge. KB was splashing Willow, who squealed and splashed back.

"Alright, fine! I give!" KB laughed, putting her hands up in surrender.

Willow grinned and shook her head at her. "I used to be a lifeguard, you know. You don't want to mess with me when I'm in the water."

"I believe you," KB laughed, and I was suddenly beyond curious what I'd missed. Especially considering that Paul, Ethan, and David's eyes were trained on them. Riveted.

My eyes drifted to the other end of the pool where Grayson and Lindsey were trying to dunk each other. Damn. This *was* high school.

Sevina lay on a lounge chair, her sunglasses perched on her nose as she pretended not to watch Lukas, who was floating on an inflatable raft around the bend of the pool with his hands behind his head.

Max was in full flirt mode with Elise, leaning in close to her as he talked. I couldn't hear what he was saying, but from the way he was gesturing, I wondered if he was continuing the conversation he'd started with me last night.

It was like watching a soap opera in real time, each of us playing our roles. The flirt, the brooding badass, the sweet guy next door, and the mysterious heartthrob.

"Do you think they're going to throw us into some sort of competition?" KB's voice interrupted my thoughts.

Willow's eyes lit up. "Like, 'Survivor' but with less island and more dancing?"

David laughed. "Or maybe it'll be like 'The Bachelor,' and you'll all have to fight over one rose." He winked.

"That would defeat the purpose of the island," Paul said, and I laughed.

"I agree, Paul!" I shouted out before anyone else could make him feel like an idiot.

～

THE SALTY BREEZE tickled my nose as I stepped onto the secluded stretch of beach with the group, my sandaled feet sinking into the warm sand. I stepped carefully and shook every few steps, trying to keep the sand from collecting against my soles.

Tall palm trees swayed overhead, their slender trunks rising up to wispy green fronds that dappled the sunlight. Colorful hibiscus and plumeria blooms dotted the tropical foliage surrounding the open-air space.

Ahead of us, the rest of the guests had already gathered near some tables laden with pots of bright paint and various sized paintbrushes. A row of mirrors stood off to one side, reflecting the ocean behind us. We were all dressed in our swimsuits as instructed, but confusion rippled through the group as we took in the peculiar setup.

"What's with the art class supplies?" Willow asked, cocking her head quizzically. Her long strawberry blond hair spilled over her shoulders as she fingered a paintbrush.

"Maybe it's some kind of tropical body painting contest," Max suggested, flashing a cocky grin. His muscular chest was already puffed out as if certain he would win such a thing.

"Ooh, kinky, I like it!" A girl who I thought was named Missy giggled, waggling her eyebrows suggestively.

"Yeah, okay." KB rolled her eyes. I was dying—*dying*—to ask her about her night with Lukas but hadn't been able to get her alone. Nor had I figured out how to ask about it without seeming. . .obsessed. Which I wasn't. Only curious. Intrigued.

Sevina pursed her lips. "What's with the mirrors?"

The others began to throw out their conjectures, the buzz of conversation rising with the palpable mix of excitement and nerves. Then it all screeched to a halt as Trinity strode into the center of our group, her brightly patterned sarong swishing around her long legs.

Her smile was wide and mischievous as she held up her ever-present clipboard like a treasured tome. "Welcome, my lovelies, to today's activity: Blindfolded Body Painting!" She paused for dramatic effect, and Max held his arms out like he was a god.

Trinity took in the laughs and "No way's," then continued unfazed. "This is all about expressing how you see each other and bonding in a fun, artistic way. You'll each take turns being blindfolded while the others paint something on your body that represents their impression of you. Then we'll switch!"

Reactions rippled through the group—nervous laughter, a few playful protests, and more than a few speculative glances.

"Body painting?" Willow whispered to me, her green eyes wide. "While blindfolded? That's intimate."

"And potentially awkward," I agreed, my own heart rate picking up. The idea of being at the artistic mercy of this group, unable to see what they were painting on my skin. Unable to watch what they were watching. . .

Lindsey raised her hand. "Are there any guidelines on what or where we can paint?"

Trinity waved a hand. "Nothing explicit, of course. Let's keep this classy, folks. And respect personal boundaries. But otherwise, let your creativity flow!"

"I'll let something flow," Max murmured, and David elbowed him.

Trinity shot him a look. "The goal is to capture the essence of the person in your brushstrokes."

I glanced around at the others, trying to gauge their reactions. KB looked intrigued. Matteo and Grayson were grinning and nudging each other. Missy looked downright gleeful.

"Can we use our fingers?" she asked.

Trinity winked. "Brushes for now, but if you want to sneak some paint back to your hut, I won't stop you." She clapped her hands. "Alright, my darlings! Let's start with the lovely ladies painting the handsome gents, shall we? Gentlemen, time to put on your blindfolds and get ready to be immortalized!"

Laughter and chatter erupted as the guys started reaching for the strips of cloth Trinity indicated, tying them over their eyes with a mix of fumbling fingers and bravado.

"My wolf doesn't like to be hidden," David grunted.

"Is that what you're calling it these days?" Adrian laughed.

High school. I swear.

My nerves jangled as the women in front of me selected paintbrushes and colors, eyeing their male canvases with calculating eyes. I grabbed a brush when it was my turn, along with a paint pot. There were four different colors and a small cup of water in the center. Quite a nifty contraption.

I beelined it to Paul first, sensing his unease even through the blindfold. He stood stiffly, his hands clenching and unclenching at his sides.

"Hey there," I murmured, keeping my voice low and soothing as I picked up a brush and considered the paints.

"Kate?"

"Yep. It's me."

Paul let out an exhale.

I tapped the brush against his upper arm. "That feel okay?" He nodded. "Just relax. This is supposed to be fun, remember?"

"Easy for you to say," he muttered back, his voice tight. "You're not the one who's blindfolded and about to be painted on by a bunch of women."

I couldn't help but chuckle. "Fair enough. But I promise, I'll be gentle." I pondered for a second, then dabbed the brush in the orange and started to paint a small, simple sunrise on his shoulder. After a minute, Paul relaxed slightly under my touch.

"Hey, Kate? Can I ask you something?" He kept his voice low.

"Sure, shoot."

He paused, then rushed out, "What do women like? Specifically when it comes to kissing."

I blinked, surprised by the question. "Oh. Um, well. . .I guess it depends on the woman. But in general, I think we like it when a guy is confident but not pushy. When he takes his time and really savors the moment."

Paul nodded thoughtfully. "How do you do that?"

I considered, thinking about some of the best kisses I'd had, then trying to describe it in a way that would make sense. "I think just make everything half-speed. Try to feel each second like it was two."

Paul's throat worked. "Got it. And what don't women like?"

I laughed. "Too much tongue right off the bat. And when a guy just kind of attacks your face without any buildup. Oh, and bad breath."

He breathed a nervous laugh. "Noted. Thanks, Kate."

"Anytime." I hesitated, then couldn't resist asking, "So . . . is there someone specific you're wanting to impress with your kissing skills?"

Even with the blindfold, I could see the blush creeping up Paul's neck. "Maybe. I don't know. It's complicated."

I smiled to myself, adding a final touch of yellow to the sunrise. "It always is. But hey, if she's the right girl, a little complication won't scare her off." I was about to step back, then a thought popped into my head. "Paul. This might be too much, so you don't have to answer. But what is your wolf like? If you've felt him."

"I've felt him."

I raised an eyebrow, tracing over the sun's edges a second time. "Do you think . . . I don't know. Do you think he could help with this? Like I said, I don't know anything about this personally, but I remember my dad saying that whenever he got nervous, he'd sink back and let his wolf take over."

Truthfully, I'd always thought he was joking. Kind of like he would always say my mom wore the pants in the family. But being here. Hearing other people talking about their wolves like that. Maybe there was something to it.

"Hmm." Paul blew out a breath.

I stepped back, surveying my work with a critical eye. The small sunrise seemed to glow against Paul's skin. "All done," I announced, then leaned in. "And for what it's worth, I think whoever she is, she'd be lucky to have you."

Paul's lips curved into a small smile.

I approached Adrian next, my brush poised and ready. He stood still, his posture relaxed despite the blindfold. I hesitated for a moment, realizing I didn't know much about him at all. What could I paint?

On a whim, I dipped my brush in the blue paint and started to create a small anchor near his ribs.

Adrian sucked in a breath as the cool paint hit his skin. "What is it?"

"I'm not telling."

"A . . . candy cane."

I snorted. "Yep. I just love Christmas."

"And you are . . . "

"Kate."

"Kate. Did you know I love Christmas?"

I dipped my paintbrush. "Considering we've never talked, no."

"Fair enough," he conceded, his tone light. "Guess we'll have to change that."

I made a noncommittal noise, focusing on the details of the anchor. Adrian fell silent, letting me work. So I guess we weren't working on that goal in the present.

Next up was Max. I rolled my eyes as I approached him, taking in his cocky stance and the smirk that played at the corners of his mouth, even with the blindfold on.

I dipped my brush in the gold paint and created a crown on his bicep. It was a bit on the nose, but it was the only thing I could think of. As I painted, Max flexed his arm, making the muscles bulge.

"Careful," he teased. "You might not be able to resist me if you keep touching me like that."

I scoffed, but a laugh escaped me despite myself. "My brush is so turned on right now."

Max laughed, spewing more flirtatious comments as I dabbed on the last of the paint and hurried on to the next in line.

I didn't realize who it was until I turned my head. I took in Lukas, and all thoughts of Max, Adrian, and Paul fled my mind. He stood perfectly still, his expression unreadable beneath the blindfold. I swallowed hard, my heart hammering in my chest as I approached him.

"Hellooo," I said awkwardly. I didn't know which was worse. Standing there staring at him or actually starting to paint.

"Hey."

Staring. Staring was worse. Lukas flinched as my brush met his skin, and I suddenly wished I had an extended brush handle. He exuded warmth. He smelled like a mix of pool and body wash.

Focus. "Good day so far?" I dipped my brush and chose a simple design—a white rectangle with red hearts in the corner and a swirl of something that could be a person in the middle. The King of Hearts because Lukas was most definitely a player. It was a joke, but halfway through, I wasn't sure he'd get it. That only heightened my nerves, building the electric current that buzzed between us every time my fingers accidentally grazed his skin.

"Mmhmm. You?"

"So good." His skin prickled in front of me, and I realized I'd said the words close enough to his shoulder that my lips almost brushed him. I yanked myself back.

As soon as I finished, I stepped back a few feet. "Okay. There you go." I bolted before he could say anything else.

A half-hour later, laughter and surprised exclamations filled the air as the men removed their blindfolds, each of them eagerly examining the designs we'd left on their skin. I watched them in the mirrors.

Max twisted to get a better look at the crown on his bicep, a smug grin spreading across his face. Paul ran his fingers over the sunrise on his shoulder, a small smile playing at the corners of his mouth. And then there was Lukas, watching as he glanced down at the King of Hearts over his chest. He glanced up, but just as his eyes met mine, I looked away and hastily shot a question at Willow.

"Alright, ladies, it's your turn!" Trinity announced, her smile mischievous. "Time to let the guys have their revenge."

A mix of nervous laughter and playful protests rose from the women as the men eagerly handed over the blindfolds.

"Oh, this is going to be good," Max said with a wicked grin, twirling a blindfold around his finger. "Payback time." He pointed to an impressively painted donkey on his right pec.

I swallowed hard as I tied the fabric over my eyes, my other senses instantly heightening in the darkness. I was suddenly hyper-aware of the heat of the sun on my skin, the grittiness of the sand against my feet, the way my bikini left me feeling exposed and vulnerable.

It was all sensation again. I could hear the men moving around us, their low voices and soft footsteps sending shivers down my spine.

Cool, wet paint suddenly brushed against my skin, making me jump. I felt the tickle of the bristles as they danced over my stomach.

"You painted an anchor?" he asked, and I grinned.

"Hi, Adrian."

"Why that?"

I shrugged. "I don't know. We're by the ocean?"

"Okay, for the record, I work for a software startup in Paris. Probably the furthest from a seafaring man you can get."

I laughed. "Got it. You like your job?"

"I like that my job allows me to travel for a month every summer."

I shivered as he added more paint. "Yeah, that would do it."

"All done," he said.

I rolled out my shoulders. "Let me guess. Something Christmas-y?"

"Guess you'll have to wait and find out."

I pouted, but before I could protest, another brush was on me. It went like that. One after another until most of my skin was covered. My thighs, the backs of my legs.

Then, a set of hands was guiding me to turn around. These hands were different—more confident, more insistent. They gripped my hips, fingers splaying across my bare skin in a way that felt more possessive than artistic.

"My turn," a new voice said, and I recognized it instantly as Patrick's. "Don't worry, I'll be gentle."

I relaxed, but just a little. "Should I be worried?"

"With me? Never." His tone was playful, but there was an undercurrent of something else, something that made my stomach flutter with nerves.

The brush touched my skin again, this time on the small of my back. I inhaled sharply, the sensation both ticklish and electrifying. Patrick worked in broad, sweeping strokes, the paint cool and wet against my heated flesh.

I pursed my lips. "That seems . . . large."

"That's what she said."

I groaned. "Are you that guy? Is that your catch phrase?"

"C'mon, you set me up for that."

I had to give him that one. It was pretty good. "What are you painting?"

He exhaled, his breath warm against the back of my arm. "You're a mystery, Kate," he murmured. "Maybe this will help me figure you out."

I swallowed hard, unsure how to respond to that. "Or maybe I'm just not all that interesting."

Patrick laughed. "Doubtful." His fingers skimmed over my hip, leaving a trail of goosebumps in their wake. He nudged me to turn around. "Nice to see you."

"Mmhmm."

Patrick stepped away, and my skin tightened as the paint dried. I listened to the conversation around me, wondering if I was off the hook for the moment.

Then, a new presence materialized in front of me, and the air thickened. My breath caught in my throat. *How?* How could my body react to something—someone—like this when I couldn't even see them?

"Hello." I twisted my fingers, suddenly very conscious of my exposed skin.

Whoever it was didn't speak, but I sensed him as he stepped closer. He was tall. The heat of his body washed over me, and I nearly gasped as he gently turned me to the side.

Heat flashed through my inner thighs at the first touch of his paintbrush. He swiped it soft and slow against my collarbone. One swipe. It should've taken a split second, but he dragged it out for at least four.

Maybe I'd given Paul bad advice. *Four times.* Make it last four times what it should.

His fingertips brushed my skin as he worked, igniting a flush of warmth that spread through my entire body. I wanted to ask who he was, but I couldn't seem to make my mouth form the words. Couldn't make my lungs drag in air. It was as if I was under a spell, trapped in a bubble where nothing existed but the brush gliding across my skin.

He worked in silence. Not a word as he spread paint slowly, tantalizingly up the column of my neck. Each stroke was deliberate, intricate. My pulse quickened, my skin tingling as his breath whispered against my ear. He was so close, he had to hear the hammering of my heart. My shaky exhales.

My cheeks burned with embarrassment, but I couldn't stop it. I wanted to melt. I wanted to lock myself in the bathroom. To stand in a cold shower for hours until I could think properly again.

And then, just as suddenly as it had begun, it was over.

Whoever it was stepped back, leaving me flushed and breathless.

"All right, ladies!" Trinity's voice cut through the haze,

bright and excited. "Time to see the masterpieces! Remove your blindfolds!"

There was a flurry of movement as the women around me scrambled to untie their blindfolds, gasps and giggles filling the air as they took in the paintings adorning their skin. But I couldn't move, couldn't bring myself to look until I heard Willow's delighted squeal.

"Holy hell, Kate! Look at you!"

With shaking hands, I reached up and tugged off the blindfold. And there, standing right in front of me, was Lukas. He still held the paintbrush, his expression unreadable as his gaze locked with mine.

I opened my mouth, a thousand questions on the tip of my tongue, but before I could speak, Lukas turned to Sevina who was stretching herself in front of the mirror.

"You like it?" he asked, that damn grin back on his face.

"It's hilarious." She pointed at a candy cane stretched across her ribs, and my jaw dropped.

"Kate?" Willow's voice was laced with concern, her hand on my arm. "Are you okay?"

I blinked, tearing my gaze away from them. "I . . . yeah. I'm fine."

"Have you looked yet? Geez." Willow grabbed my arm and yanked me toward the mirrors.

I turned, my heart pounding in my chest. I stared first at the giant Santa Claus on my stomach and laughed. Thanks, Adrian. Willow turned the mirrors so I could see the massive night sky and constellation Patrick had put on my back. I took in the rose on my calf, ocean waves, a butterfly.

"Who did *that?*" Willow turned me back around and pointed at my neck.

I held my breath and took in the design that started at my collarbone and spread over the left side of my neck. They were flowers, but none I'd ever seen before. White fluffy petals in a star like shape surrounded tiny pale yellow dots. The flower heads were dotted amongst twisted, delicate stems that wrapped over my skin in an intricate pattern of lines and curves.

"Damn." Willow folded her arms over her chest. "Someone here is an artist."

I didn't tell her who it was. I didn't like sharing a secret I didn't understand. It was beautiful. Breathtaking, even. But what did it mean?

Probably nothing. It was likely a random flower he saw outside our huts.

I followed Willow to the outdoor showers and found a spot next to KB. The cool water was a shock against my heated skin, and I let out a gasp as I stepped under the spray. *Hadn't I been wanting exactly that ten minutes ago?*

Around me, the others were laughing and joking, splashing each other as they scrubbed at the paint on their bodies. Willow chased Alec with a stream of water, her blond hair plastered to her face as she giggled. Adrian reached over, trying to help KB get the paint out of her hair, his brow furrowed in concentration as he worked at a particularly stubborn spot.

But even as I watched them, even as I tried to lose myself in the playful chaos of the moment, my mind kept drifting back to Lukas. To the way his hands had felt against my skin, the intense energy swirling as he painted me. The way my body had responded to his touch, like a live wire sparking to life.

I didn't want that. Right? I didn't want to be here. I didn't want a mate. But was that what Lukas was saying when he partner-propositioned me? Neither of us wanted a mate, so did he think I wanted something else?

Heat flushed through me again, and I was suddenly grateful for the cold. When most of the paint was gone, I stepped away from the showers, wrapping a fluffy white towel around myself as the sky deepened into shades of lavender and indigo. The air was still warm, but a cool breeze whispered against my damp skin, sending a shiver down my spine.

KB and Willow were waiting for me, their hair wet and slicked back, their faces flushed from the heat of the water. "That was wild." KB appeared almost as shell-shocked as when she'd looked at the board last night.

I started to walk. "How were your nights?"

"Fine," KB answered.

"Fine?" I teased, willing her to give me some details.

She shrugged. "We were both tired. Lukas was on a phone call for a while."

I gaped at her. "What? He has cell service?"

She shook her head. "No, it was from someone at the resort. Something about his family."

I chewed on my lower lip.

Willow adjusted her towel and leaned closer. "Well, I may or may not have kissed Enzo."

KB laughed. "So, you *did* kiss Enzo?"

Willow grinned. "But I've been *dying* for tonight. My friend who came here last year? She said the moonlight confessionals are the best part of the whole month."

I felt a flicker of nervousness in my stomach. "How so?"

Willow grinned. "Just make sure to wear good underwear."

EIGHT

I held out my hands to the flames of our personal bonfire. The staff had it going before we arrived at the beach. The walk had only taken fifteen minutes or so, but it felt like we were on a completely different island. There were no signs of modern civilization, only driftwood on the white sand beach and moonlight sparkling over the soft ocean waves.

Trinity had divided us into two groups of twelve upon arrival, and now we were here, waiting to see what happened next.

Patrick rubbed his hands together and sat on one of the logs near the fire. "Now this is more like it."

Max grunted from across the fire, his muscular arms crossed over his broad chest. "As long as no one expects me to sing Kumbaya or some shit." His voice was a low rumble, his gray eyes narrowed as he surveyed the group.

Sevina arched one perfectly sculpted brow. "Charming as ever, Max," she quipped, her crisp British accent making even her insults sound polished. She tossed her long, dark hair over one shoulder, the firelight catching the hints of violet in her eyes.

The flickering firelight danced across designer dresses and pressed slacks as we lounged around the bonfire, still riding the buzz from dinner cocktails.

Trinity appeared like a specter on the other side of the flames. "Glad you could all join us this evening." She held up a bottle made of blue glass. "Tonight you will be breaking down walls."

I shivered. I didn't like the sound of that. My walls were exactly where I wanted them to be. Tall. Strong. Well, they could be stronger, considering how much I was still thinking of the flowers Lukas had painted on my neck.

That made me want to throw up. I didn't *think* about men. I didn't respond like that to them in the first place. I crossed my legs and folded my arms over my chest, staring at the flames.

"This bottle will move around the circle, and you'll each get a chance to spin it. Whoever the lip points at, they'll need to choose truth or dare," Trinity explained.

"And we get to choose the question? Or the dare?" Max asked, his eyes glinting.

Trinity nodded. "The goal is to push out of your comfort zone."

"Why?" Elise asked. My thought exactly.

Trinity smiled. "Most of you have grown up comfortable your entire lives. We believe that's why many of your wolves remain dormant. There's no threat to protect you from."

It made sense, but I still couldn't understand why they were trying to draw our wolves out. If we didn't need them, then why fight to wake them up?

I glanced over to see Lukas staring at the sand, his brow furrowed. Trinity lifted the bottle with dramatic flair and set it in Willow's hands, then motioned to the servers to deliver drinks for the night.

Willow grinned, then set the bottle in the sand in front of her and spun it with a flick of her wrist. As it slowed to a stop, the neck pointed directly at Patrick.

His crooked grin widened. "Lay it on me, Wil. I'm an open book."

"Truth, then?" Willow tapped her chin thoughtfully. "Most embarrassing childhood memory."

Max groaned. "Too easy."

Willow scoffed. "I'm just warming things up."

Patrick ran a hand through his tousled hair. "Okay, fine. When I was seven, I thought I could impress my crush by jumping off the high dive at the community pool. I didn't jump far enough, and my ass hit the board as I dropped. Ripped my suit. Got a concussion and mooned my entire fifth grade class."

My laughter was strained. I felt like I'd just chugged a Red Bull. How long did I have to stay? They had the board for the night, and if I pled illness, I could probably get my assignment early and crash.

Patrick reached for the bottle, giving it a spin. It landed on Max, who raised an eyebrow in challenge. "Truth or dare, big guy?" Patrick asked.

Max smirked, his muscular arms crossed over his broad chest. "Dare. I'm not afraid of a little action."

Patrick's eyes gleamed. "I dare you to give Barnes a lap dance."

The group erupted in a mix of gasps and hoots, all eyes turning to Max and Barnes. Max stood up slowly, a predatory grin spreading across his chiseled features. "Get ready, pretty boy," he growled, stalking toward Barnes with exaggerated swagger.

I couldn't tear my gaze away as Max began to move, his

hips swaying to the beat of some imaginary song. Barnes leaned back on his elbows, making a kissy face. As Max's dance grew more risqué, the group dissolved into raucous cheers and wolf-whistles. He twerked. He gyrated. When Max finally finished his performance with a dramatic bow, Barnes tipped an imaginary hat in his direction.

Max chuckled good-naturedly, settling back into his spot as he reached for the bottle. "Alright, who's next?"

The bottle made its way around the circle, and when Barnes spun it, it landed on Elise. She let out a nervous giggle.

"Alright, Elise," he drawled, a mischievous glint in his eye. "Truth or dare?"

She hesitated for a moment, biting her lip. "Dare," she said finally, her voice wavering slightly.

Barnes's grin widened. "I dare you to remove a piece of Lukas' clothing without using your hands."

My stomach dropped as a chorus of "oohs" erupted from the group. Elise's cheeks flushed scarlet, but she stood up determinedly, smoothing her dress.

As she made her way over to Lukas, I watched for his smile to falter. It didn't. Something hot and bitter clawed at my insides, but I pushed it down, taking another swig of my drink.

Elise squared her shoulders, her blush deepening as she approached, but she managed a flirtatious smile. Lukas remained relaxed, his arms crossed over his chest, watching Elise with that same infuriatingly calm expression.

Elise stopped in front of him, her eyes darting to his broad shoulders and the neckline of his T-shirt. "Can you stand?"

Lukas nodded and pushed up from the log. She took a breath, then crouched and leaned in closer, her hands held deliberately behind her back. She bent at the waist and dipped her head, her face even with his crotch as she used her teeth to catch the hem of his shirt, tugging gently. The fabric stretched under the pressure, and Lukas, to his credit, stayed perfectly still, only arching one eyebrow as Elise worked to maneuver the shirt upward.

A ripple of laughter and cheers filled the air as she managed to drag the edge of the shirt up over his abs, revealing the taut lines of his stomach.

My cheeks were red hot, and something swirled in my gut. The image of me marching over and pushing Elise away from him flashed in my head, and I blinked. I wasn't a violent person. I'd never pushed anyone in my life. Well, besides my brothers, but that didn't count.

When Elise couldn't lift any higher, Lukas slowly dropped to his knees, then lifted his arms to help. Elise wrinkled her nose with concentration, her face brushing against his chest as she tried to inch the fabric up over his head. Lukas' breath hitched, but his cool demeanor remained intact, even as the shirt finally slipped free, falling to the ground beside them.

With a triumphant smile, Elise took a step back, catching her breath as the group erupted into applause and hoots. Lukas reached down to pick up his discarded shirt, giving her a nod of acknowledgment that was more polite than enthusiastic. The entire display left me feeling restless, the burn in my chest flaring up as I watched them.

I forced a smile onto my face, pretending to enjoy the spectacle as I tried to ignore the tight knot of jealousy twisting in my stomach.

The bottle spun again, landing on David. Elise grinned mischievously. "Truth or dare?"

David hesitated for a moment, then shrugged. "Truth."

Elise's eyes sparked with challenge. "Tell us a secret you've never told anyone before."

David hesitated for a moment longer, the firelight reflecting in his eyes as he seemed to weigh his next words.

Finally, he looked down at his hands, turning them over as if searching for the right thing to say.

"Alright. You want a real secret?" He paused, swallowing hard before continuing. "My wolf found a mate a few weeks before I came here. A woman from my town. But she rejected me. Told me I wasn't what she wanted."

The air seemed to grow heavier, the quiet that followed his confession thick enough to cut through. My breath caught in my throat, the unexpected rawness of his admission hitting me like a punch. Around the fire, the others shifted on their seats.

David rubbed the back of his neck, his gaze fixed on the ground, as if he couldn't quite bear to look any of us in the eye. "It's not something you get over easily. The whole thing's messed me up more than I'd like to admit. Coming here was supposed to be a fresh start, I guess. A chance to forget. But I don't know if that's really possible."

His voice cracked on the last word, and he quickly cleared his throat, forcing a lopsided smile that didn't quite reach his eyes. "So yeah, that's my big secret. Not exactly the fun party confession you were hoping for, huh?"

For a moment, no one spoke.

Then Sevina exhaled. "Well. Obviously she's an asshole."

The group erupted, and even David cracked a smile. He was next in line, so he grabbed the bottle and spun it, and the lip pointed through the fire at Chariya. She let out a small squeak of surprise, her dark eyes going wide.

David grinned, the wheels turning in his head. "I dare you . . . to take a shot of tequila from Enzo's belly button."

The group erupted into hoots and laughter.

Enzo was already sprawling himself out on the sand, hiking up his shirt to expose his toned abs and a dark trail of hair. "Belly button shot glass, at your service!" he announced, sending Chariya a playful wink. "Don't worry, I showered."

More laughter rippled through the group as David found a server and carefully poured a splash of tequila into the little divot of Enzo's navel. Chariya covered her face with her hands, her shoulders shaking with embarrassed giggles.

A cheer went up as she crawled across the sand to hover uncertainly over David's prone form. He grinned up at her, doing his best to hold perfectly still even as barely suppressed laughter shook his frame.

She bent, dark hair curtaining her face, and in one swift move, slurped the tequila up with a quick swipe of her tongue. Enzo let out a hoot as she popped back up, face flushed but triumphant.

I cheered and laughed along with everyone else, still internally calculating how long I had to stay. I was next in line to spin even though it hadn't landed on me yet, and I breathed a sigh of relief. *At least I wouldn't be next.*

I spun the bottle over the sand, my heart leaping when it pointed to Paul. He'd been quiet all night. Observing. Taking it all in. I knew I couldn't give him something easy, or the group would revolt, but I also didn't want to give him a mental breakdown.

"Truth or Dare?" I asked.

Paul hesitated. He was probably doing risk analysis in his head. Surprisingly, it didn't take him long to answer, "Dare."

I smiled, as an idea occurred to me. "Kiss Willow."

Paul blinked, and Willow let out a breath next to me. It was kind of perfect. Willow was happy to kiss most people, and Paul needed to try out his new theoretical skills.

The chatter around the bonfire died down to a hushed anticipation as everyone watched, waiting to see if he'd go through with the dare. Willow, for her part, looked equal parts amused and apprehensive. She tucked a strand of blonde hair behind her ear, her blue eyes widening slightly as Paul wiped his palms on his slacks and stood.

Paul walked over and put out a hand, pulling her up from the log where she sat. "Are you okay with this?" He adjusted his glasses.

Willow nodded, wetting her lips, and Paul leaned in. I saw the moment he remembered my advice, because he slowed his approach. He put a hand on her waist, and almost in slow motion, carefully made his way to her lips. The kiss started off tentative, almost chaste. But then something shifted, and Paul seemed to throw caution to the wind. His hand came up to cup Willow's cheek as he deepened the kiss.

Willow let out a small, surprised noise, her hands fluttering uncertainly for a moment before coming to rest on Paul's shoulders. I couldn't tell if she was trying to push him away or pull him closer. But then she relaxed into the kiss, her eyes drifting shut as she started to kiss him back.

It was like watching a scene from a movie. After what felt like an eternity, they finally pulled apart. Willow's cheeks were flushed, her lips slightly swollen and curved into a dazed, bewildered smile. Paul looked equally stunned, like he couldn't quite believe what he'd just done.

For a beat, everyone just stared. Then, the dumbfounded moment of quiet broke. The group erupted into a cacophony of hoots, hollers, and claps, punctuated by Max's good-natured whistle of approval.

"Damn, Professor!" Barnes crowed. "Didn't know you had it in you!"

Willow dropped back to her seat. "That was a good kiss, Paul. Like, a really good kiss."

Paul ducked his head, clearly embarrassed but also fighting back a pleased grin. He glanced at me and barely tipped his head. I got the message and grinned.

The bottle spun and wobbled, slowing its orbit until the neck pointed at Barnes. I let out a relieved breath, but Willow's grin was pure mischief, glowing in the firelight. "Okay, Barnes, I've got a dare for you," she announced, glancing between us. "Draw a temporary tattoo on Kate's inner thigh."

My jaw nearly dropped. "Willow, seriously?"

"What! You made Paul kiss me!" She smirked, leaning back on her hands like she was enjoying every second of my discomfort.

Barnes smirked. "I'll need something to draw with."

Willow called out to Trinity, and within seconds, had a fine-tipped Sharpie in her hands.

Barnes stalked over and took it from her, a slow, teasing smile lighting up his face. "You heard her, Kate. I'm the resident tattoo artist tonight." He motioned for me to lift my dress.

I shot Willow a look. She had warned me to wear good underwear. With a sigh, I tugged up the hem of my dress and butterflied my left leg to the side. It wasn't any worse than someone seeing me in a bikini, but the angle. . .

I glanced up and found everyone's eyes on us except Lukas. His arms were crossed, the flames reflecting in his eyes as he stared straight at them. His smirk was gone.

Barnes leaned closer, his breath whispering over my knee as the marker touched the soft skin of my thigh. "Hold still, now," he said, his voice low and teasing. "Wouldn't want this masterpiece to get all smudged."

"Just don't make it anything I'll regret."

Barnes laughed, then bent his head and got to work. The group watched, curiosity mingling with laughter as Barnes made slow, deliberate strokes with the marker. I stared anywhere but Barnes's head between my knees.

Barnes finally pulled back with a satisfied grin. "There you go, Katie-girl. A little something to remember me by."

I looked down at my thigh and stifled a laugh. He'd drawn an arrow pointing toward my underwear with the phrase, "Barnes was almost here."

Willow threw back her head and chortled, which meant the entire group had to get up and take a good look. Everyone except Lukas.

Barnes handed the marker back to Willow. "Hey, we even spent the night together. I tried my best."

I rolled my eyes. Not true. He'd been a perfect gentleman.

Enzo was next. Willow handed him the bottle, and he spun it without fanfare. When the lip pointed at Sevina, my breath caught in my throat.

"Dare," she said.

Enzo glanced at Lukas. "Sit in his lap. For the next two turns."

Sevina grinned. "Easiest thing I've done all night." She swayed across the sand and, instead of dropping to his lap, she faced him, sliding forward, straddling his hips.

And that's when something inside of me erupted.

KATE

Zara: Are you feeling better this morning?

Kate: Mmhmm. Thanks for asking.

Zara: What happened?

Kate: Too much to drink. Just a really full day.

Zara: What was happening when you left?

Kate: Not sure. It was right after Barnes drew his tattoo.

Zara: Right. I heard that was funny.

Kate: It was.

Zara: And then. . .I think Sevina was sitting in Lukas' lap?

Kate: Again, not sure. I left pretty quick after that.

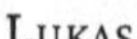

LUKAS

. . .

Zara: What the hell happened last night?

Lukas: I'm sure you already know.

Zara: I know Sevina sat in your lap and Kate nearly shifted for the first time on the sand.

Lukas: That's not what happened.

Zara: Trinity was there. Someone at the other fire saw Kate's wolf.

Lukas: . . .

Zara: You don't believe me?

Lukas: I think people will say plenty to get attention.

Zara: So you don't think it's possible that Kate feels something for you? Sevina definitely—

Lukas: Kate doesn't know me.

Zara: Hmm. But Sevina does?

Lukas: Have you heard anything else from my mother?

Zara: No.

Lukas: Good. That's good news. He must be getting better.

Zara: Lukas, if your father dies—

Lukas: He's not going to die.

Zara: . . .

Lukas: Sorry. I didn't mean to raise my voice.

～

Willow

Zara: I heard you had quite the kiss last night.

Willow: Uh, yeah. Wasn't expecting that. Paul seems so quiet, but yeah. Wow.

Zara: Would you do it again?

Willow: Kiss him? Absolutely.

Zara: Have you two been paired up yet?

Willow: Not yet.

Zara: Challenges start Monday. You could always change that.

~

PAUL

ZARA: Paul, you certainly made an impression last night.

Paul: Yes, well. I took Kate's advice.

Zara: Kate gave you kissing advice?

Paul: I asked her about what women like.

Zara: And it worked.

Paul: Willow seemed. . .pleased.

Zara: Yes, she did.

Paul: Hmm. Well. That's nice.

CHAPTER

TEN

A hot, searing sensation tore through me, clawing its way up from the pit of my stomach. My breath hitched, my vision blurring around the edges as I watched Sevina slide into Lukas' lap, her hands resting on his shoulders like she owned him. The firelight danced over their bodies and Sevina's smile widened with smug satisfaction.

Something inside me snapped.

Heat flared under my skin, burning and restless, like my own blood was trying to boil me alive. I clenched my fists, nails digging into my palms as I fought to keep control, but it felt like my thoughts were slipping through my fingers like water. The edges of the world blurred, and I heard a low, rumbling sound—deep and guttural, barely human—before I realized it was coming from me.

What the hell was happening?

The sensation was unlike anything I'd ever felt—like my skin was too tight, too confining, like I was splitting open from the inside. My muscles trembled, my teeth ached.

But I couldn't move, rooted to the spot as if the earth itself had wrapped around my ankles. The air was alive with scents I'd never *noticed before—the salt of the ocean, the charred wood of the fire, the musk of adrenaline from the others. And Lukas. His scent stood out like a beacon, deep and rich, pulling me toward him even as my mind screamed at me to stay away.*

Mine. The word pulsed through me as I was forced to stand there and stare at Sevina, smug and triumphant, pressing herself against Lukas, acting like she had a right to him.

PAIN LANCED through my head as my eyes flew open. I stared at the ceiling above my bed, panting, my body drenched with sweat. I turned my head, praying that I hadn't said or done anything in my dream to wake Ethan up. I exhaled with relief when I saw him still slumbering in the bed across the room, his arm draped over his pillow.

I slipped on my indoor flip-flops, tiptoed through my darkened hut, and flicked on the light in the bathroom, confronting my reflection in the mirror. Messy dark hair, shadows under my eyes. I went through the motions of my morning routine, trying to let the mundane tasks soothe my frayed nerves.

I squeezed mint toothpaste onto my brush and scrubbed my teeth. After rinsing, I splashed cool water on my face, relishing the refreshing sensation on my skin. Patting my face dry with a soft towel, I inhaled the clean scent. I needed to pull myself together.

My first step was to avoid Lukas. I couldn't make sense of what had happened by the fire, but it was linked to him. Second step . . . well. Pretty much, it was just the first step.

The next few days passed in a blur of solitude and distraction. I found myself withdrawing from the group, seeking out quiet corners of the resort where I could be alone with my thoughts. The pool became my refuge whenever it was empty. I took long walks along the beach, my calves burning as I watched the waves crash against the shore, the salty breeze whipping through my hair.

Even my yoga practice became a solitary pursuit, my mat unrolled in the shade of a palm tree rather than in the bustling group sessions. I did my best to maintain a semblance of normalcy, chatting with KB and Willow over breakfast or in passing, but I was strategic about my time. I did a minimum of three talk backs with Zara a day to get WiFi access and numb out on my phone.

I lost myself in contract readings and email correspondence with my professors. The familiar language of legalese was a comfort, a reminder of the world I'd left behind. I scrolled through upcoming course materials and internship applications.

It was the first time in a long time I looked forward to messaging my family. My mom sent cheerful updates about her garden back home, detailing the progress of her tomato plants and the new bird feeder Dad had installed. My Dad forwarded me news articles about a recent Supreme Court ruling, trying to connect.

The weekend blurred by in a jumble of forced conversations and awkward interactions with two new partners. Matteo, though undeniably sweet, was a bit too eager. We chatted about our favorite childhood books, finding some common ground in our love for The Chronicles of Narnia. Adrien, on the other hand, was more confident and self-assured. Our conversations flowed easily, touching on topics from our hometowns to our career aspirations.

Saturday night brought the karaoke party, a whirlwind of lively energy and colorful chaos. Neon lights glinted off the microphone as contestant after contestant took their turn belting out pop hits and classic ballads. I participated, reluctantly of course, taking my turn on stage with Willow and KB in a rendition of "Sweet Caroline" that earned us roaring applause.

Lukas was impossible to miss. He sat at the back and didn't get up to the mic. I pretended that side of the room was lava. But my mind still flickered back to him sitting at my table on the beach saying the two of us should team up. To be allies since neither of us wanted to find a mate.

He must've forgotten all about that. It had only been a week, but it felt like a year with all that had happened.

Sunday night, the dining area was transformed, the usual casual beach vibe replaced by an air of elegance and sophistication. Tables draped in crisp white linen dotted the space, each adorned with a centerpiece of tropical flowers in vibrant hues of fuchsia and tangerine. The scent of the ocean breeze mingled with the mouthwatering aroma of grilled seafood and freshly baked bread.

As I made my way to my assigned seat, I couldn't help but marvel at the effort that had gone into the evening. Soft strains of music from a string quartet filled the air, blending with the gentle laughter and murmured conversations drifting from table to table. Luna Bay went all out. It was impressive.

I took my seat, shoving my thoughts and emotions down deep. I only had to survive. One month. Hundreds of thousands of dollars. That became my mantra once again.

The first course arrived, a delicate seared tuna paired with a creamy avocado puree. I took a bite, savoring the interplay of flavors on my tongue. As the courses progressed, from a rich lobster risotto to a refreshing mango sorbet, I found myself getting lost in the artistry of each dish.

The clink of silverware against porcelain faded into the background as Mac Hastings took to the small stage at the front of the restaurant. The string quartet's gentle melody came to a close, and a hush fell over the gathered crowd.

Tension thrummed in the air, a current of anticipation and uncertainty that set my nerves on edge.

"Good evening, everyone," Mac began, his rich baritone carrying easily over the assembled diners. "I hope you've all enjoyed the delicious feast our chefs have prepared for you tonight. But now, it's time to reveal the new pairings for the next phase of our journey together. Tomorrow our challenges begin, and you will compete with your partner from the night before."

I swallowed hard, my heart hammering against my ribcage as Mac began to read out the names. *Just not Lukas.* I kept my gaze fixed on the tablecloth in front of me, my fingers twisting nervously in my lap.

Mack called my name, and my head snapped up, my breath catching in my throat. "You'll be paired with Patrick."

Relief washed over me, so strong it left me dizzy. I risked a glance across the room and caught Patrick's eye. He grinned at me, then stood to retrieve our keys.

I set my napkin on the table and left with him. We talked on the path up to our new hut. So strange that this had begun to feel normal.

I stopped in front of the door as Patrick pulled out the key card the staff had given him. Mine was still in my purse. He unlocked the door and pulled it open, then waited as I stepped over the threshold.

I let out a slow breath and stepped into our own private beach house. Each one was a little different. This one had bar stools at the counter.

"Nice." Patrick walked in to stand next to me.

I set my purse on the chair and walked through the door on the left into the bedroom. Our luggage had already been delivered.

Patrick leaned against the doorframe for a moment, then

walked past me, and I turned to follow his eyes. The beds with their white duvets and soft, fluffy pillows.

"Should we push these together?" Patrick raised an eyebrow.

I walked to my suitcase.

He chuckled. "C'mon, I was kidding."

"Mmhmm." I rolled my bag to the end of the bed on the right side of the room. I unzipped the top and pulled out my toiletry pouch, then a pair of pajamas and a change of clothes. I left the rest, knowing I'd likely be moving to a new room the next day.

Patrick unpacked a few things, then flopped back on his bed. "So, what now?"

"I'm not looking for a mate." I turned to him. "I'm here because my father is my pack alpha." I'd been telling each guy one by one. I hadn't wanted to announce it, but after a couple of them started getting a bit frisky, I needed to be frank.

Patrick nodded and sat up. "Okay."

"Okay?"

He walked up to the window and peered through the blinds. "Want to get drinks and swim?"

I nodded. "Sure."

I followed him back to the front door and slipped on my sandals. Patrick led me down the path to the bar next to the pool. We ordered, then grabbed waters with lime and sat at a two-top table away from the other guests at the bar already getting raucous.

His response in the room had taken me off guard. He didn't seem to care in the least, and I couldn't tell if that was a good thing or not. At least he knew I wasn't interested. That allowed me to relax a little.

Patrick leaned forward, elbows on the table. "So, Kate from Minneapolis. What do you like to do in your spare time?"

I blinked. We'd had plenty of conversations, but hadn't really gotten to know each other. "I—" I didn't have spare time. I liked to hang out with my mom and study? "I like reading."

Patrick nodded. "Okay, reading. What else?"

I shrugged. "I like to go on hikes—"

"Oh, I love hiking. Where are your favorite places?"

"I love the Willow River State Park in Wisconsin."

Patrick's eyes lit up. "Wisconsin's beautiful. I had a friend who lived in Milwaukee, and we used to visit him every summer."

"You've been to Milwaukee?" I stared at him.

"Texans do travel. When it's worth it."

I smiled. "I forgot you and Barnes were both from Texas."

"He's a real Texan. I'm a transplant."

"Fair enough." I fished out a piece of ice with my straw. "Same question for you. Go."

Patrick exhaled. "Well, I play poker with friends on Friday nights. I play a mean game of street hockey."

"Hockey?"

"Weird, that caught the Minnesotan's interest?"

I rolled my eyes. "What position?"

"Mostly left wing, but I fill in wherever they need me." Patrick leaned back in his seat. "I enjoy cooking, believe it or not. And I love live music. There's a little pub near my place that has local bands every weekend."

I assessed him. He seemed normal. He was good looking. He had interesting hobbies. "Why the hell are you at an island matchmaking retreat, Patrick?"

Patrick laughed. "Should I take that as a compliment?"

"Or a sign that your Tinder profile is a little too perfect."

The waiter brought our drinks, and we paused our conversation for a moment. When he left, Patrick leaned in. "Yeah.

Well, our pack is small. We're kind of in the middle of nowhere."

"And you can't travel *if it's worth it?*" I felt a surge of adrenaline rush through me. I'd never been this forward with men before. Since I had zero desire to impress any of them, it opened me up to saying what was on my mind. It was intoxicating.

Patrick grinned. "Our pack doesn't have the best reputation."

I raised an eyebrow and picked up a chip myself. "Now I'm intrigued."

"Then I better stop talking."

I took a sip. "Yeah, save your secrets for one of the other actually eligible maidens."

Screams broke out to our right, and I glanced up to find two women in bikinis chicken fighting in the pool, their thighs pressed against the ears of two men who were grinning like idiots. One of them was most definitely Lukas.

That tracked.

"You could have fun, you know. Even if you don't want a mate." Patrick's thumb slipped down the side of his glass.

Fun. I'd tried that hadn't I? I'd done everything Luna Bay had asked me to, and the only thing it'd gotten me was a panic attack.

I continued to scan the pool area. It had gotten busier since we'd come out. People milled about, chatting and laughing as they lounged on deck chairs. A group was playing some sort of drinking game at a table near the bar, and two couples sat in the hot tub, steam rising around them like they were in a tropical snow globe.

"I could." I tapped my glass. But having fun was dangerous. It meant heightened emotions and . . . . expectations. "But I think I'm good."

"Kate!"

I looked up. Willow and KB waved at me from a set of loungers. They had changed into swimsuits, Willow in a bright coral bikini and KB in a sleek one-piece that looked like it belonged in a sportswear catalog.

"Mind if I—?"

Patrick shook his head, a flicker of disappointment crossing his face. "No, of course."

I thanked him, then grabbed my glass and left the bar area and crossed the pool deck, plopping down on the lounger next to my friends.

"This place is growing on me." KB sighed dramatically.

Willow nodded. "Right? I feel like I'm in a movie or something." She took a sip from her drink, which was some kind of tropical cocktail with a slice of pineapple and a cherry on top.

I crossed my legs. "If they had cell service, I'd be sold."

"I thought about leaving my phone at home, but figured it was at least worth having for the flight."

I frowned. "Wait, you knew there wasn't going to be WiFi?"

Willow raised an eyebrow. "You didn't know that?"

I shook my head.

KB smirked. "Yeah, the whole point of this place is to unplug. No phones, no emails, no distractions. Disconnect so you can connect. Just you and your mate."

I drank as Willow and KB spilled the tea on their partners for the night. They knew about as much as I did about Patrick, but Willow was at least interested in Alec.

The poolside area started to empty out as the night grew late. The crowd thinned, and the lively atmosphere shifted to a quieter, more subdued ambiance. Patrick had long since left our table, and when I glanced over, he met my eyes from the bar.

I gripped the edge of my lounger, my palms sweaty. "We

should probably head back to the hut." My voice sounded more casual than I felt. Willow nodded, and KB put out a fist.

"Solidarity."

I laughed and bumped it, then stood and walked along the edge of the pool.

Patrick was already there waiting for me. He gave me a questioning look, but I strode past him and made a beeline for the path that led back to our hut. Before I knew it, we were standing in front of the door.

I didn't wait for Patrick to open it. His eyes were glassy, and he was struggling to pull the card from his pocket. I grabbed the key from my purse and unlocked the door myself.

The space felt smaller now that it was fully dark out. I went straight to the bathroom, not even bothering to turn on the light as I washed my face. Patrick moved around behind me. I heard the sound of his shoes hitting the floor, the rustle of fabric as he changed out of his clothes.

I used a towel to pat my skin dry, then grabbed my toothbrush from the toiletry bag.

"That was fun, right?" Patrick's voice was unexpectedly close. I jumped, dropping my toothbrush into the sink.

"Yeah, totally." I picked it up and rinsed it off, then squirted toothpaste onto the bristles.

Patrick leaned against the doorframe, his arms crossed over his chest. "You looked like you were having *fun* with your friends."

I nodded, my mouth full of minty foam. "Mmhmm."

Patrick watched me for a moment, then sighed. "I'm not going to bite, you know."

I spit into the sink, then rinsed my mouth. "I know. It's just —" I gestured vaguely, not sure how to explain the knot of anxiety that had been growing in my chest since we'd left the pool.

Patrick raised an eyebrow. "Just what?"

I turned off the faucet and wiped my mouth on a towel. "Just weird. That's all."

Patrick chuckled. "You mean an adult summer camp isn't normal?"

I smiled in spite of myself. He was funny. Easy to talk to. If this was my normal life, we'd probably be friends at least.

I thought of the way his hands had felt on my hips when he turned me around and spread paint on my back. *You're a mystery, Kate.*

I'd be lying if I said a part of me didn't consider moving closer to him. I was sure he'd feel good. That he'd be willing to make me feel good for the night.

But the idea of being with anyone made my stomach twist. Well. Not *anyone.*

I shivered as he pushed off the doorframe and walked over to his bed, plopping down on top of the sheets. "First challenge is tomorrow."

"Yeah. What do you think it will be?" I turned off the bathroom light and walked over to my bed, slipping under the cool sheets. I curled up on my side, facing the wall, and tried to calm my racing heart.

"No clue. But we're definitely going to win."

I turned my head and smiled.

Patrick stretched out on his back, his hands behind his head. "You know, if you wanted to make this less weird, you could always come over here and—"

"Goodnight, Patrick."

Patrick laughed. "Goodnight, Kate."

CHAPTER

ELEVEN

The next morning, I finished my breakfast and stood from the table as Patrick quickly shoved a sausage link and scrambled eggs into his mouth. He swallowed and caught up to me and Willow as we strode toward the door. "What special skills do you have? We didn't get the chance to talk about it last night."

I stopped, frowning. "What are you talking about?"

"It's you and me. Bestie. We need to know who can do what."

"We don't even know what the challenge is."

Patrick made a point to sound exasperated when he said, "You're not taking this nearly as seriously as I am."

I shot him a look as we walked onto the beach. I stepped up next to Willow who looked like she was in her element. I had at least transitioned over to wearing khaki shorts and tank tops instead of business casual.

Willow scanned the line of contestants and grinned when she found Alec, who stood next to Lindsey. She waltzed over to him, and within a few minutes, everyone was standing in their pairs from the night before.

A light breeze rustled the palm fronds above, and I breathed in the fresh morning air. Patrick was practically bouncing on his toes next to me. "What do you think it'll be?"

"Hopefully making mixed drinks."

He shot me a look. "Maybe we have to wrestle a crocodile or something. They said they were trying to reconnect us with our wolves."

"I don't think crocodiles live in the Bahamas."

He scoffed. "They'd fly it in. Obviously." Patrick laughed at his own joke, and I couldn't help but absorb a bit of his infectious energy.

I glanced up, scanning for KB, and that's when I saw him. Lukas. He was standing next to Elise, and they were talking animatedly. Or, she was talking animatedly? He was nodding and occasionally looking in her direction.

That winning smile was back on his face. His fingers looped in his pockets. Was he *that* into her?

Lukas must have felt my gaze because he looked up. Our eyes locked, and for a moment, it was as if the world narrowed to just the two of us. My heart skipped a beat, and I quickly glanced away, pretending to be interested in a seashell on the sand.

I could still feel his eyes on me, but I refused to give him the satisfaction of looking back. Thankfully, Trinity walked out in front of us, standing next to a flag emblazoned with the Luna Bay logo. Her brightly colored island wear fluttered in the breeze, her long braids swaying as she raised the megaphone to her lips. "Good morning! I hope you all slept well because today, we're starting with a bang."

The sound of ocean waves crashing against the shore mixed with the murmur of excited voices.

"Today, you're going to be stranded on an abandoned beach," Trinity announced, her eyes sparkling with mischief. "But don't worry, we're not that cruel. We're giving you tandem kayaks."

My heart skipped a beat. *Tandem kayaks?* I'd never even been in a regular kayak, let alone one where I had to coordinate with another person.

Patrick nudged me. "This is going to be epic."

I nodded, not trusting myself to speak.

Trinity continued, "You'll start on the beach, and your goal is to paddle through a series of checkpoints in the ocean. Each checkpoint will require you to solve a puzzle or complete a physical task before you can continue. The first couple to reach the final checkpoint and solve the final puzzle wins."

The crowd buzzed with excitement, and I couldn't help but feel a twinge of competitiveness. Not that I cared about winning for the prize. Who would I choose to room with? Probably just Patrick again, honestly. At least I knew he wouldn't bother me, and I did have an extremely restful night of sleep.

"But here's the catch," Trinity added, her grin widening. "This isn't a calm lake. This is the ocean. You'll need to be in perfect synchronicity with your partner to navigate the waves and currents. And remember, safety first. Life jackets are mandatory."

I swallowed hard, imagining the open water stretching out before us. The thought of paddling into the unknown, relying on Patrick and him relying on me, sent a thrill down my spine.

Trinity waved us forward. "Alright, everyone. Head over to the speedboats. They're going to drop you off at the starting point. Good luck, and may the best couple win!"

Speedboats waited along the dock, their hulls bobbing gently in the water. The captains helped each of us in, presenting us with bottled spring water and reef-safe sunscreen.

KB sat next to me on the leather seats. Orion, her partner, and Alec sat on our opposite sides.

"This is going to be interesting," I murmured, squeezing out a dollop of SPF 50 into my palm.

KB nodded, her eyes scanning the horizon. "I don't know about you, but I'm already regretting my life choices."

I laughed, spreading the sunscreen across my arms.

KB shook her head, her dark hair swaying. "Seriously. And the whole tandem kayak thing? I can barely coordinate with myself, let alone another person."

I grinned. "Well, at least we get to bond with our partners over our mutual incompetence."

Patrick took off his shirt, rubbing the sunscreen over his toned chest. It's not that he wasn't good-looking. He was. But he didn't grab me. Not like. . .

I turned my head, taking in the boat next to us as the staff pushed us free of the dock. Lukas threw his head back and laughed. His partner put a hand on his bicep. I turned back to KB and swallowed hard.

A man wearing a Wolf Island shirt handed us blindfolds, and I raised an eyebrow. "Seriously?"

"Seriously." He grinned. "No peeking."

I'd worn more blindfolds in the last week than the rest of my life combined. I pulled the fabric over my eyes, and the world went dark. The smell of sunscreen filled my nostrils, mingling with the sea breeze. The boat rocked gently beneath me, and I gripped the edge of the seat.

"This is like a trust fall exercise, but with more potential for drowning," I muttered.

Patrick chuckled beside me. "Don't worry, if you go overboard, I'll notice the lack of complaining and come after you."

KB snorted, and I couldn't fight back my smile.

The engine roared to life, and the boat surged forward. My stomach did a little flip, and I took a deep breath, trying to steady my nerves. It was disorienting to only hear water splashing against the sides of the boat and feel the hum of the engine vibrating through the seat.

"Ugh. This is not making her happy."

I laughed. "Making who happy?"

KB—at least I thought it was KB—put a hand on my thigh as she leaned in. "My wolf."

I tensed, not quite sure how to respond. My thoughts plinked around like the inside of a kaleidoscope. She could feel her wolf? She had enough experience feeling her wolf that she knew how to interpret it?

"Kate?" KB felt around to make sure it was me and nearly grabbed my right boob.

I laughed. "It's me, sorry, that took me off guard."

"Why?" She still had to yell over the sound of the engine and the rush of water.

"I don't feel mine."

"Your wolf?"

I nodded, then realized she wouldn't be able to see the motion. I swiped a strand of hair from my lips and said, "Yes. I've never felt her."

Lie.

I blinked, wondering where that thought had come from. I hadn't, had I? Maybe a little here or there, but any inkling that she existed had quickly faded. It had been easy to push it away.

For the briefest moment, I wondered if anyone else was listening in on our conversation, but then figured if I could barely hear KB sitting directly next to me, I doubted they'd be able to make our words out.

"Never?" KB sounded shocked.

"I think it's pretty common." I suddenly felt defensive. *Or jealous?* No, not that, but I couldn't put my finger on what was making my chest cinch so tight. I didn't want my wolf. I'd seen what came with that in my parent's generation. They never quite seemed to fit in with the world around them. They had responsibilities as a pack, but also responsibilities to their wolves. They were gone on random nights of the month, they performed rituals in the woods behind our house that I wanted nothing to do with. All of it was mystical and strange.

At school one day—I think I was in seventh grade?—a kid named Tony Mack said he saw my dad naked at the lake. I called him a liar, but deep down I suspected it was probably true. When he showed me the picture on his cell phone, I knew it was.

Back then, I just wanted to fit in. Maybe our genetic abilities were a boon fifty years ago, but in this day and age where everything could be captured by a cell phone camera? Not so much.

But there was a small part of me that wondered. That tiny burst I'd felt back in the lounge. *Was that her?* Was she buried there deep within me?

My parents always talked about how connected they were to their wolves, how it was this monumental moment when they first shifted. And here I was, twenty-one, and I couldn't distinguish between my wolf and a gas bubble.

"It is common." KB's voice snapped me back to the current boat, blindfold situation. "I was surprised when I first shifted."

I swallowed hard, my throat suddenly dry. "When did it happen for you?"

KB sighed. "Only two years ago."

I wasn't totally sure how old she was, but my guess was that we were within a year of each other in either direction.

The boat hit another wave, and I gripped the edge of the

seat tighter. "Is there any benefit?" It's the question I would never have asked my parents. They spoke all the time about how they couldn't live without their abilities. But I wanted to hear about it from someone who hadn't been shifting for forty years.

I nearly jumped when KB leaned into me. "Sorry." She laughed as we jostled against each other. "I just didn't want to announce this to the whole boat."

"Sure." I wrapped an arm around her waist so we were at least bouncing together.

"Full disclosure. It's not always easy. But I do have one thing that I think is because of my wolf."

My ears perked. "What's that?"

KB hesitated. "I have this ability to sense the strength of the shifters around me. It's like I can feel their presence, even if I can't see them." She paused a moment. "It doesn't happen all the time. Only when I'm really in tune with my wolf, which, let's be honest, is almost never."

"Still." I wondered what it would be like to have that kind of private information about someone. "Just their wolves?"

She shook her head. "I don't know yet. Yes? Maybe? It sounds cheesy, and I will never admit to saying this, but I think it's more the strength of their soul. I don't know. Never mind."

"No, it's not cheesy." Somehow having this conversation with my eyes closed felt easier, but I couldn't believe I was hearing it from KB and not Willow. She seemed like someone who would be completely in touch with her spiritual side. "Thank you. I don't know anything about this stuff." For a second I felt like I had in eighth grade when Marci Wood told me what a blow job was.

"I wouldn't even be thinking about this, but she flared up this week," KB said.

I frowned. "When?"

"At the reception. Before I came to your table that first night."

I frowned. "Do you know what caused it?"

She exhaled. "I think it's a couple of people, actually."

"Who?" My heart picked up speed. I didn't even need to hear her answer. Somehow I already know that she was going to say—

"Orion. Paul. Lukas."

I pondered that. It made sense. Maybe that was why I'd responded the way I had? If he was a strong alpha, of course I'd felt that energy.

Relief washed over me as the drone of the engine lowered in pitch, and then we were dropped at the beach. Our blind-folds were removed and all of us were outfitted with life jack-ets, hats, more sunscreen, snacks, and water. I slathered the white cream over my arms and legs, watching the sun glisten on the water. Gulls cried out in the distance, and my pulse quickened. I hadn't competed for anything since my applica-tion to law school, and the excitement and nerves were a heady combination.

Patrick and I grabbed our kayak as soon as we were given the go-ahead, then carried it down to the water. He kept up the commentary as we set it along the shore. I laughed and nodded, even though my stomach was twisting into knots. Whoever won got to choose their partner for the night, which didn't exactly feel monumental. Honestly, seeing so many others obviously interested in finding a mate here on the island sent a pang of guilt through my middle. Anytime they were partnered with me, they were wasting a night.

So who would I choose if we won? That sent enough anxiety shooting through my veins, I almost wanted to refuse to get in the damn kayak.

"We're going to win this, Kate." Patrick stretched his arms

over his head as we lined up next to the other contestants. I groaned internally.

Trinity stood on the back of one of the speed boats. She did a little dance and held up the megaphone. "Contestants ready?" Cheers erupted around me, Patrick's included. "On your marks, get set, go!"

CHAPTER

TWELVE

The next few minutes were a chaotic blur. Everyone scrambled to get into their kayaks and push off from the shore. Sevina slipped on the wet sand and went headfirst into the water, her curses echoing in the morning air. I froze, wondering if I should help her, but then Patrick was pulling me into our kayak. "No mercy! Time to go!"

I waded in as he held it steady, then climbed in and grabbed the paddle. Patrick jumped in behind me, and we were off. "Left, right, left, right!" he chanted, trying to get us in sync, but our paddles kept clacking against each other.

"Crap, sorry!" I huffed out a breath. I hadn't been in a kayak since I was twelve. Maybe thirteen? We had them at our cabin, but I was more interested in books than going out on the lake during my teenage years.

It took a few minutes to get in a rhythm, but once we did, we started to pull ahead. A few of the other kayaks struggled, but we were mostly in an even heat. Sevin and Lukas were just ahead of us. She was trying to wring out her clothes while

Lukas paddled hard enough for the both of them. *Okay, show off.*

The water was cool against my arms as I dipped my paddle in and pulled. My muscles burned, and as much as I hated to admit it, it was a good burn. A satisfying burn. I gritted my teeth and pushed harder. This wasn't at all about winning for me, but I didn't want to be the crappy partner. As much as I didn't care about impressing Patrick, I also didn't want to let him down. He'd been nice to me. That was worth something.

I spotted the flag first. It bobbed on the water, a vibrant red against the shimmering cerulean blue that stretched out to the horizon. "There!" I pointed with my paddle. Patrick grunted and dug his paddle into the water, increasing our speed.

The flag grew larger, and soon, we were close enough to see the floating raft it was attached to. Along with all the others. The red flag coordinated to the red stripe on our kayak. I frowned, immediately working to piece things together. Were we all getting the same clues? Were they just trying to prevent a traffic jam or paddle war?

Patrick guided our kayak alongside it, the wood bumping gently against our hull. "Steady," I murmured, trying to keep my balance as I reached for the object sitting on the raft.

The sun glinted off the water, sending sparkles dancing in my eyes. I squinted and pulled out a small locked box with a keypad and a piece of damp paper taped to the top.

I turned the box over in my hands. "It's locked."

Patrick leaned over and the kayak wobbled. "What does it say?"

I unfolded the paper, and my eyes immediately narrowed. I cleared my throat dramatically, reading aloud: "The more you take, the more you leave behind. What am I?"

Patrick frowned, then lifted a hand and rubbed the back of his neck. I gave him a second. I didn't want to make him feel like an idiot if he didn't know what it was. Since I most definitely did.

He looked up, distracted by the sound of other kayaks approaching their rafts. He clenched his jaw. "I don't know. Any guesses?"

Willow and Alec pulled up to the raft next to us, their kayak gliding gracefully. Next came Orion and KB, their paddles slicing through the water with precision. Orion reached for the clue, but KB beat him to it, her eyes scanning the paper quickly before shoving it at him.

I wet my lips. *Focus.* "Umm, yes. I think the answer is "steps.""

His eyes shot up to mine. He blinked. "Holy shit. Yeah. That makes sense. How did you—?"

I was already typing the word into the keypad on the front of the box. There was a soft click, and the lid popped open. Inside was a small piece of rolled-up parchment.

"Ta-da!" I pulled it out and grinned.

"Kate. Are you one of those people who has the New York Times game app on your phone?" Patrick assessed me.

"We don't have time for this, but yes." I held out the paper so he could read it.

Paddle toward the sun until you see the twin palms. There lies your next clue.

Patrick squinted toward the horizon, then pointed. "Sun's that way. Twin palms, here we come."

Max and Elise cut us off. "We're going that way," he barked, pointing in the opposite direction from where we were headed.

"I think—" Elise started, but Max was already paddling. The other groups had already started splitting off, each heading in a different direction.

"Wait, are none of them going the same way as us?" Patrick glanced over his shoulder at me.

"Don't question it. We have our clue."

Patrick nodded and we started off. It did make me nervous that we seemed to be heading off alone, but that clue couldn't be interpreted any other way. It had to be part of the challenge—see if we're stay true or question ourselves. I loved psychological games like that.

Something warm bloomed in my chest as we paddled. It could've been the sun. Or because Patrick called me a genius at least twice. Most likely it was the fact that he flipped off KB and Orion as we passed and KB splashed him in the face with a paddle full of water.

Was I having fun? Damn it. I wasn't supposed to be having fun, but I couldn't help myself. We paddled around the island, the sun climbing higher in the sky. My arms burned, the muscles in my shoulders and back screaming for relief. We kept hydrated, applied more sunscreen, and ate a few of the snacks Luna Bay provided. The waves were gentle, but persistent, lapping at the sides of our kayak and making every stroke feel like I was pushing against a wall of water.

I gritted my teeth and kept my strokes steady, trying to match Patrick's rhythm.

"Come on, we need to pick up the pace," he called over his shoulder.

I grunted in response, my paddle dipping into the water with a splash. "I'm going as fast as I can. Contrary to popular belief, I'm not a professional rower."

He laughed. "Sorry. I'm a bit competitive."

"Never would've guessed." I panted. "How are you keeping this up?" Patrick hadn't taken one break.

"Hey, bartending requires a lot of arm strength. You try shaking cocktails for eight hours straight."

I laughed. Secondary *damn it*. I was starting to think Patrick was *okay*.

For a solid twenty minutes, the only sounds were the splash of our paddles. The shore was a blur of green and gold, the palm trees swaying in the breeze. Finally, Patrick spotted something bobbing in the water ahead of us. "There!" he pointed with his paddle, and I followed his gaze. A buoy with a small treasure chest attached to it floated on the waves, the wood dark and weathered.

We paddled closer, and I reached out, my fingers brushing against the damp wood. I grabbed the chest and pulled it onto the kayak, the saltwater dripping onto my legs. I popped open the lid and pulled out a scroll of parchment, tied with a piece of twine.

I untied the twine and unrolled the parchment. The words were inked in that familiar, swirling script:

WHERE THE ISLAND'S *heights greet the sky,*
And shadows fall from something tall,
Find the one that stands like a knight,
And look beneath where echoes call.

PATRICK RAISED AN EYEBROW. "WORK YOUR MAGIC."

I laughed. "I don't think this one takes a genius. 'Where the island's heights greet the sky.' Sounds like cliffs."

Patrick squinted out over the water. "Yeah, but there are cliffs all around. What about the 'something tall'? That could be anything."

I glanced around, trying to make sense of it. From where we were floating, I could see a few distinct cliffs towering over the shoreline. "Okay, let's just paddle toward the most obvious cliffs. Maybe we'll figure it out when we get closer."

Patrick shrugged, digging his paddle into the water. "Worth a shot. Let's head toward those ones over there." He gestured to the south, where the cliffs rose higher than anywhere else on the horizon.

We started paddling, the kayak cutting through the water with each stroke. My muscles burned, but there was a determination in my strokes now—the thrill of solving the puzzle pushing me forward. As we drew closer to the cliffs, I squinted at the jagged rock formations. Something about the way one of them jutted out caught my attention.

"Hold on." I paused mid-paddle. "Look at that." I pointed toward the tallest cliff. "Does that rock formation look a little like a person to you?"

Patrick cocked his head, following my line of sight. His eyes widened. "It looks like he's holding a sword." He turned back and grinned.

We paddled closer, the towering rock formation looming above us. From this angle, the resemblance was uncanny. The cliff did look like a knight, tall and proud, his head tilted forward as if watching over the sea.

"Okay, so look beneath where echoes call?"

I scanned the base of the cliff, my eyes narrowing as I spotted something. "There." I pointed toward a dark opening just above the waterline.

We paddled closer, approaching the mouth of the cave. "The roof is way too low," Patrick muttered, his brow furrowing. "There's no way we can paddle the kayak inside."

I sighed, staring at the dark water lapping at the rocks. The cave opening was barely large enough for a person, let alone a kayak. The only way to get in was to swim. "One of us is going to have to go in."

Patrick turned, his usual cocky smile slipping back into place. "You might be a genius. But I can hold my breath for over a minute."

"Umm, how do you know this?"

He winked. "Maybe I'll show you later."

I rolled my eyes. Such a flirt. "Just get the clue and try not to get eaten by anything, alright?"

Patrick tossed off his shirt, leaving it in the kayak, and slipped into the water, his muscles rippling as he swam toward the cave's entrance. I watched, my breath catching slightly as he disappeared beneath the shadow of the cliff.

I gripped the side of the kayak, my knuckles white, trying to keep my impatience in check. The gentle bob of the water did little to calm me, and my eyes stayed fixed on the shadowy entrance where he'd vanished. Every ripple, every small splash in the distance had me holding my breath.

"Come on," I muttered under my breath, glancing up at the cliffs looming above me. It was safe in there, right? They wouldn't ask us to do something that wasn't safe. Unless that was how they were going to try and force our wolves out of us? The blood drained from my face.

Was this one of those stories? We go to an island seeking love, and then one by one, we're killed off? I ran my hands through my hair. I'd watched way too many movies. This was fine. *He was fine.*

Seconds felt like minutes. Minutes felt like hours. I shifted in the kayak, adjusting the paddle in my lap, my eyes darting back to the cave again. What was taking him so long?

I started to panic. I was not capable of dragging a dead, bloated Patrick from the ocean floor. My breathing started to become erratic when, finally, a ripple broke the surface of the water, and Patrick's head popped up near the mouth of the cave.

"That was longer than a minute!" I shouted, half relieved, half annoyed.

Patrick swam toward the kayak, grinning like a kid who'd just found a secret stash of candy. "You're gonna love this." He held up something small and shiny.

He grabbed onto the edge of the kayak, treading water. I leaned closer. He held a small, ancient-looking coin. Etched into its surface was a symbol of some sort, and underneath it, in elegant script, were the words: *Return to beach.*

I frowned. "That's it? No more clues?"

Patrick shook his head, flipping the coin over in his hand. "Nope. But there's this." He pointed to the back, where a few simple directions were scrawled, leading us back to what had to be the resort.

I threw out my hands. "We did it?"

Patrick laughed. "We did it." He hoisted himself up, nearly flipping the kayak in the process. I leaned as far as I could to the other side while he scrambled in. He flicked the water out of his hair, not even bothering to put on his shirt or life jacket.

We paddled hard, heading toward the beach with Patrick giving directions. Just as we rounded the bend, I caught sight of another kayak up ahead, closer to the shore. My heart sank. Willow and Alec.

Patrick spotted them at the same time I did. He turned with a competitive gleam in his eyes. "Race you to the beach?"

I didn't need to be asked twice. We both threw our weight into the paddles, our kayak slicing through the water, closing the distance between us and Willow's boat. They turned to us, their eyes wide. Willow's laugh carried over the water, and Alec's voice rang out as they scurried to build momentum.

But they didn't stand a chance.

Patrick and I paddled in sync, our kayak gaining speed with every stroke. My arms felt like jelly, but I refused to stop. We overtook them just as we neared the shore, the nose of our kayak scraping against the sand a split second before theirs.

"Woo!" Patrick raised his paddle in the air, grinning from ear to ear. "We did it!"

I couldn't help the satisfied smile that spread across my face. I stood up shakily, my muscles burning protest as I stepped out of the kayak and onto the beach.

But my victory high didn't last long.

I glanced up toward the beach chairs, expecting to see excitement or maybe some applause. Instead, my heart sank as I spotted Lukas and Sevina already lounging by the water, looking impossibly relaxed. Sevina was sipping something fruity with a little umbrella in it, while Lukas was reclined with his hands behind his head, a tray of food at his side.

"Oh, you've got to be kidding me," I groaned, stopping in my tracks.

Patrick followed my gaze, his grin faltering. "No way. How did they beat us?"

I shook my head, feeling a mix of disbelief and frustration bubble up inside me. "I don't know, but apparently, they've been here long enough to order drinks."

Lukas caught my eye and, of course, flashed me a smug grin from his lounge chair as if to say, *is that energetic enough for you?* He raised his glass in a silent toast, his eyes glinting with amusement.

There was that twinge again. I swallowed hard, then turned and worked with Patrick to drag the kayak and our paddles far enough onto the sand for them to stay put. We slumped next to it, catching our breath. I bent over, hands on my knees, and then ran a hand through my saltwater-damp hair. My skin was gritty with sweat and sea spray, and I longed for a hot shower.

"Great work, guys!"

I looked up to see a crew member holding out bottles of water. I accepted one gratefully and twisted off the cap. I took a quick swig, then poured the rest over my head and scrubbed my face.

Patrick did the same, and we both sat there, dripping and breathing heavily.

"Looks like we have a buffet waiting for us." Patrick nodded toward a table set up under a palm tree at the edge of the beach. It was loaded with tropical fruits, grilled seafood, and what smelled like coconut rice.

My stomach growled loudly. "I'm starving."

We trudged up the beach as Willow and Alec were bringing their kayak up onto the sand. KB and Orion were nearly to the beach, but I didn't see anyone else.

"Do you think they had trouble finding the clues?" I asked as we reached the table and grabbed plates.

Patrick shrugged. "Who knows? Maybe they didn't solve the riddles as fast." He nudged my elbow and I grinned.

I scooped a pile of shrimp kebabs onto my plate and added a serving of pineapple and mango slices. I didn't realize how famished I was until I took the first bite. The shrimp was perfectly grilled, with just a hint of smokiness, and the pineapple was juicy and sweet.

Patrick and I found a spot in the shade to sit and eat, and we watched as the other couples started to arrive. KB and Orion dragged their kayak onto the beach, then joined Willow and Alec at the buffet.

I finished my last bite of shrimp and leaned back, wiping my hands on the wet hem of my t-shirt. The sun felt good on my muscles, and for a moment, I let myself relax, just listening to the sound of soft chatter and the hush of waves.

Not the worst.

"Attention, everyone!" Trinity's voice snapped me out of

my reverie. I sat up, squinting against the sunlight, and saw her standing next to the rock outcropping at the end of the beach. The last couple was pulling their blue-striped kayak up onto the sand.

Patrick and I sat up.

"Congratulations on finishing the challenge! You all did an amazing job. Did you all have fun?" She paused, and impressively, the cheers were almost as loud as they were first thing that morning. Trinity's eyes sparkled. "As you know, there can only be one winner."

Groans sounded around us, and someone tossed a used napkin at Lukas. He batted it away with a grin.

Trinity took a deep breath, then smiled. "I'm pleased to announce that the winners of today's challenge are Lukas and Sevina!"

I couldn't help but notice the way Sevina's eyes lit up as she looked at Lukas.

"Do we choose in order?" Patrick asked.

"Hmm?"

"Like, after they choose, do we get to choose next?"

I blinked. That had never once occurred to me. My heart started to race, and I turned back to Lukas and Sevina walking toward Trinity at the front. Lukas looked completely composed. His dark hair was tousled from the wind and water, and his shirt clung to his chest.

I waited for Trinity to say something else—to make it clear that only the first place winners had a choice in partners for the night. Then I started thinking about who I'd get paired with if I didn't choose, and my vision started to blur. *Lose, lose.*

Trinity held up a hand for silence. "As the winners, Lukas and Sevina get to choose new partners for tonight's pairing. Sevina, who would you like to partner with?"

Sevina looked like she was about to say something, but

before she could, Lukas stepped forward. "Sorry, Trinity, if you don't mind, I'd like to choose first."

Trinity smirked and nodded. "Of course. Go ahead, Lukas."

Sevina gave a smug grin. I rolled my eyes. Classic. He wanted to impress her and—

"Kate." My head snapped up. Lukas was staring directly at me. "I'd like to partner with Kate."

THIRTEEN

TALKBACKS

O RION

ZARA: So Orion, tell me about that kayak challenge with KB. Looked like you two were getting pretty cozy out there on the water.

Orion: Yeah, KB's great. We really hit it off during the challenge. We may have gotten a little . . . distracted at one point.

Zara: Hmm. Distracted?

Orion: She's got strong energy.

Zara: Willow seemed to think you weren't interested in her.

Orion: Uh, not sure about that.

Zara: Any reason?

Orion: Hmm. Willow felt awkward. I was trying to make sure she knew I wasn't entangled.

Zara: Are you entangled now?

Orion: It's only the second week, so.

Zara: But you do want to find a mate?

Orion: If it happens it happens, I guess.

~

PAUL

ZARA: Hey, Paul. How are—

Paul: Do you have any statistics on how often the couples here typically work out?

Zara: Nearly a hundred percent. When the mating bond snaps into place.

Paul: Right.

Zara: Do you know anyone who's experienced a mating bond?

Paul: My parents.

Zara: I think that's most people here. No friends, though?

Paul: No.

Zara: Maybe you'll be the first?

~

ELISE

Zara: Elise. How are you doing?

Elise: Just a little overwhelmed by everything, I guess. The full moon isn't helping.

Zara: Don't worry, we have plans for that.

Elise: Ooh, what kind of plans?

Zara: We'll announce it—

Elise: I'm great with secrets.

Zara: Are you?

Elise: Absolutely. I know so much about the people here, and I haven't told a soul.

Zara: Oh, what do you know?

Elise: Ha. I see what you're doing.

Zara: No, I already know everything. Your secrets are safe with me.

Elise: Then you know Max brought mushrooms? Or that David once got arrested for having sex in the back of an apple cart?

Zara: . . .

~

MAX

Zara: Max. How are you?

Max: Great. How long ago did Kate go in there?

Zara: Oh, she didn't do a talk-back this afternoon.

Max: Hm. I thought I saw her come in here. She kind of lives here, doesn't she?

Zara: She may have come into the building. I've been—

Max: No, that's fine. Just curious.

Zara: About Kate?

Max: Not about Kate, per se. More about why Lukas chose Kate.

Zara: Right. I heard about that. What do you think?

Max: Uh, he wanted to bag the most difficult she-wolf here? That's my guess.

Zara: You think Kate's difficult.

Max: She obviously doesn't want to be here. And Lukas only wants a conquest.

Zara: Oh?

Max: He has that face, you know?

FOURTEEN

Sevina's violet eyes widened in shock as Lukas announced he was partnering with me for the night. She frowned and leaned over to Trinity, then pointed at Patrick. Trinity called his name, and I turned to him, my mouth agape.

"Well, that was unexpected," he said with a half-smile. His green eyes danced with amusement, but I could see confusion underneath.

"Mmhmm." *Did Patrick look a little disappointed?* "You were a good partner today." I put out my hand, and he awkwardly shook it.

He glanced up at Lukas, then turned back to me. "Do you— is there something going on with you two?"

I shook my head. "Not in the least."

"Huh." Patrick adjusted the plate on his lap.

Nerves churned in my stomach. What was Lukas playing at? He'd barely looked at me since that night around the fire. Though I hadn't made myself easy to find. I picked at the rest of my lunch, barely tasting it as my mind spun. As I stood to place my dishes on the cart, KB and Willow came over and linked their arms through mine.

"Come on, let's go for a walk," KB said, her braids swinging. "I need to digest before I explode."

Willow laughed and tugged me along as we made our way out of the open-air dining room and onto the white sand beach. The afternoon sun was warm on my shoulders as we strolled along the shoreline, the turquoise waves lapping gently. I tried not to make a big deal about shaking out my sandals every few steps.

"So, Alec is like, insanely hot," Willow gushed. "Kayaking with him was . . . " She pursed her lips together. "I thought I might combust when he took his shirt off."

I grinned, grateful they weren't immediately wanting to talk about what just happened. And while I personally wasn't interested in finding love, I was thrilled that Willow was getting the experience she wanted.

KB fanned herself dramatically, and Willow tried to reach across me to smack her hand. She missed. We walked far enough away that the conversation and music were hushed.

Then Willow bumped my hip with hers. "Can we talk about what just happened?"

I pursed my lips. What was there to say?

"What did you do that made him pick you?" KB gave me a look.

I let out a huff of air, wondering how much I should say. "Last week, he asked why I was here, and I told him the truth. That I'm trying to get my law school tuition covered and have no interest in finding a mate. But we haven't had a real conversation since."

At least not with words. I imagined his paintbrush on my skin. His eyes watching me through the flickering flames. *It was only his alpha energy.*

KB laughed. "Rookie move, Kate! You may as well have said, 'Look at me! I'm a nut that needs cracking!'"

I scoffed. "I was being clear—"

"Clear that you'll be a challenge! He's an alpha. Men like him love that shit. He's not going to stop until he gets you in bed." KB stopped next to a palm tree while I worked to keep the panic off my face. Is that what had happened? Had Lukas suddenly become interested in me because he thought *I* was untouchable?

Willow was reigning in the giddiness. "Kate, I don't care if you want a mate. You have to at least—"

"I'm not doing anything with Lukas!" I planted my hands on my hips to keep my hands from shaking. Just the idea of Lukas wanting anything physical was giving me heart palpitations. What was it about him? KB watched me, and our previous conversation on the boat played back in my head. *I wouldn't even be thinking about this, but she flared up last night . . .*

Willow twisted a tendril of hair around her finger. "The other night. At the bonfire."

I nodded. We hadn't talked about it besides me claiming to have the flu. "I'm fine. I think I drank too much."

Willow glanced at KB, then smiled. "Well, just enjoy the eye candy, at least! Even if nothing else happens, getting to ogle that specimen all night is reward enough."

I laughed, but my stomach flipped at the thought. An entire night, just me and Lukas. I needed a drink. I needed two drinks.

As we walked back into the sprawling resort complex, KB and Willow peeled off toward their rooms with cheerful waves. "See you at dinner!" Willow called. "Wear something sexy!"

I rolled my eyes but couldn't help grinning as I made my way to the room I had shared with Patrick last night. Thankfully, he wasn't there when I entered. I wasn't in the mood for awkward small talk. There was a note on the door with instructions for leaving our luggage for the porters to be moved to our newly assigned huts. It was impressive that they were going to clean and organize everything in just the few hours we were at dinner.

I stepped inside and switched my sandals. Grabbing a notepad from the desk, I scribbled a quick message:

Patrick - Grabbing a shower. Nothing personal, but not looking for company while I'm in my birthday suit. I'll be fast. Great paddling today.
- Kate

I STUCK the note to the outside of the bedroom door and gathered a plush towel and some toiletries. As I stepped under the hot spray of the rainfall shower head, I tried to calm my jittery nerves.

It's just dinner. And drinks. And an ENTIRE NIGHT. With a guy you barely know but who makes your heart race in a way you've never felt before. No big deal.

Determined to at least look good, even if I was a mess on the inside, I took my time getting ready. I dried my dark hair until it fell in loose waves down my back. I chose a strappy sundress in a rich teal hue that complimented my olive skin and put on some light makeup—just enough to make my eyes pop.

I didn't want to impress him. Maybe punish him a little? If he thought he could call my name and I'd fall into bed with him, he was gravely mistaken. Or was he serious about his deal? About us sticking together to avoid finding mates?

Something inside me screamed that was a terrible idea, but there was nothing to do about it now. At least not tonight.

Surveying myself in the mirror, I took a slow, deep breath. Then I stepped out into the bedroom, packed my last few things, and threw my dirty clothes into the laundry bag. I crammed a few toiletry essentials into my purse, then placed my bags by the front door. Steeling my spine, I walked out to meet the others at the pool for cocktail hour.

The sun was just starting to dip towards the horizon, painting the sky in streaks of orange and pink. Twinkling fairy lights were strung up around the patio, and the gentle splash of the infinity pool mingled with the laughter and chatter of the other guests.

I spotted Lukas immediately, his tall frame and dark hair unmistakable even turned to the side. He was listening to something Orion was saying, a half-smile on his chiseled face. Sevina and Elise were draped over the arms of his chair, their swimsuit cover-ups leaving little to the imagination. Lukas didn't seem to be distracted in the least.

Tearing my eyes away, I went to where Willow was perched on a stool at the outdoor bar. She grinned at me and patted the seat next to her.

"Look at you, gorgeous! Lukas won't be able to take his eyes off you."

"Not exactly what I was going for," I muttered, climbing up beside her. "I don't think it matters, though. He hasn't even glanced my way."

Willow signaled the bartender. "Two mojitos, please! Who knows. Maybe he's trying to play hard to get."

"It won't work."

Willow raised an eyebrow.

I frowned. "What's that supposed to mean?"

"Nothing." She put her napkin in her lap, then winked at me and turned to the server approaching our table. This place had the fastest drink service I'd ever seen.

He set them down on the table, and I took a sip from the swirled glass.

Willow leaned over the table. "You never told me much about your life back home."

I latched onto the distraction gratefully. "Mmm. Not much to talk about."

"Which means there's *so* much to talk about."

I laughed. "Okay. I have three siblings, an older brother and sister, then one younger brother." I immediately skipped over Lee in my head and moved to the safer topic of Rachel. "My older sister lives in Omaha—"

"Mated?"

I shook my head. "She's in her residency. Pediatrician." I wasn't the only one scared off from finding a mate. I didn't know if Rachel even dated.

Willow exhaled. "I'm officially intimidated by your family."

"Oh, you shouldn't be. We're massive disappointments."

She laughed. "Because you're single?"

I motioned around us. "My dad offered to pay three years of law school tuition for me to be here." As I said it, that guilt settled back in. *I didn't owe him anything.* This was the deal. Just because he wanted me to find someone didn't mean it was the right choice for me. I said I'd come, I didn't say I'd try.

Willow's eyes widened. "Your dad sounds intense."

"My parents are the alphas of our pack."

"That's a lot of pressure."

I took another drink. "That's why I moved to Minneapolis."

She lifted her glass and clinked it against mine. "Here's to having fun then. At least for the next couple of weeks."

We ended up ordering another round and chatting until the sun fully set and the stars emerged, and I, at least, tried to pretend this was just a normal girls' night. Not the prelude to yet another arranged date with a man I barely knew.

Finally, as the outdoor lights brightened and a soft bell rang out across the patio, Willow set down her empty glass. "Guess that's our cue. Ready?"

I took one last fortifying sip, the alcohol settling warm in my belly. "As I'll ever be. Let's do this."

We hopped down from our stools, wobbling only slightly in our heeled sandals, and followed the crowd streaming into the open-air dining room.

The dining room was a vision, all gauzy white curtains billowing in the warm breeze and twinkling fairy lights strung up in the wooden rafters. Each table was set with flickering candles, artfully mismatched china, and small glass vases bursting with tropical blooms. It looked like something straight out of a wedding magazine spread.

I was so busy admiring the decor that I barely noticed the seating chart until Willow elbowed me. "Looks like this is where we part ways. Try to have fun, okay?" She gave me a quick hug before heading off to join her assigned group. She looked a bit nervous, and I felt bad I hadn't even thought to ask her about her possible pairings tonight.

Taking a deep breath, I scanned the elegant place cards until I found my own name. Table six. As I approached, I recognized David and Elise. I was starting to put most names with faces. They were leaning close together, whispering and laughing. And across from them, Paul. He looked up as I arrived, his eyes widening slightly as he took in my outfit.

"Hi." He stood to pull out my chair.

"Thank you." I took my seat, already dreading the next hour of conversation. Not because of Paul, but because of the others. Might as well start off getting them talking so I didn't have to. "Have you all had a chance to explore the island much?"

David leaned forward eagerly. "I went snorkeling this afternoon. The reef is incredible—I swear, I've never seen so many colors in my life."

"It's true," Elise chimed in. "We even swam with a couple of sea turtles. Though we had to be careful not to touch. They're quite skittish around shifters."

They went together. Interesting that David made it sound like he'd gone alone. Who else had been there?

This was who I'd become on this island. A nosy, drama-seeking missile since my brain had nothing else to focus on. I needed a good textbook.

The conversation flowed easily—a welcome surprise—as our first course arrived. I devoured the bright mango and avocado salad artfully arranged like stained glass on the plate while David and Elise shared stories of their packs. I tuned in anytime one of them mentioned their wolf. Clearly KB wasn't the only one who had experience with that.

Paul told us about his work as an environmental lobbyist, passionately describing a recent success in getting a parcel of land preserved from development. It was surprisingly interesting.

I forced myself not to look for Lukas even though the curiosity was killing me. The more I tried to ignore the compulsion, the more my mind circled back around to it. Finally, I gave myself permission to glance up as the main course of fresh seared fish arrived, fragrant with lime and chili. He was telling a story. His hands gesticulating. Totally focused and engaged. Maddening.

The fish was delicious, and dessert provided the perfect distraction as the waitstaff set down plates of passion fruit mousse topped with edible flowers so delicate, they looked like they might dissolve on contact. I closed my eyes in bliss at the first tangy-sweet spoonful, feeling some of my nerves settle.

The feeling was short-lived. No sooner had we set down our spoons than Mac took the small stage at the front of the room, megawatt smile firmly in place as he raised the mic.

"Let's hear it for the incredible Luna Bay staff!" he boomed as we all burst into applause. "Now, the moment you've all been waiting for—time to reveal tonight's special pairings!"

My stomach flipped as Mac began to call out names, but not because I was listening. Because Lukas was striding toward the stage. As he approached, Trinity leaned down and handed him two key cards. He whispered something to her and she laughed. When he turned he was still smiling, and then he looked up. For the first time, he met my gaze head-on.

He nodded his head toward the exit to the patio, and the muscles in my legs turned liquid. Lukas didn't wait. He strode out of the restaurant, and I quickly grabbed my purse.

"It was nice talking with you," I murmured to my table mates, surprised that I actually meant it, then made a hasty exit. Lukas was standing next to the pool, his hand in his pocket. My heels clacked on the stone, and when I was close, Lukas turned. His expression was unreadable as he extended an elbow. "Shall we?"

Heart pounding, palm almost slipping on the smooth fabric of his dress shirt, I took his arm and let him lead me toward the path. I was touching him. *Why was I touching him?* Something about the way he asked, it hadn't even occurred to me to say no.

Neither of us spoke as we followed the winding path through the swaying palms and flowering bushes, the tension stretching thick and heavy. I had so many questions for him, but considering the last time I spoke, I'd given him unneeded hangover advice, I opted to keep my mouth shut.

The heat of his body warmed my side, and I tugged on the hem of my dress. It was too short. I should've worn a full-length body suit.

"This is us." He pointed to a hut tucked back in the trees on the opposite side of the pool from where I'd stayed with Patrick the night before. Again I couldn't help but notice how his mouth moved around his vowels in foreign ways. I still couldn't quite place his accent. French? Eastern European? My breath caught in my throat as he dropped my arm and scanned the key.

Lukas pushed the door open and stepped aside, gesturing for me to enter. I crossed the threshold and moved forward so the door could click shut behind me. Suddenly, the reality of being alone with him hit me like a rogue wave, and I couldn't stop the nervous energy from skittering down my spine.

My luggage would be waiting in the bedroom, but I couldn't bring myself to move further into the bungalow. Instead, I watched as Lukas sauntered past me, completely at ease, and kicked off his shoes before settling onto the loveseat in the cozy living area.

The space was similar to the one I'd shared with Patrick—all beach chic and understated elegance, with clean lines and tasteful decor—but the atmosphere couldn't have been more different. I chewed on my bottom lip.

Lukas said nothing. Not a damn word. He leaned back against the sofa and closed his eyes. Anger built in my chest, and I couldn't take it anymore. My hands twisted together in front of me. "Why did you pick me, Lukas?"

He looked up at me, his blue eyes unreadable in the soft light. A heartbeat passed, then two, before he leaned back, draping an arm along the back of the loveseat. "Do you want to sit down?"

I hesitated, then crossed the room and perched on the edge of the cushion, angling my body toward him. He watched me, his gaze so intense I could almost feel it on my skin.

"We already talked about this," he said, his voice low and smooth.

I bristled. "No. You talked about it. Then didn't mention it for a week."

He shrugged. "I thought we were on the same page."

"That we don't want mates?" I scoffed, and he frowned.

"You changed your mind?"

I blinked at him. "No, Lukas. You flirt with everyone."

Lukas let out a puff of air. "I don't flirt."

"All you do is flirt. Constantly."

"With everyone?"

"Everyone except me." I squeezed my knees together. "That —that came out strange. I don't care. It's good. I'm glad you don't flirt with me."

Lukas assessed me. "Okay."

I nodded. "Okay." What the hell kind of answer was that? I thought back to him sitting between Sevina and Elise. How he didn't seem bothered by the cleavage two inches from his face. It was impressive. Or . . . *he wasn't interested.*

"Wait. Are you gay?" I couldn't believe I asked it out loud, but it made so much more sense than the alternative.

Lukas laughed out loud, then turned to me. "No." He ran a hand through his hair, relaxing back against the cushions.

"But you don't want a mate."

He nodded, assessing me. "You don't want a mate. Are you gay?"

I opened my mouth, then closed it again. "No, but—"

"But what?"

I gave an exasperated huff. "But I'm not—" I motioned to him. "I don't inspire the opposite sex the way you do."

He raised an eyebrow, and my cheeks flushed. "Or the members of the opposite sex you inspire are too insecure to do anything about it."

My lips parted, and for a moment, I couldn't breathe. Nobody had ever said anything like that to me before. Sitting there with his arm slung over the side of the chair, the dim lighting making his skin golden, saying things like that? He could *not* have been any more attractive.

Maybe I'd spoken too soon to Willow. If he was playing hard to get, he had a higher chance than I'd thought of being successful. I turned my body away from him, desperately trying to communicate to my lady parts that there was nothing of interest to our right.

Lukas let out a slow exhale. "When you said you were only here for the free tuition, I figured we could help each other out."

Surprise rippled through me. *He'd listened when I said that?* "Let me get this straight. You're acting like you want to sleep with everyone here—except me, as previously mentioned—but you actually aren't interested?"

"Not interested."

I swallowed. "In any of it?"

He turned his head. "I'm not celibate. If that's what you're asking."

My cheeks flamed. "No. I didn't think—"

"Are you blushing?"

My eyes widened. "Don't say that."

Lukas sat up. "Say what?"

"If someone's blushing you don't ask if they're blushing. It makes it worse."

The corner of his lip curled. His eyes slipped to my flushed skin. "What are you getting tuition for again?"

I wet my lips. "Law school." I liked it better when he was staring at his phone screen.

"Hmm." He leaned forward, clasping his hands over his knees. "So what do you think. Could we make a good partnership?"

No. We would not make a good partnership. He was too . . . everything.

But as I tried to form the words to turn him down, that same heat flared inside me, and I sucked in a breath, trying to calm the fluttering in my chest. And then I completely lost control over my tongue. "What would that look like?"

What the hell? I broke out into a cold sweat.

He shrugged. "We pretend to be interested in each other, keep winning challenges, and enjoy a month in paradise without any expectations."

I couldn't believe what I was hearing. It was like he'd read my mind, offering me the perfect solution. So why did I feel like I was roasting over a spit?

"Why are you here? If you aren't looking for love?" I asked. He knew my reason. Maybe if I understood more about his story, I wouldn't feel so off-kilter. *Alpha energy. It was only his alpha energy.*

He exhaled, the sound sending shivers down my spine. "Let's just say I have responsibilities back home that make a relationship impossible right now."

I raised an eyebrow. "Responsibilities? Like a girlfriend?" I sat up straighter. "Wait, is this a forbidden love situation? You love someone but your parents don't approve?" I could get on board with helping him there.

"Sure. Something like that."

"You're not going to tell me?"

His grin widened, and my heart stuttered. "Are you my partner or my therapist?"

"You wouldn't want me as your therapist."

Lukas' eyes dropped just a fraction, then landed back on mine. "Partners, then."

I nodded. Mmhmm. Sure. I could definitely do partners and not lose my shit every time he was close to me. Simple.

Lukas stood and started to unbutton his shirt.

"What are you doing?" I snapped.

He paused, looking down at me. "Getting ready for bed. Do you care which side of the room I take?"

I shook my head, and he continued opening his shirt, then sauntered into the bedroom.

CHAPTER

FIFTEEN

I blinked awake, the warm sunlight filtering in through the wooden blinds of our private beach hut. Across from me, Lukas stirred, his chiseled features softened by sleep. The awkwardness of our arrangement settled over me like a heavy blanket as we both sat up, avoiding eye contact.

"Good morning." Lukas' voice was gravelly.

"Good morning." I was grateful he wasn't looking at me. I was fairly sure I'd forgotten to wash off my makeup the night before. I probably had raccoon eyes.

Our discussion from the night before flooded through me. *Partners.* "We should probably talk about expectations," I ventured, my voice immediately tight.

Lukas raked a hand through his tousled hair. "Right. Ground rules." He met my gaze, those piercing blue eyes unreadable. "What do you think?"

I drew a deep breath, looking down at my hands. "We need to look like we're into each other, but nothing physical. Meals together, hanging out during the day." I tried to ignore the flutter in my stomach at the thought of playing at being a couple but was grateful for the absence of guilt. Pretending with Lukas meant I wasn't ruining anyone else's time here. They could all find their mates while he and I opted out, and I'd still get my tuition paid for.

But if he was just playing hard to get . . . *The brush on my skin. The pull of his gaze.* Then the image of Sevina sliding onto his lap.

I clenched my jaw and glanced up. "You'll probably need to tone down the—" I waved my hand at him.

He cocked his head. "The what?"

I swallowed hard. "All of that. You know. Your flirty energy."

His mouth curled. "Flirty energy?"

I groaned, dropping back to my pillow. I'd made a big deal out of this twice now, and he was still making me spell it out. "You know what I'm talking about."

He paused, then stood. "Got it. Tone down all of this."

I turned my head just in time to catch Lukas adjusting himself as he stood in front of the bed. I quickly snapped my head back.

"Do you need the shower?" He asked.

I shook my head, then regretted it instantly as he stalked into the bathroom. I didn't need the shower, but my bladder was about to burst. I stood and made my bed as soon as he disappeared behind the door, then laid out my outfit for the day.

A day off. I had no idea what we were going to do with all our time, but I hoped it would involve plenty of other people. I sat down on the bed and waited, but when I heard the shower turn on, I worried my lower lip. I could walk over to the restaurant and use the bathroom there, but that would require me to show my makeup smeared face and possibly pee myself on the path over.

I squinched my face and forced myself to walk to the bathroom door. I knocked lightly.

"Yeah?"

"Hey, can I use the toilet really quick?"

Lukas paused. "Uh, let me just get in the shower first."

My whole body tensed. He was naked behind the door. I dropped my hand to the handle. How long was I supposed to wait? And wasn't the toilet visible from the shower?

Just as I was about to exit the hut and find a bush or something, Lukas called out, "Okay."

My heart beat against my ribs as I opened the door. Just keep your eyes down. I walked in and turned left, my eyes boring into the floor tile. The splashes of water sent my blood thrumming. The toilet was tucked far enough back that I didn't think Lukas would be able to see me. I yanked down my pants and underwear and sat, and as soon as I lifted my head, I realized my mistake.

The mirror.

Lukas stood reflected there from head to toe. He angled his face into the spray, rubbing his hands through his wet hair. It was only a split second before I lowered my head, but that image was burned into my retinas. Hard muscle. The strong lines of his back. His upper thighs and—

I peed as fast as physically possible, praying he didn't turn around and look up. When I was finished, I pulled up my pants and rushed to the sink, keeping my eyes glued to the counter.

"You want to do breakfast?"

I jolted, and my eyes flicked up, catching another glimpse of him, this time looking directly at me. "Ummm, sure." I dried my hands, then spun and rushed to the door.

A few minutes later, thankfully after I'd finished changing, Lukas exited the bathroom, a towel wrapped around his waist. "Sorry. Forgot to grab clothes."

"It's fine. I'll give you some privacy." I slipped out of the room and closed the door behind me, then waited for Lukas to join me in the living room. He appeared a few moments later in a white polo and charcoal shorts. All I could see was tanned skin behind the shower glass.

"Ready?"

I nodded once, then walked to the door and slipped on my sandals.

We walked together to the restaurant, the salty sea breeze teasing my hair. As we entered, a few heads turned our way—Zara and Sophie, the member of the kitchen staff I'd met the day before, offered friendly waves.

And then Lukas was swarmed.

"Lukas, darling!" Sevina air kissed his cheeks as Elise simpered beside her. David and Max clapped him on the back like old chums.

I stood there awkwardly, no one seeming to notice my existence. Which was fine. Totally fine. I wasn't here to make friends anyway. I was about to turn when I felt a hand on mine. I glanced up as Lukas pulled me to his side, not breaking his conversation with David as his arm slid around my waist.

He was touching me. *He was touching me.* The ticker tape flashed on repeat in my head. I'd specified nothing physical, hadn't I? Though, literally never touching each other probably wasn't how he'd interpreted it.

Sevina let out an overly loud breath, and when Lukas pointed at the buffet, the whole group moved with him like a school of fish. He stayed next to me as we filled our plates with tropical fruits, flaky pastries, and crispy bacon. Lukas chose a large table, the opposite of what KB, Willow, and I had been looking for the past couple of days.

As people filled in around us, Lukas leaned in. "So, what's on the agenda today?" He popped a grape into his mouth.

I chewed my lip, considering. "I'm pretty boring."

"Boring is good."

"Like reading on the beach, boring."

A slow grin spread across his face. "I'm in if we can people watch with commentary. That's the only reason I pretend to read books at the cafés back home."

Cafés. That was a clue. *Because all of Europe wasn't covered with cafés.* I only assumed that from watching Emily in Paris, so. Not an expert.

A surprised laugh escaped me. "Deal. But I get to choose the book you hold." I was imagining something with a bare man-chest and preferably a satin-wrapped heaving bosom.

"Fine, but afterward, we're doing my thing." His eyes held a mischievous gleam.

"Okay. I'm nervous." I took a bite of bacon.

"I don't think you told me where you were from."

His accent made even a simple statement sound sexy. "Minnesota."

"Not by the beach."

I smiled. "Plenty of lakes, but no ocean."

"Perfect."

I set my fork down. "Very nervous."

"You'll be fine."

I gaped at him. "You're not going to tell me?"

He took a drink of his coffee. "You promise you won't back out?"

I swallowed hard. I wanted to reserve that right, but the way he was looking at me . . . "I won't back out." *What was happening?* I never felt the need to please people. Peer pressure for me wasn't a thing. Which meant friends were often also not a thing, but I've never cared much. I always found my people.

"Surfing."

My stomach dropped, and I nearly choked on my mango.

THE SUN BEAT down on the white sand as we made our way to the shore, surfboards tucked under our arms. Reading hadn't lasted long, mostly because after I'd read a paragraph four times and still had no idea what the words said, I decided even making a fool of myself was better than stress-sweating on a lounge chair.

After lying on our boards on the beach and paddling in the sand, our surf instructor Riley deemed us ready for the ocean.

I was so not ready for the ocean.

I spotted a few other familiar faces—KB and Paul were already out on the waves. KB seemed to be getting the hang of it at least. Poor Paul appeared to be overthinking it, his movements stiff and awkward.

I was basically looking into a crystal ball at my own imminent future.

Because I made a promise, I applied sunscreen to any skin that my sun shirt and bikini bottom didn't cover, waited a few minutes, then walked into the waves with Lukas and dropped my board to the surface of the water. I lunged forward and slid it under my chest.

My arms were still sore from paddling the kayaks, but at least my legs were fresh. Although I spent most of my time in front of a computer screen back home, I did used to play sports. Soccer. Volleyball. If there wasn't current muscle there, my legs at least had the memory of it.

Once we got out past the breaking waves with the others, Riley began explaining the basics. I listened intently, absorbing every tidbit like I was studying for an exam. But that wouldn't help me here. If I could just take a multiple choice test, I'd pass with flying colors, but having to actually put it into action?

That thought stopped me cold. As the water lapped against

my calves, I thought about how little action I'd gotten over the past three years. Not just *that* kind of action, but any action. When was the last time I'd gone on a trip? Taken a day off? Partied with classmates or friends on the weekend? It seemed there was always another essay or exam to prepare for, especially since I'd taken classes summer semester of my last year before starting law school.

It felt good to be out in the sunshine. It felt good to use my body. For the first time, I wondered if my dad had sent me here for more reasons than just the one.

I was jolted back to the present as Lukas took to the waves like he was born in the ocean. His arms flew in strong, even strokes through the water, and then his tanned, muscular form lifted to his board with breathtaking ease, the salt spray making him glitter.

Another clue. He clearly lived by an ocean or was wealthy enough to visit one regularly enough to be a surfing god.

"Your turn, Kate! Another set is rolling in." Riley motioned for me to move closer to her. She reiterated the technique and said she'd help give me a boost.

She boosted. I missed the wave. On the second try, I actually caught it, but when I tried to get up, I slipped off my board and face planted, downing saltwater like I was shotgunning at a party. By the time I settled back in our wave-waiting line for the fourth time, I was panting and my eyes burned like I'd been maced.

I straddled my board, pressing my palms against the smooth surface. "Okay. I did your thing."

Lukas swiped the hair from his forehead. "Are you giving up?"

My eyes widened. "I just ate it three times, and you're asking if I'm giving up?"

"Takes at least eight to get up for the first time." He turned to me, his stomach flexing as his shoulders curved forward.

Daaaamn it. My nostrils flared. He was doing this on purpose. He had to be. Always striking a pose or running his hands through his hair before trying to get his way.

"This isn't fair," I hissed.

He gave me a quizzical smile. "What's not?"

I decided to leave the fact that he was an expert at this activity, and my choice of activity required no prior training, out of my argument and went straight to the crux of the matter. "You know the effect you have on women, yes?"

For a moment, it looked as if he was going to play dumb, but he saw my eyes flash and exhaled. "I do."

"And you use it to your advantage." It wasn't a question. I didn't need to lead this witness. "That's a problem for me." I glanced over his shoulder to make sure we were out of earshot from the others. "If we're doing this for a month, then we have to be on equal footing. You can't just wave that around to get what you want." I motioned to his stupidly defined six pack.

"You're saying you aren't strong enough to withstand this?" He glanced down at his stomach, then looked up innocently.

Even when he was teasing me, I wanted to touch it. "I'm asking you not to make it hard for me—" I stopped mid-sentence as the words hit my ears, and Lukas' grin widened. "Oh. My. Hell. What are we, twelve?" I dropped to my board and paddled past him.

I might've glowered, but I wasn't mad at him. I was mad at myself because he was exactly right. It wasn't his fault he looked the way he did. It *was* his fault that he knew he was using it for his benefit, but I couldn't blame him. Didn't we all use whatever tools we had in our arsenal to try and get what we wanted?

"Kate!" Lukas paddled after me, and it only fueled my frustration that it took him all of two strokes to catch up. He cut me off with his board. "I won't make it hard for you." He winked. "Promise."

I rolled my eyes. "Fantastic."

He dropped into the water next to his board so all I could see were his hands and his face. "But I still think you should try again."

I groaned and watched KB catch her second wave of the morning. "Even if I do, I don't think I'm strong enough to get up."

Lukas shrugged, and was about to stretch his hand up to mess with his hair, but stopped. The grin he kept plastered to his face slipped an inch. "I think it's brave that you came out here. I don't remember the last time I did something brand new publicly. Really. It's impressive." He glanced back at the shore. "I'll come back in with you if you're done."

And just like that, the storm left my sails. That was nice. Lukas had just paid me a genuine compliment, and I didn't quite know what to do with it. I followed his eyes to the sand. Did I want to go in? *Takes at least eight to get up the first time.*

I didn't give up on things. I had plenty of other shortcomings, but determination and drive were not on that list.

"I'll try again." I fluttered my feet and started paddling.

"You don't have to—"

"I want to." I curved in an arc to sit next to Riley. She grinned at me and started watching over her shoulder until she found another set she liked, then gave me a boost.

I tried four more times with no luck, but on the fifth, my board somehow stayed under me. I wasn't able to fully get to my feet, but with one knee down and one lifted, I rode the wave, laughing like a crazy person for a few exhilarating seconds before toppling off with a splash.

"Did you see that?" I sputtered, paddling back to Lukas with a grin splitting my face.

He dove off his board and swam to me, pulling me into a hug under the water. The breath whooshed from my lungs, and if my hand hadn't been on my board, I would've sunk like a rock.

"Lucky number eight." Lukas grinned at me, his hands still on my skin under the crystal-clear water.

The spell broke as Sevina paddled over. "Lukas, can you help me with my foot placement?" She motioned to Riley, who was working with Paul, as if to justify her interruption.

Lukas dropped his hands and gave me one last look before paddling back to his board.

After a few more runs, my muscles started to protest and my stomach grumbled. I caught Lukas' attention as he was paddling back from another ride and motioned to the beach. He didn't hesitate, just flipped his board and headed back. After turning in our equipment and rinsing at the outdoor shower, we strolled back to our cabin. Not in silence that time. Any tension I'd felt had slipped away after that moment in the ocean.

"So you grew up near a beach?" I asked.

Lukas nodded. "My mother is from Sylt."

He said it like I should know where that was. "That's in Europe somewhere?" I winced, wondering if I was even close.

Lukas grinned. "Yes, Northern Germany."

"Is that where you live now?"

He shook his head, his jaw tensing. "We live further south."

South Germany. Okay, that was something. "I've only been to Europe once," I admitted. "A choir trip in high school. We did one of those whirlwind ten countries in ten days tours."

"Ah, the American way," he teased.

"What's that supposed to mean?"

He shrugged. "You can always tell the Americans. They have a checklist."

I frowned. "How is that a bad thing?"

"It's not bad."

I scoffed. "You made it sound bad."

Lukas paused at the door of our hut. "When we travel, we go to enjoy. To sit and eat and talk." He pulled the key from his pocket. "Americans race around like there's a prize or something."

I tilted my head, studying him. "So you go to a new place and just sit?"

He pushed the door open. "With good food. And good people."

I considered this. "Huh." I walked in and took off my shoes.

Lukas offered to let me use the shower first since our beach showers were really only to keep us sand-free. I glanced at the clock and couldn't believe it was already three. I rinsed the salt and sand from my body, reveling in the feel of the cool water against my sun-baked sink.

I couldn't stop the smile tugging at my lips. Today was fun. More fun than I'd had in longer than I could remember. It was a confusing swirl of emotions. I didn't want to be there. But it was good. Better than I expected. Especially now that I had an ally. It would've been better if he looked and moved a little more like Paul, but beggars couldn't be choosers.

Freshly showered and dressed for dinner, the glow of the day still warming my cheeks, we both took some time in the WiFi lounge after a talkback with Zara, then made our way to the main restaurant as the sun started its lazy descent.

Dinner was delicious as usual. More perfectly prepared seafood, I ordered the pasta and decadent side dishes. We were assigned tables, but somehow, Lukas and I ended up together with Willow and Orion. The three of them kept me laughing with stories of their college antics. I contributed a few of my own. By the time we finished, my face hurt from smiling so much.

Just as we were finishing our coconut cake, a clinking glass silenced the chatter. Our hosts stood at the front of the room, gleaming smiles plastered on their faces.

"You've had a day of fun in the sun," Mac announced, "but first thing tomorrow, you have another challenge!" A surge of nervous energy zipped through the room.

"Each couple must select one representative to report to the reception area at eight sharp tomorrow morning," Trinity instructed. "Choose wisely!"

Lukas turned to me. "What do you think? Brains or brawn for this one?"

I laughed. "You think I have brains?"

He shrugged. "Patrick couldn't stop talking about how fast you solved that riddle."

My eyebrows shot up. Patrick was talking about me? "Didn't help us much."

He gave a cheeky grin.

"I'm going," Willow said. "If it's something on the water, I'll be the best option."

Orion frowned. "I'm not bad with water sports."

"Oh, I wasn't saying that." She put a hand on his. "It's just that this is my natural habitat."

I loved how confident she was. All the men here were strong and capable, and she didn't doubt for one second that she could match up with them. I, on the other hand, doubted plenty.

I turned to Lukas and kept my voice down. I loved Willow, but my comfort on this island now depended on us winning. "I don't think it's going to be something on the water. They'll probably do something different. And if they're splitting us up, my guess is it's some sort of teamwork exercise."

"Obstacle course?"

I nodded, chewing my lower lip. "Something like that. If that's the case, I'd rather guide."

"So we just have to decide if the person showing up at eight is the one they'll put in the maze." Lukas licked his fork and set it on his plate, then picked up his wine glass.

"What do you think?"

He took a drink. "Fifty-fifty."

Willow got up from the table to sign herself up. I glanced over to find Sevina shooting daggers at me.

I leaned into Lukas. "Did you two sleep together? That first night?" I asked. She was acting like I'd killed her dog.

Lukas cleared his throat, and I glanced over at Orion who looked just as interested in his answer as I was.

"Sorry," I muttered. "None of my business."

Orion frowned in disappointment.

I leaned back in my seat. "Maybe you sign up for the morning?"

Lukas nodded, then pushed his chair back. He stood and lowered his head to my ear. "No. We didn't."

SIXTEEN

TALKBACKS

ILLOW

Zara: So Willow, tell me about your experience being paired with Orion last night. How did that go?

Willow: Oh man, it was a little weird at first, not gonna lie. He had just been with KB. And Orion kept going on about how KB was kind of a prude, which made things a bit awkward. Since we're friends.

Zara: I can imagine that would be an uncomfortable situation. Did things get better as the night went on?

Willow: For sure! Once we got past the initial weirdness, it was actually pretty fun. We ended up in the hot tub and let's just say . . . things got steamy. Orion's a great kisser.

Zara: You don't have to tell me about—

Willow: Got it. Sorry, I thought I was supposed to be candid.

Zara: It's fine, you can tell me whatever you want, I just don't need details. So overall, you'd say you had a good time with Orion, despite the rocky start?

Willow: Totally. I'm looking forward to one more night.

Zara: Well, I'm glad to hear things took a positive turn.

Willow: *Very positive.* Oh. Sorry. Was that too much?

KB

Zara: KB, thanks for taking the time to chat with me. How was your night with Max?

KB: Not like I have a choice. It was great.

Zara: Great. Did you do anything special?

KB: We went to the pool. Max had a rousing conversation with Sevina.

Zara: I see. And how did that make you feel, him talking to Sevina?

KB: It didn't bother me. Max can talk to whomever he wants. It gave me time to soak in the hot tub.

Zara: He didn't sit with you?

KB: For a bit.

Zara: I noticed you weren't with him today.

KB: He didn't want to surf. Paul did.

Lukas

Zara: You look pleased with yourself.

Lukas: I'm talking with you, aren't I?

Zara: [pretends to gag]

Lukas: How are you doing?

Zara: I'm talking with you, aren't I?

Lukas: Touché

Zara: So. Kate.

Lukas: What about her?

Zara: You tell me. You said she didn't know you, but—

Lukas: She's got this air of mystery about her like she's got secrets just waiting to be uncovered. She's gorgeous. Who wouldn't want to get to know her better?

Zara: Wow. That's some world-class bullshit.

Lukas: Are you allowed to say that?

Zara: Are you going to tattle?

Lukas: Depends.

Zara: . . .

Lukas: . . .

Zara: You went surfing.

Lukas: I did.

Zara: It's been three days hasn't it?

Lukas: Elise knows now. Sevina told her.

Zara: Oh. But they haven't told anyone else?

Lukas: Keeping it a secret was to their advantage, but now that I chose Kate—

Zara: Not so much.

Lukas: Exactly. Not so much.

Zara: . . . I told him you were the life of the party when he called, by the way.

Lukas: Of course he called.

Zara: Sorry.

Lukas: Not your fault.

∽

Kate

Zara: So Kate, tell me about Lukas. How are things going with you two?

Kate: Lukas is very charming.

Zara: He is. Did you enjoy time together last night and on the beach today?

Kate: It was very relaxing. Except for the surfing. That sucked. Mostly.

Zara: You seem relaxed. That's a change from when you first arrived. You seemed pretty set against the whole 'finding a mate' thing. About the whole island in general.

Kate: Well, I've had some time to think about it. Maybe spending time here is just what I need.

Zara: Hmm. That's good to hear. What about Sevina? I noticed some tension there when Lukas chose you.

Kate: Who didn't notice.

Zara: So, not great.

Kate: Honestly, she's never said two words to me. I have no problem with her, but she seems . . . fine.

~

Sevina

Zara: It must have been disappointing to see Lukas choose someone else. How are you feeling about it?

Sevina: How am I feeling? I'm pissed.

Zara: At Lukas?

Sevina: He's playing a game. I just need Kate to understand she can't swoop in and take what's mine.

Zara: Yours?

Sevina: Not like that. I just meant we're supposed to be together. Obviously.

Zara: Obviously.

Sevina: . . .

Zara: One of the staff said they found you in, ah, a compromising position with Max last night.

Sevina: I was paired with *Paul*. What did you expect?

CHAPTER

SEVENTEEN

The waxing moon glowed over the beach as Lukas and I made our way back to our private hut, our sandals brushing against the sand-swept stone. My head buzzed pleasantly from the drinks at dinner, and I swayed slightly, bumping into Lukas. His hand shot out to steady me, his touch warm through the thin fabric of my dress.

"Careful there," he murmured.

I felt giddy and lightheaded, though I couldn't tell if it was more from the alcohol or Lukas' proximity. I voted for the alcohol. "I'm fine." I moved away from him as he opened the door.

Soft silence wrapped around us like a blanket as we stepped into the hut. We orbited each other as we got ready for bed. Lukas' hand brushed mine as he reached for his toothpaste, and I audibly sucked in a breath. He froze. And I hissed air through my teeth, pretending I stubbed my toe.

Lukas' words played back to me from the water. I would've been more than annoyed if he was ogling me all the time. Commenting on my body. Despite his godly physique, it wasn't fair for me to objectify him.

So. I was trying to see past the abs. And the shoulders. And the hair.

It wasn't helping. Because the more I saw of Lukas when he wasn't putting on a show, the more I liked. He was funny. Surprisingly gentle. I thought all alphas were rough and aggressive, though my dad wasn't. He was kind and thoughtful, only asserting dominance when he had to.

He slipped out of the bathroom so I could use the toilet, and when I was finished, re-entered to take his turn. I exited and slid under my sheets. I closed my eyes, willing myself to drift before Lukas re-emerged, but I had no such luck. My head was buzzing, and my filter was down.

"You know, you're like two different people sometimes," I whispered. Lukas shifted in the dark across from me.

"What do you mean?" His voice was low.

I rolled to face him, making out the angles of his profile in the moonlight filtering through the window. "I don't know how to describe it. Once when I was a kid, I did a commercial for a local grocery store."

"Your an actor?"

"Hell, no. It was the most stressful experience of my life. But when we were there, I remember I was supposed to smile at my fake mom as she helped me select canned peaches from the shelf. Or applesauce? I don't know, I can't remember. But every time they'd yell "cut" I felt like my face was going to crack. My cheeks ached, and it was take after take." I paused, realizing I was rambling. "Anyway, that's what I mean."

"That you're concerned I enjoy canned fruit?"

I sighed. "Yes, Lukas. Two different you's. One with a healthy bowel and one without."

Lukas laughed, then scrubbed a hand over his jaw and lay back on his pillow. I could barely see him, so I knew that motion wasn't supposed to be for me. My pulse sped anyway.

"Can I tell you something?" he asked.

I nodded, shifting closer to the edge of my bed.

"I grew up in the public eye—"

"Wait, *you're* an actor?"

He shook his head. "No, but my family was well known. It was difficult for me to go out without being noticed, and my parents told me that someone would always be watching."

Lukas lay there with his hand behind his head, staring up at the ceiling.

"When did you get to call cut?" I asked, my mind spinning. What kind of family did he have if there was that much scrutiny on his life?

"Only at home. Alone in my bedroom."

"Were you there often?"

He shook his head. "Hardly ever."

I blew out a breath. "Brutal. I'm sorry."

Lukas tossed off his covers and sat on the edge of his bed. "There are two different you's, too."

I frowned. "What?"

He leaned over his knees. "You act like all you are is serious. But you had fun today."

I groaned, covering my eyes with my arm. "I did. And now I'm not going to be able to go back."

"Go back to what?"

"My life!" I felt as if I was an observer to my own answers. Where was this coming from? "All I do at home is work and study. I thought that was all I wanted, all I needed to make myself happy. I mean, of course, at some point I want to finish school and move on to only working, but I didn't think I needed more than that."

"Hmm." Lukas held still. Watching me. "And now?"

I turned back to my side to face him. *Why was I telling him this?* Because I was tipsy. And a little riled up, if I was being honest. Elise and David had been making out in the hall when we left. It looked like fun. "I don't know how to have balance back home."

Lukas blew out a breath. "I know the feeling." He stared at his hands a moment, then pushed up from the bed. "I'm going to go out for a bit."

I frowned. "Out, as in—"

"I need to run my wolf."

My mouth snapped shut. "That's—you do that?" I'd only ever heard my parents say that out loud. It wasn't something our generation talked about.

He paused at the door. "You don't?"

I lifted up to my elbow. "No." I left out the part about me not having a wolf to run in the first place. "Do other people here do that?" I glanced at the window. The moon was waxing. *Was it almost full?*

"You can come if you want."

I shook my head, fear suddenly gripping my throat. "I'm tired, and we have the challenge tomorrow."

He tapped his fingers on the door. "Goodnight, then. Partner." With that, Lukas slipped out of the room.

SUNLIGHT STREAMED THROUGH THE CURTAINS, jolting me awake. I blinked groggily, disoriented, before the events of the previous day came rushing back. I turned to look at Lukas' bed, but it was empty. Either he died in the jungle last night or he had already left for the challenge.

Fumbling for my phone, my stomach dropped as I registered the time. 9:30 AM. I was supposed to be at the main building by ten o'clock sharp. I cursed under my breath, leaping out of bed and scrambling for my suitcase.

I threw on the first outfit I could find, jean shorts and a tank top, and dragged a brush through my hair. Thankfully I'd showered the night before. The real bummer was no time for a trip to the WiFi lounge to check my texts and emails.

Still, I shoved my phone in my pocket to snap a few quick photos of the room. I'd totally forgotten to take any at the kayak challenge yesterday. Mom would never let me hear the end of it if I came home without documenting my "grand island adventure." Though she'd only be looking for pictures of potential alpha's.

I brushed my teeth and rushed out the door, breaking into a light jog as I made my way down the path. The resort was stunning in the morning light, all lush greenery and turquoise water, but I barely had time to appreciate it, focused on not face-planting on the sand-dusted stones.

I stopped in front of the main building with two minutes to spare, breathing hard. The other contestants were milling about outside, looking various degrees of nervous and excited. No sign of Lukas.

"Cutting it a bit close there, aren't we?" A voice chirped near my elbow. I turned to see Willow grinning at me, bouncy as ever despite the early hour.

"I'm out of practice," I replied, trying to catch my breath. During the regular semester, I was up at six-thirty every morning. Even on weekends so I didn't disrupt my Circadian rhythm. *I was such a nerd.*

Willow laughed. "Well, I hope you're hungry at least. I hear they're serving us breakfast on the beach before the challenge."

My stomach rumbled on cue. "Ravenous, actually. Nerves always do that to me." We still had no idea what the challenge was, and my mind was spinning like a top at the possibilities.

As if summoned, a resort staff member emerged to usher our group around the side of the building. There, a beautiful breakfast spread awaited us, laid out on crisp white tablecloths in the sand. The smell of coffee and something sweet and fruity wafted over the ocean breeze.

I followed behind Willow as we both loaded up our plates with eggs, tropical fruits, and some kind of cheese drizzled with honey.

"You ready to get your asses handed to you?" Patrick fell into line behind us.

Willow rolled her eyes. "What place did you come in on the kayaks?"

Patrick shrugged. "Hey, second isn't bad." He gave me a wink.

We didn't have long to enjoy the meal before the doors to the building swung open with a dramatic flourish. I craned my neck, trying to see what the morning had in store for us.

What I didn't expect was the sight of our partners decked out in full chef's attire—white coats, hats, and aprons. Lukas somehow managed to make the get-up look runway-worthy, a glint of mischief in his ocean-blue eyes as they met mine across the sand.

"Umm." Willow looked down at her plate. "Did they make this or something?"

I frowned. The food tasted like it had the other two mornings.

Our partners came and retrieved us one by one, and as we filed into the restaurant, I had to do a double-take. The space had been completely transformed overnight. Where there had once been cozy tables and chairs, there now stood rows of gleaming stainless steel cook stations, each equipped with cutting boards, knives, and an array of ingredients. It looked like a professional kitchen had sprouted up in the middle of our island getaway.

"Welcome, welcome!" Trinity greeted us with a mega-watt

smile. Her braids were piled atop her head in an intricate updo, and she practically vibrated with energy. "I hope you're all ready for this morning's challenge!"

A ripple of nervous laughter went through the group. I glanced up at Lukas, and his expression didn't breed confidence.

"Did you all enjoy breakfast?" Trinity waited for us to nod our heads. "That was only the appetizer." She clapped her hands together. "Each of you will have to eat your way through a series of four dishes. Some of the most prized delicacies from around the world!"

Okay. Food. I could do food. But why was Lukas in a chef's getup? Was this going to be some kind of eating competition? I'd slammed pizza with my siblings, but I was no Kobayashi.

Trinity gestured to a table at the front of the room, where four covered platters sat ominously. With a flourish, she whipped off the lids, revealing the so-called delicacies.

"First up, we have balut from the Philippines—a fertilized duck egg boiled and eaten in the shell." The embryonic duck curled in on itself, its bones and beak visible through the gelatinous white. My stomach lurched.

"Next, Nordic hákarl. That's fermented shark meat, folks. A true Icelandic specialty!" The greenish hunk of fish glistened, emitting a staggeringly pungent odor that made my eyes water.

"Third, we've got some delightful casu martzu, a Sardinian sheep's milk cheese filled with live insect larvae. The maggots are said to enhance the flavor." The cheese wriggled and squirmed, and I had to look away.

Lukas put a hand on my shoulder as Trinity pulled the last lid free.

"And last but not least, how about a heaping portion of Cambodian fried tarantulas? Crispy, hairy, and full of protein."

The arachnids were enormous, splayed out on the plate in a nightmarish tangle of legs.

The reaction from the contestants was immediate and visceral. Willow turned an alarming shade of green. KB looked like she might faint. Even Patrick appeared vaguely queasy, his earlier bravado wavering. I fought back my own wave of nausea, breathing through my mouth to avoid the symphony of smells wafting from the table.

Trinity, on the other hand, seemed positively gleeful at our horrified expressions. She let out a tinkling laugh. "But wait, there's more! Your partners will have access to a variety of ingredients to help enhance the dishes. To make them a bit more palatable, if you will. They'll be your culinary guides on this wild gastronomical journey!"

Lukas walked with the others behind our individual prep center. He looked up and mouthed, "I'm so sorry."

I groaned, still staring at the unpalatable display in front of me. Lukas wasn't American. Wouldn't this have been far easier for him? Why didn't I volunteer?

I scanned the line of unlucky guests. Max glanced over from his chef getup and smirked. Sevina stared at her plate, determined. What would happen if we didn't win?

I had no idea who I'd end up with, but Lukas would be snapped up instantaneously. He'd never get to relax backstage. But while I wanted to help him and myself, I was inhaling a stomach-churning amount of fermented fish.

"Aaaaand . . . begin!" Trinity crowed, brandishing a timer. I surveyed the grim options before me, my stomach already staging a revolt at the thought of ingesting any of it.

Lukas leaned forward, an apologetic grimace on his handsome face. "I'm so sorry, Kate. If I'd known it would be this gnarly, I would've volunteered to do the eating myself."

I couldn't even force a smile. "How could we have known, right?"

Patrick was already holding two tarantula legs. He shoved them into his mouth, the crunch reverberating across the room.

I shuddered but couldn't fault his technique. That did seem like the least offensive option. "Get me one."

Lukas nodded, then turned to the display. He discussed briefly with Trinity, then returned with two legs on the plate. "You have to eat a minimum of two. There are different amounts for each item."

My eyes widened. Was I going to have to eat this much of the fish?

"Do you want ketchup or . . . " Lukas inspected his prep table. "I have hot sauce or mustard—"

I reached out and grabbed both legs at the same time, then dropped them. "Are there hairs?" I clapped a hand over my mouth, dry heaving.

"I don't—no, I don't think so." Lucas' throat bobbed as he inspected the plate.

I nodded, then closed my eyes and tried again. French fries. *They were just french fries.* "Get me ketchup."

Lukas nodded and squirted some on the plate. I dipped, then took a bite and chewed as fast as I could. After a few seconds, my eyes flew open. Lukas was staring at me.

"It's not bad." I licked my lips. "It's like fried chicken skin?" I shoved the rest of them in my mouth and chewed, hope building in my chest. Maybe all the foods were like that. They looked disgusting, but they didn't taste horrible? Maybe they were delicacies for a reason?

"Get me something else!" I shooed Lukas back to the display.

Around us, the challenge was in full, chaotic swing. KB was hunched over her plate, dry heaving between bites. I couldn't tell what she'd just ingested, but that wasn't promising. Alec and Elise were already arguing, their voices rising above the general din. Willow, to my amazement and envy, stood in front of two empty plates, chugging water like her life depended on it. At the far end of the line, I saw Max berating his partner, a petite redhead named Lindsay, for not eating fast enough.

I had to hurry.

Lukas returned with a chunk of fish the size of a teaspoon. His face pinched. "Sorry. I think this one might be the worst. Figured we could get it over with."

I nodded, then reached up and plugged my nose.

He winced as he caught a whiff. "Do you want me to do anything to it? Hide it in . . . puff pastry?"

I shook my head. That was only going to make it worse and waste time. "Put it in for me."

Lukas picked up a fork and scooped it up. I closed my eyes and opened my mouth. As soon as it hit my tongue, I gagged. The taste was indescribable, a mix of rotten onions, turpentine, and raw sewage that coated my tongue and throat. I sealed my lips shut, refusing to let anything out. I was not going to do this more than once.

Lukas handed me a glass of fruit juice, and I gratefully chugged it, washing the putrid fish down my throat. The sweet juice really only made the flavor worse, but at least it was in my gut. I drank the rest of the glass and whimpered, searching for anything else that could get the flavor off my tongue. I motioned to a bag of wafer cookies, and Lukas ripped open the package.

Just as I shoved two of them in my mouth, a commotion erupted from Paul's station. I looked up just in time to see him convulsing, his body twisting and contorting. With a ripping sound, his human form melted away, replaced by a massive, snarling wolf.

CHAPTER

EIGHTEEN

"Holy shit." Lukas set down our plate and ran to him. Screams filled the air as the wolf that was Paul thrashed and writhed, upending tables and sending dishes flying. I sat frozen, my mouth still full of half-chewed wafer cookie, as I watched the unbelievable scene unfold.

I had never seen another shifter my age before, let alone mid-shift. It was both terrifying and strangely exhilarating, a visceral reminder of the wild power that lurked beneath my own skin.

Lukas gripped Paul's wolf with both hands, holding his jaws closed. "I'm going to lead you outside, okay? You'll be able to run."

The wolf's eyes blazed, but with Mac at the wolf's flank, they got him out the door. Strong emotions. Whatever Paul had felt had woken up his wolf, and I was suddenly shaking. Not from the fermented fish.

Lukas ran back in, panting. "Sorry. Let me—"

"How did you know how to do that?"

He blew out a breath. "Had to do it with my little brother once."

He and his brother both had wolves that presented? None of my siblings had. Not that I knew of. A pang of insecurity hit my already roiling gut. I didn't want to be a shifter, but knowing that I others had embraced their wolves? That I'd barely ever felt mine? Maybe even if I wanted to, I'd be too weak to find her.

"Kate!" Lukas' voice cut through my daze. His hands were on my shoulders, his blue eyes intense and urgent. "Stay with me, okay? We're almost through this."

I nodded mutely as he returned with both the third and fourth plates.

Shit. The maggot cheese. "How could you think the fermented shark was worse than that?"

"It's cheese. How bad could it be?"

My eyes flashed. "How bad—"

"Okay, yeah. Sorry. Here." He set the plates down. "We'll do these two together." Lukas ran back and got two more servings.

"You don't have to—"

"Right now." Lukas picked up the chunk of cheese and waited for me to do the same. He counted us down, and I shoved it in my mouth. I did not even chew before I forced myself to swallow and chased it with another drink of juice.

I was still choking and gagging when I realized Lukas had the fourth and final plate in his hands. He watched KB. She was already digging into the barut with a spoon.

I cursed under my breath and grabbed my plate, then shoved the little yolky gremlin in my mouth. Tears streamed down my face. I had to chew, and the crunch made me shudder and heave. Finally, Lukas handed me a chunk of straight-up raw onion, and I shoved it in my mouth like a slice of apple.

And then, miraculously, it was over. I clapped a hand over my mouth just in case as Lukas raised his hands in the air seconds before KB did.

Trinity strode toward us. "Kate and Lukas, congratulations! Kate, if you keep that down, you two have not only won the right to choose your partners for the next two nights but also an exclusive night out at the hottest club on the island. You can choose two other couples to go with you."

I blinked, not trusting myself to speak.

Lukas looked ready to jump for the trash can.

"Any thoughts?" Trinity motioned to the other couples, half of whom were hunched over, gagging or crying.

Lukas pointed to Willow and KB. "We'll take them."

I wanted to tell him he didn't need to defer to my friends, but there was no way I was allowing my lips to part. I sent him a silent thank you through my now-watering eyes.

I kept my hand over my mouth until we got outside. I kept satan's breakfast concoction inside my stomach until we arrived back at the hut. Then Lukas held my hair back while I heaved into the toilet.

THE CLUB WAS a small but vibrant oasis tucked into a corner of the island, a low-slung building with thatched roof and neon signs that flashed in sync with the pulsing beat. Inside, the air was thick with humidity and the scent of coconut rum. Bodies packed the dance floor, moving in rhythm to the music that pounded through the speakers, the bass line so deep it felt like it could rearrange your heartbeat.

After a day spent lounging—okay, mostly recovering—by the pool after making sure Paul was okay, the six of us had slipped into something a little flashier and made our way to the club. As VIPs, we'd been ushered past the line that stretched outside, straight into a cordoned-off section with plush couches and our own server. The whole place had that carefree Caribbean vibe: dim lighting, strings of lights tangled around palm trees that peeked through open windows, and bartenders who seemed like they went from their surfboards to the bar and then back again.

Drinks were flowing, laughter filled the air, and everything felt warm and alive. We started the night with shots—fruity, colorful things that went down too easy—and quickly moved on to the club's signature cocktails served in hollowed-out pineapples. It didn't take long for the alcohol to work its magic, turning the slightly awkward tension between all of us into loose, carefree camaraderie. Even Max, who rarely smiled, cracked a few jokes while Lukas leaned back against the bar, looking effortlessly cool as usual.

I sipped my drink now, feeling the pleasant buzz spreading through my limbs, mixing with the adrenaline from the night. Beside me, Willow laughed and twirled, her blonde hair flying around her face as she danced, her cheeks flushed and her eyes bright with tipsy joy. She tossed back the last of her drink and grinned, mischief sparkling in her eyes.

"Let's dance!" she shouted over the music, and before I could protest, she grabbed my wrist and tugged me back onto the dance floor.

The crowd moved as one, swaying and spinning beneath the strobe lights that painted the space in flashes of electric blue, red, and gold. My feet moved to the beat, my head light with the rhythm, the alcohol, and the heady feeling of being far away from reality.

I never drank much at home. I couldn't afford to feel terrible even one day out of the week, and while I didn't plan to make it my new personality, it was fun to let loose for once.

Willow spun in front of me, her laughter blending with the thumping music, and I couldn't help but join her. The club had a way of making everything feel like it was happening in slow motion and high speed at once, like we were floating through a vibrant dream that might disappear if we blinked too hard.

I caught sight of KB and Orion at the edge of the dance floor. KB, normally composed, was swaying with her arms above her head, a lazy smile on her lips as she chatted with Orion, who looked almost relaxed for once. Max had found a group of tourists and was charming them with some ridiculous story, his hands gesturing animatedly, while Lukas leaned against the wall near the bar, his eyes tracking the dance floor with that cool, unreadable look.

Willow tugged me closer, her smile infectious. "Don't worry about him!" she yelled, barely audible over the music.

I laughed, tipping my head back and letting the beat pulse through me as I moved to the music, the strobe lights painting the crowded dance floor in a kaleidoscope of colors.

Before the song ended, a pair of hands landed on my hips, pulling me back against a solid chest. I turned, expecting to see Lukas, but instead, I found myself face-to-face with Max.

"You're more fun than I thought at first." His breath was hot against my ear. I tried to pull away, but his grip only tightened, his fingers pressing against the waistband of my jeans. He began to grind against me, his hand trailing over my ass.

"Max, let go," I said, my voice sharp with warning. "I don't—"

Max's eyes widened, and his hands dropped. He stepped back as Lukas appeared at my side.

Max chuckled. "You think you own her or something?"

"Eff off, Max." Willow's eyes flashed.

Lukas' expression was hard. "She can do what she wants. But in this case, I don't think she wants."

Max shook his head. "A whole month to sample different flavors, and you're already locking in?" He raised an eyebrow and slunk back into the crowd.

I shivered. KB spent two nights with him? I made a mental note to check in with her and make sure she was okay.

Lukas turned to go back to the wall, but I caught his arm.

"Do you want to go?" I asked, leaning in so he could hear me over the bass. Someone bumped me from behind, and I caught myself against his chest. Lukas was warm, and his shirt smelled like sunshine.

"I'll stay if you want to."

I dropped my hands, but too many people pressed against us for me to step back. "This isn't really my scene either." I glanced over to see Willow dancing with two locals. She seemed completely in her element.

Lukas nodded, pulling me closer as a group moved past us toward the bar. He lowered his head. "It just makes my wolf nervous. All the light and sound."

My cheek brushed his stubble, and a jolt of electricity pulsed through me. "I can't say I know that feeling." I thought about pulling back. Of walking to the bar and telling our driver that we were ready to head back to the resort, but my feet didn't move.

I couldn't stop thinking about what happened in the kitchen that morning. Paul just shifting out of nowhere. Or Lukas leaving the night before to run.

The words spilled out of my mouth. "What is it like? Can you sense your wolf all the time?"

Lukas' hands still brushed my waist. "Yep. Sometimes he's more insistent, but he's always there."

I tilted my head to look at him, and my nose nearly brushed his. "So I was right. There are actually two of you."

A slow smile spread across his face. "I guess so."

"Not the two I saw, though. Wait, have I ever seen him? Does he tell you what to say or—" I wobbled on my heel, and Lukas gripped me.

"How much have you had to drink?"

I shrugged. I could already feel the buzz beginning to dissipate. "I'm fine. I don't wear heels very often." My curiosity burned brighter than ever. "When did you first shift?"

Lukas pulled me closer, his hands sliding around to the small of my back. "I was thirteen," he said, his breath warm. "It was terrifying."

I tried to imagine it—the sensation of your bones reshaping, your skin giving way to fur. "And what about now?"

Lukas' lips twitched. "If you're so curious about my wolf, why don't you ever let yours out?"

I scoffed. "First of all, it's not something I can just do. Second, even if I could, there are so many reasons."

"Like?"

"Like I'm going to law school. I live a normal life. I don't want to be forced to live outside the city or hear another voice in my head or get antsy around the full moon . . . " I paused, last night suddenly clicking into place. "It's almost the full moon, isn't it?"

Lukas pursed his lips. "Yeah."

"That's why you had to leave. That's why Paul shifted." My eyes widened. "Is it going to get worse? Are people going to start prowling around the resort at night, or . . . " I turned my head looking for Max. I knew enough to know that the full moon heightened all emotions and energy. Alpha's got more aggressive. Their sexual drive increased. My father had broken up more fights than I could remember over she-wolves when I was a teen.

My throat worked as the crowd around us surged, jostling us even closer together. Suddenly, I was acutely aware of every point of contact between us—his hands on my waist, my chest pressed against his. A wave of heat rushed through me, and I felt that strange, magnetic pull again, stronger than ever.

I swallowed hard, trying to steady myself. But it was like trying to hold back the tide—the more I fought it, the more I felt like I was drowning. I needed space, air, anything to clear my head. "I think I need to get some air." I pulled away as best I could, searching for an exit.

He nodded, his expression unreadable. "Of course. Let's head outside."

The cool night air was a shock to my system as we stepped out onto the club's patio. I took a deep breath, trying to calm the riot of emotions swirling inside me. What was happening to me? I'd never felt so out of control.

"You okay?" Lukas leaned against the railing beside me.

I forced a smile. "Yeah, I'm fine. Just needed a breather."

He studied me for a moment, his gaze intense. "It's getting late."

"Yeah," I agreed, taking in the nearly full moon rising over the trees.

We gathered the others and after finally dragging Willow away from the dance floor, slid back into the car. Max and Willow started kissing before the car even got out of the parking lot. Orion's hand sat on KB's upper thigh, his fingers flirting with the hem of her dress.

"Are they allowed to switch it up?" I whispered to Lukas.

He gave me a look that said, "Who's going to say anything?"

I certainly wasn't. If Willow wanted Max's attention, that was on her.

By the time we got back to the resort, I was able to ask enough questions to know that Willow and KB were both sober enough to make rational decisions, even if I questioned their critical thinking skills. We hugged, then made our separate ways to our huts.

Something inside me still felt wrong, but I was blaming it on the food challenge that morning and the alcohol. I could sleep it off, and everything would feel fine in the morning.

I stepped through the door of our hut, my heart still racing, my skin flushed despite the cool sea breeze. My eyes immediately landed on a folded note sitting on the kitchen counter. I snatched it up and unfolded the crisp paper.

"What's that?" Lukas asked, his voice low and rough.

"It's . . . a gift. From some anonymous benefactor." I cleared my throat, trying to keep my voice steady as I read the elegant script. "They've gifted us a private couple's massage on the beach tomorrow night."

He frowned and stepped closer, reading over my shoulder.

I set the note down, wondering who in my life would do something like that. Anonymous benefactor? I'd barely had time to text my parents and siblings, let alone friends. And while they knew I was on a beach, they didn't know why.

I blew out a breath and turned to Lukas. His jaw was set. His eyes hard. Okaaay, maybe not a massage guy. "I'm going to go shower. Wash the club off me."

Lukas nodded and followed me into our room. I flicked on the lights and stopped cold, grunting as Lukas ran into my back.

He gripped my shoulder and froze, taking in the scene in front of us. Our beds—our beautiful individual beds—were gone. Replaced by one large, plush King in the middle of our bedroom.

CHAPTER
NINETEEN

Lukas' face was unreadable as he stood by the bed. My breath caught in my throat. *What the hell, Luna Bay?*

I tried to steady the flutter in my chest, but it was next to impossible. If I wasn't fully sober before, I was at that exact moment.

"Well," I said, aiming for casual. "This is new."

Lukas ran a hand through his hair, his jaw clenched tight. The muscles in his neck tensed, and the way his fingers raked through those dark strands made me feel like I was on a playground swing. "I'll take the floor."

I scoffed. "Don't be ridiculous." The words left my mouth before I could stop them. "I didn't mean anything by that."

"You mean by the look of disgust written all over your face?"

I clenched my jaw. "We're both adults. We can share."

The silence stretched between us, thick and charged. His eyes met mine, dark and intense in the dim light, and a shiver tickled the length of my spine. *Why had I said that?* Again, I felt like I wasn't fully in charge of my own tongue. Which, sharing a bed with Lukas, was a dangerous problem.

A heartbeat passed. Two. His expression softened just a fraction, as if he was considering something he shouldn't. Then he nodded once. "Fine."

I turned quickly, busying myself with taking off my heels. My fingers fumbled with the clasps, and my heart thudded so loudly in my ears that I barely registered the soft thuds of Lukas pacing the room in front of me. He moved like a caged animal, restless and wound tight.

I watched him out of the corner of my eye, my chest tightening with each sharp turn he made. My senses buzzed, sharp and raw, as if something inside me was straining to reach toward him. It felt primal, instinctual, like a pull from deep within that I couldn't rationalize away. And that scared the hell out of me.

It was the dancing. The drinking. Maybe it was the full moon, or maybe it was just this place. Every day I seemed to feel less like myself and more like . . . I couldn't even end that sentence. It wasn't someone I didn't know. It felt more like someone I had forgotten. That was even more terrifying.

Lukas grabbed a t-shirt and shorts from his bag, then headed for the tiny bathroom. "I'll change in here." His voice was gruff, tighter than usual.

"Okay." I kept my eyes on the pajamas I'd pulled out, but felt his gaze on me, heavy and heated, as he lingered for a moment before shutting the door. My pulse stuttered, and I let out a shaky breath, the tension coiling tighter in my stomach.

He seemed upset by the beds, and I couldn't blame him. But it didn't have to be a big deal. I couldn't let it be a big deal.

I tried to think about KB and Willow. I hadn't even stopped to ask who they were going to be paired with. At least it wasn't Max.

I pulled off my dress and slumped to the bed. *Our bed.* My thighs burned. Ugh. What was happening to me? I wasn't like this. I didn't get weak in the knees over a guy, even a specimen like Lukas.

I changed quickly into a tank top and sleep shorts, hyper-aware of every sound from the bathroom. The rustle of clothes, the creak of the floorboards. The sudden rush of water as he splashed his face.

The bathroom door creaked open, and I jumped, my heart leaping into my throat as Lukas emerged, his hair damp, droplets glistening on his skin. His t-shirt clung to his broad chest, outlining the sculpted lines of muscle beneath, and the air between us crackled like static. I averted my eyes, but the heat rising in my cheeks betrayed me.

"Which side do you want?" His voice was rough, strained, like he was struggling to keep it even. The tension in his body was palpable, and it seeped into the space between us, tightening around my ribs. *Was he angry that I suggested we share?*

"I don't care." My voice came out too breathy, too uncertain. I tried to swallow the lump in my throat, to ignore the way my body seemed to hum with a strange, urgent energy. "Whichever."

We slid under the covers from opposite sides, the bed vast and yet not nearly big enough. I could feel the heat of him, even with a foot of space between us, and every nerve in my body felt like it was on high alert. My skin tingled, and my breaths were shallow and uneven. It was maddening.

I wanted to blurt it out. To talk about it. Normally, Lukas and I could say whatever was on our mind, or at least it felt that way to me, but this wasn't a topic we'd breached. And I couldn't do it tonight. Something was different about tonight.

I lay stiff as a board, staring up at the ceiling, trying to ignore the way my heartbeat echoed in my ears. Why did it feel like everything had changed since the club, like I was on the edge of something I couldn't pull back from? It wasn't just attraction—it was a pull, like gravity, drawing me toward him, even though every logical part of me knew better.

I tried to relax, forcing myself to focus on the sound of the waves outside, the faint rustle of palm fronds in the wind. But all I could hear was Lukas' breathing, steady but strained like he was struggling with his own thoughts. Like he was fighting the same battle I was.

Just sleep, I told myself. *Sleep, and forget this ever happened.* But my body had other ideas, every inch of me hyper-aware of the man beside me, of the way his chest rose and fell, of the heat radiating from his side of the bed. I turned on my side, facing away from him, hoping the distance might give me some peace.

But it didn't. If anything, it made the ache worse.

And then, like the snap of a string, a sudden rush of energy jolted through my body. Like an electric current igniting every nerve. My eyes flew open, my breath catching in my throat. *What was this?*

Panic and awe warred as the sensation surged through me —wild, raw, a force I couldn't control. It was unlike anything I'd ever felt before—primal, visceral, like something deep and ancient was clawing its way to the surface, refusing to be ignored. It wasn't pain, but it wasn't comfortable either. It felt like being burned and freed all at once.

Beside me, Lukas turned. "Kate?" The sound of my name on his lips sent a shiver down my spine, adding another confusing layer to the chaos inside me. "What's going on?"

What was going on? I didn't even know how to put it into words. My mind reeled, thoughts spiraling in all directions as I tried to make sense of the strange, untamed sensations coursing through me. *Ummm, well, you see, Lukas, every part of me wants to reach over and tear your clothes off.*

I bit my pillow. It felt like a beast within me was awakening —stretching, flexing, testing its strength for the first time—

Holy. Hell.

I pressed a trembling hand to my chest, trying to calm the wild beating of my heart. No. No, no, no, no, no.

Was this what it was like? *Was she—?*

It was as if I was being split open, my senses heightened to a painful degree.

Lukas sat up beside me, his presence steady and grounding in the swirling darkness. His warmth radiated toward me, an anchor in a storm. His hand found my shoulder, strong yet gentle, but the contact sent another wave of agony—*pleasure?* —through my body.

"Kate, talk to me. What's happening?"

"Mmm. I don't know," I whispered, my voice trembling, barely able to get the words past my dry throat. My mind felt scattered, like I was trying to grasp at fog. "It's like . . . I don't know. I'm burning up." There. That was normal. Make it sound like a fever. *Maybe it was a fever?*

His grip tightened, his thumb brushing over my collarbone, sending sparks skittering across my skin.

"I think I'm sick," I eeked out.

"You're not sick." His voice rumbled through me.

"You don't know that, Lukas."

He blew out a breath. "Yeah. I do."

I gripped my pillow tighter. "Lukas—"

"I can feel her, Kate. Your wolf. Just like at the bonfire."

The bonfire? *Your wolf.* The words hung between us.

Lukas brushed my hair from my cheek. "She's waking up, and she's a little pissed off."

I couldn't breathe.

I couldn't—

Lukas yanked me up from the bed, folding me over and rubbing my back. "Breathe. Now, Kate."

I forced my lungs to expand, and tears pricked at my eyes, blurring my vision as the reality of it crashed over me. I was raw, exposed, and I wanted to scream. To hide.

"Why?" I gasped. "Why is this happening to me?"

Lukas' hand slid down my arm, his fingers intertwining with mine. "It's not happening. It's part of you."

"I don't want this to be part of me!"

"Yeah," he murmured, his lips brushing my ear. "I get that."

I turned into him, burying my face in the crook of his neck. His scent filled my lungs—woodsy, earthy, like the forest after a storm. It grounded me, and I clung to it, to him, as silent sobs wracked my body.

Lukas held me close, his arms wrapped around me, his heartbeat a steady rhythm against my cheek, a counterpoint to the erratic thudding of my own.

This is real. The thought sank deep into my bones. I wasn't dreaming, wasn't imagining it.

As the wave of heat and thunder reached a head, I clung to Lukas, sure my ribs were going to flay open, and then I heard —*no, felt*—thoughts layering over my own.

My wolf assessed her surroundings. Her senses sharp and focused. She was agitated. Hungry. Restless. *A little pissed off.*

I'm sorry. I sent the thought without even realizing it was possible. Grief washed over me, replacing the layers of terror and frustration.

Had she really been there all along? It felt like an empty cupboard inside of my heart was suddenly full. I hadn't even realized it was vacant until suddenly, it wasn't.

You should be. She stretched, breathed. Raised her head and flashed her golden eyes, then honed in on him. She pressed against my consciousness, and Lukas' arms went slack.

"What the hell is this," I whispered.

"Shh." Lukas didn't move. Didn't speak. We sat there together as our wolves inspected each other. Assessing. Judging.

And then she retreated slightly, and I melted against him, my body sapped of strength. I became acutely aware of every point of contact between us—the way his fingers brushed gently against my spine, the solid warmth of his chest beneath my cheek, the steady rise and fall of his breaths.

With great effort, I lifted my head, finding his eyes in the shadowed room. They were dark and intense behind his long lashes.

And then it was like a string tied to my spine was suddenly tugged, and I moved forward, tilting my chin, flexing into him like he was the case I was meant to fit into.

Lukas' gaze dropped to my lips, his own parting slightly. The movement was subtle, but it sent a shockwave through me, my breath catching in my throat. For a suspended moment, we hovered on the precipice, and I didn't remember anything outside of that bedroom. That bed. Those sheets and his arms.

My hand lifted of its own accord, fingers trailing lightly over his jaw, feeling the roughness of his stubble beneath my touch.

One kiss. The thought came unbidden, treacherous. *What would it hurt?* My lips tingled, blood rushing in my ears.

Then, from outside, a commotion shattered the quiet of the night—a distant shout, the crash of something falling. Lukas jerked back, his head snapping toward the sound.

Another yell. A grunt and a second crash.

"Something's happening by the pool," he growled, already pushing back to stand.

The loss of his touch was a physical ache, like something vital had been ripped away. But the urgent tone in his voice broke whatever spell I'd been under. I nodded, though my tongue felt tangled and useless, unable to form words.

Lukas hesitated at the door, his hand on the knob. He glanced back at me, his eyes conflicted. "Kate, I . . . " His voice trailed off, his jaw tightening. "We'll talk later."

And then he was gone. The door closed softly behind him, leaving me alone with the storm inside me. I sat motionless on the bed, my fingers pressed to my lips, still feeling the warmth of his skin. But as the seconds ticked by, reality came crashing back with a force that made me want to scream.

I didn't want this. I didn't want a mate. I didn't want the complicated tangle of emotions and instincts that came with it. I wasn't ready for the weight of that responsibility, the pull of something deeper than attraction. I didn't want my life to be tethered to someone else, to give them the control to ruin me. I wasn't open to feeling any of it, but especially not . . . *her*.

My wolf. She was there now, prowling beneath my skin, awake and restless, agitated by Lukas' absence. She was curious. Interested. The thought sent a cold rush of panic through me, and I pushed her down, tried to shove that primal part of me back into the dark where she belonged.

She was the reason I wasn't in control. *She was risking everything.*

I stood abruptly, pacing the small confines of the hut. My breath came in shallow gasps as my mind raced, tumbling over the implications of what had just happened. My wolf was awake, and nothing in my life would ever be the same. *Shit.* Nothing was going to be the same.

I should never have come. No amount of tuition money was worth this. The thought of returning home with my wolf in my head—trying to do my work, trying to succeed as a lawyer—

And then another thought derailed the first. *What if my parents were right?* The fear clawed at my insides, gnawing away at my resolve. My parents had always suspected this would happen, had professed this day would come, but I'd been hell-bent on proving them wrong.

They'd always said we weren't whole until we embraced our wolf, but I wanted to show them that I could be normal. That I could have the life I wanted without bending to this magic that lay dormant inside me.

But now? What if everything they said was true? What if I found out I'd wasted the last ten years of my life? What if nothing I loved or cared about mattered? New fear unlocked, and it was enough to make me dry heave.

I stopped pacing, my heart racing as I stared at the bed, at the space where Lukas had just been.

I wasn't ready for this. I wasn't ready for my wolf, for the pull toward Lukas, for the shift in my very identity. I wasn't ready to let go of the person I'd spent my whole life trying to be. *I wouldn't end up like Lee.*

"I can't do this," I whispered into the empty room, my voice shaking with fear. "I won't."

But even as the words left my lips, I knew they were a lie.

Something had changed tonight, something fundamental and irreversible.

And I didn't know what in the hell I was supposed to do about it.

TWENTY

TALKBACKS

M^{AX}

Zara: You look better than you did last night.

Max: They won't let me call my lawyer.

Zara: You have a lawyer?

Max: My family does. What Orion did last night? That should put him in prison. I'm going to send pictures as soon as we're done here.

Zara: You tried to touch his mate.

Max: I didn't know shit about KB being his mate! We got back and found out our pairs were all changed, and I made a joke.

Zara: But he was with KB on the way home from the club even though he was paired with Willow.

Max: Yeah. I thought we were swinging.

Zara: He said he gave you a warning?

Max: Pft. I didn't know he was serious.
Zara: Seems like you know now?

PATRICK

ZARA: Hey, Pat—

Patrick: What the hell happened last night?

Zara: You'll have to be more specific.

Patrick: I saw Max's face outside. Did that happen at the club? Are the others okay?

Zara: By others . . .

Patrick: Yeah, I mean Kate. Did something happen?

Zara: She's fine. Max got his ass handed to him by Orion.

Patrick: . . . Seriously? Orion? Damn.

Zara: Back to Kate—

Patrick: Oh, not a big deal. She was my last partner before the challenge. Just making sure she's okay.

Zara: So you're fine that she's been paired with Lukas for three nights now?

Patrick: Hmm. Weird that he keeps choosing her.

Zara: Weird?

Patrick: I wonder if she's okay with it.

Zara: You could probably ask her.

Patrick: Yeah. I could.

KB

. . .

Zara: I'm surprised to see you here this morning.

KB: Surprised? Why?

Zara: I know what it's like to be newly mated.

KB: Oh, Orion wasn't happy about me leaving.

Zara: He's still at your hut?

KB: Hell, no. He's pacing outside the door.

Zara: You find that funny?

KB: Umm mostly hot.

Zara: So you're good with this. That he felt the mating bond?

KB: I felt it before he did. Why do you think I was all over him at the club?

Zara: Oh, I guess I assumed—

KB: All good. People always think the males are stronger, but female alpha energy just presents differently.

Zara: . . . You're an alpha? And—

Orion: Hey. I'll stand over here.

Zara: That's my door. You just broke down my—

Orion: They wouldn't let me in.

Zara: . . .

Orion: I'll replace it.

TWENTY-ONE

The coral sunrise glowed over the ocean as I knocked on the door to KB's hut, my thoughts churning like the ocean behind me. The air was cool but already promising heat, the kind that clings to your skin and makes everything feel heavier. KB emerged a moment later, her dark hair tousled and her eyes bleary with sleep. "Hey. What's up?"

"I need to talk. Surfing?" My voice was tighter than I intended, and understanding dawned in her eyes. Likely because she'd seen my surfing performance.

She yawned. "Okay, just give me five."

I waited on the step, mulling over the night before. I didn't hear Lukas come back into the room. I was so emotionally exhausted. Then when I woke, he wasn't there in the bed. Anger had flared in me, then. Why would he act that way—hold me like that, be there for me—and then just leave?

The door swung open, and KB appeared. We crossed the sand in our swimsuits. Riley handed us two surfboards with a friendly nod, and we paddled out past the waves. I had no intention of trying to catch one, but it was quiet out here. Nobody around to listen in.

The salt spray misted my face, and the cool water lapped at my limbs, but it did little to soothe the unease coiling in my stomach. Seabirds wheeled overhead, their cries mingling with the rhythmic white noise. For a moment, I tried to focus on the beauty around me—the way the sun kissed the horizon, turning the water into liquid gold. But even out here, the thoughts gnawed at me, relentless and insistent.

What happened last night? I couldn't shake the feeling of my wolf, that strange, wild presence waking up inside me, reaching out toward Lukas with a pull I didn't understand. It was like she had a mind of her own—no, it was like I had become someone else. Someone I barely recognized. How could so much happen in so little time?

We sat straddling our boards, bobbing gently on the swells. KB swept her hair back, giving me a searching look. "So, what's on your mind?"

I tried to focus on her, but my thoughts were a tangled mess. "Umm, we could start with Max. What an arrogant jerk."

KB snorted. "Seriously."

"What set him off, though?" By the time I'd gone out to the pool deck, everyone had dispersed.

KB dragged in a breath. "Is that what you wanted to talk about?"

I chewed my lip, hesitating as the unease bubbled back to the surface. No more small talk. "KB, can I ask your advice about something? It's about my wolf."

Her expression softened. "I wondered."

"Did you notice anything? At the bonfire?"

KB nodded. "I felt her. Even though I was across the beach."

I wanted her to say more. To say something about what she felt, but couldn't bring myself to ask.

KB turned her board. "That was the first time?"

I took a shaky breath, the words tumbling out before I could stop them. "I didn't shift. Just—there were lots of feelings. But then last night . . . " I shook my head. "She's there now. I can feel her. She *talks* to me." I winced, waiting for KB to laugh at me, but she didn't.

"That's so great!" Her eyes lit up. "Not everyone can hear their wolf, so you're lucky."

Lucky? That was the last thing I felt. "I just don't get why it's happening now, you know? Like, why here on this island of all places?"

KB threw her head back and laughed, and for a second, I felt a flash of annoyance. This wasn't funny—didn't she get that I was terrified? But then she met my eyes again, her gaze kind. "Oh, Kate. Think about it. You're feeling so much right now—excitement, nerves, attraction. That's why this place works. *Of course* your wolf is stirring awake. She feels everything you feel, only amplified."

I swallowed hard, trying to absorb her words. My wolf *was* me, but she was also *not* me, and that scared me more than anything. I didn't want to be ruled by instincts, by some ancient force I barely understood. I'd always been the one in control. *What if I couldn't be that person anymore?*

"So what do I do? How do I handle this?" My voice cracked, and I hated the desperation I heard there. So pathetic.

KB's expression turned thoughtful, her eyes distant, like she was remembering something from long ago. "The key is not to fight it. Embrace your wolf, get to know her. She's a part of you." She offered me a small, encouraging smile. "When I first shifted, it was overwhelming. Like every nerve ending was on fire. But over time, I learned to channel that energy, to work with my wolf instead of against her."

I nodded slowly, trying to believe that it could be that simple. "What if I can't?"

"What do you mean you can't?"

I exhaled and told her about Lee. Explained how for the last two years, I'd watched him shrink into a shell of of the man he'd been before. "I can't do it. I didn't want to embrace that side of myself before, but now? I don't see how that's worth it."

KB nodded. "Don't you think he had a choice?"

I frowned. "No, she was in a car crash—"

"I mean after." She turned and looked at me. "I'm not saying it wasn't devastating, but maybe . . . I don't know. Maybe he's doing the same thing you are."

"Which is?"

She gave a small smile. "Fighting it."

An image of Lukas flashed in my head. *Mine.* My hands started to tremble.

"I'm fated." KB said it so fast, I almost missed it.

"Wait, what?"

She exhaled, her cheeks staining pink. "To Orion."

My eyes bugged out of my head. "What—when did this happen?"

"Last night. It just—" She clapped her hands together.

"He knows?"

Her blush stained crimson. "Uh, yeah. He knows."

"Do you . . . do you want this, KB?" The question slipped out before I could stop it. We were only halfway in. *How could so much be happening in a couple of weeks?*

KB glanced out at the water, the sun glinting off the waves. "It's not about wanting or not wanting it, Kate. It's about accepting it. My wolf chose, and I choose to trust her." She turned back to me, and there was a fierce light in her eyes, something wild and untamed. "And yes, I do want it. Because the alternative? Living half a life, denying a part of who I am . . . That's not living at all."

"But you said—"

"I know what I said," she groaned. "But I was wrong. It's— I don't know, Kate. Like my world was in black and white and now it's—" She spread her arms out like she was giving the sky a hug. "I know it sounds ridiculous. I would have made fun of me a week ago."

"But what about your life? What are you going to do?"

KB shrugged. "We haven't gotten that far."

"How far did you get?"

"Mostly just sex. A lot of sex."

I laughed and splashed her. As we paddled back toward shore, the tension coiling tighter with each stroke. I wrestled against the voice in my head—the one that whispered that maybe I should trust my wolf. That I should recognize how she came alive with Lukas. But I couldn't accept that. Not yet. Maybe not ever.

The beach came into view, and my thoughts skittered like the foam across the waves, unable to settle. The island was beautiful, sure, but it felt like a trap—like a place where everything I'd been running from was catching up to me, faster than I could outrun it.

One month. Hundreds of thousands of dollars.

Maybe it wasn't worth it.

We reached the beach and hopped off our boards, carrying them up the sand. As we made our way back toward the pool area, a knot of unease twisted tighter in my gut, my brief respite from reality fading with each step.

But as we rounded the corner, I was jolted out of my thoughts by the sight of Sevina standing by the pool bar, surrounded by people. Even from a distance, I could see the tension in her shoulders, the tight lines of her face. She looked upset, almost angry.

Exchanging a curious glance with KB, I quickened my pace, the soft sand shifting beneath my sandals. The closer we got, the clearer it became that something was wrong. Sevina's normally pale complexion was flushed, her violet eyes flashing as she spoke to the group in low, urgent tones.

"What's going on?" I asked as we reached them, a sense of foreboding trickling down my spine like icy water.

Sevina's gaze snapped to mine, and in that moment, I saw a flicker of something that looked almost like pity. "Oh, Kate. I'm sure you're so disappointed."

I frowned. "About what?"

"That Lukas had to leave."

My heart stuttered in my chest. "What are you talking about?"

"Well, what did any of us expect, really. It's not like the prince of Rheinhardt would be able to take an entire month off." Elise grinned, folding her arms over her chest.

The prince of—what? Blood rushed in my ears. Rheinhardt. The high alpha. Wasn't that the article my dad had sent to me earlier in the week? I never paid attention to them, to any hierarchies within the shifter world, but now . . .

Sevina stepped forward, her expression softening. "Kate, are you okay? This isn't a surprise, right? Lukas *must* have told you."

TWENTY-TWO

The WiFi lounge was a stark contrast to the rest of the resort - sleek white furniture, cool air conditioning, and the soft glow of computer screens instead of tiki torches and ocean breezes. I tried to focus on the steady hum of the AC unit, hoping it would calm the churning storm inside me. But as I paced in front of Zara's desk, my hands clenched at my sides, it was impossible to push down the anger and confusion boiling up from my gut.

Zara sat perfectly poised, her dark hair sleek and not a strand out of place despite the island humidity. She regarded me with a polite but distant expression, her professional mask firmly in place.

"I'm sorry, Kate, but as I've said, I'm not at liberty to discuss the personal details of any of our guests, including Lukas. We have strict non-disclosure policies in place." Her tone was measured. Rehearsed.

I stopped pacing and leaned on her desk, meeting her gaze directly. "Cut the corporate shit, Zara. This isn't about some random guest. This is Lukas. He's my partner—"

"Are you trying to tell me he's more to you than an assigned pair? Are you fated?"

"No, I—no." I ran my hands through my hair.

Zara's expression softened. "I understand this must be difficult for you, Kate. But my hands are tied. The best I can suggest is that you speak directly with Lukas about any concerns you have."

I let out a harsh laugh. "Speak with Lukas? He's gone, Zara. Disappeared without a word." Not exactly without a word. I had found a note in our hut that said:

Family emergency. L

"And now I find out he's some kind of royalty?," I continued. "That everyone knew who he really was except me?" Each word tasted bitter on my tongue.

Zara sighed, her professionalism slipping for just a moment. "I truly am sorry, Kate. Not everyone knew. He wanted to keep it quiet for obvious reasons. I wish I could say more. But this is a complicated situation, and there are factors at play that I simply can't discuss."

I pushed off from her desk, my anger deflating into a hollow ache in my chest. "Right. Of course. Forget I asked."

I could still feel his arms around me. Hear his voice whispering against my ear. Why hadn't he said something? Probably because I was absolutely losing it. When would he have had time?

And it didn't matter. Lukas didn't owe me anything. *Are you trying to tell me you're more than assigned pairs?*

I groaned and stalked to the door, then paused, slipping my hand in the pocket of my shorts. *WiFi.* That was my key, my only connection to the outside world. I snatched it up, my fingers trembling slightly as I navigated to the browser.

I turned back to Zara. "Do you think we talked for ten minutes?"

Zara opened her mouth, then shut it. She motioned for me to go into the lounge.

Thirty minutes. That was all I had.

I took a deep breath, steeling myself for what I might find. Then, with a sense of grim determination, I began to type.

The minutes ticked by, each search result adding another piece to the puzzle. Royal engagements, charity events, press releases—a life so far removed from the carefree existence we'd shared on the island that it was hard to reconcile the two.

But there he was, staring out at me from the screen. Andrew Lukas, heir to the Nachtwald Dynasty. The High Alpha's son.

I have family responsibilities.

No shit. Everything dropped into place. The way he put on a show, how he always looked so polished, his accent.

I set my phone on the table, my breath coming in shallow gasps. My wolf stirred within me, responding to my agitation, the need for action. She prowled beneath my skin, urging me to move, to run, to give in to the primal instincts that had always been there to guide me. The instincts I'd ignored.

But I still couldn't relent. Not here. Not now.

I stalked out of the WiFi lounge, barely registering the startled looks from the other guests. My legs carried me towards the pool, the laughter and splashing of the guests a jarring contrast to the storm raging inside me. I skirted the edge, keeping to the shadows of the palm trees, my eyes fixed on the path that led to my hut.

Sevina's voice drifted over to me, smug and gloating, each word a dagger twisting in my gut. "Of course Lukas is playing games," she said, her tone dripping with condescension. "He's the heir. He can't just mate with anyone. It has to be strategic."

I froze momentarily, then forced myself to move. I reached my hut, the door slamming behind me.

~

I woke from my nap in a cold sweat.

My skin felt too tight, stretched thin over a frame that could barely contain the tempest within. The heat built beneath my flesh, a fever that had nothing to do with the tropical climate and everything to do with the war raging inside me. I paced the confines of the hut, my footsteps echoing the frantic rhythm of my heart.

I couldn't breathe. Couldn't think. Couldn't focus on anything but the overwhelming need to escape, to break free. I had to get out. Had to move, to run, to do something—anything—to quiet the screaming in my head. With a burst of desperate energy, I lunged for the door, nearly tearing it off its hinges in my haste to escape.

The night air hit me like a slap, the humidity clinging to my skin. I gulped in deep breaths, filling my lungs with the heady scent of the jungle—a mix of damp earth, exotic blooms, and the faint, salty tang of the distant ocean.

For a moment, I just stood there, letting the symphony of nocturnal sounds wash over me. The chirping of insects, the rustle of leaves in the gentle breeze. Everything was brighter. Louder. More intense.

I stared up into the sky and found it. The moon. Round and swollen. Without a second thought, I plunged into the foliage, letting the shadows swallow me whole. The undergrowth tugged at my clothes, scratched at my skin, but I barely felt it. All I could focus on was the pounding of my heart, the rush of blood in my ears, the frenzied energy propelling me forward.

I ran. I ran like the hounds of hell were on my heels, like I could outpace the demons nipping at my soul. I ran until my lungs burned and my muscles screamed, until the physical pain eclipsed the emotional anguish, and in that moment, I felt a shift deep within me, a stirring of something ancient and primal.

The pain hit me like a tidal wave, crashing over me with a force that stole my breath. It started deep in my bones, a searing ache that radiated outward, consuming every inch of my being. I doubled over, my fingers digging into the damp earth as a scream tore from my throat.

But even as the agony threatened to overwhelm me, there was a strange undercurrent of rightness, of inevitability. It was as if my body had been waiting for this moment, yearning for the transformation that now took hold.

My bones shifted, realigning themselves with sickening cracks and pops. My skin stretched, itched, as fur sprouted along my spine, racing across my body in a wave of heat. My senses sharpened, the jungle coming alive around me in a dizzying array of scents and sounds.

The pain reached a crescendo, a white-hot blaze that consumed every fiber of my being. I was torn apart and remade, my human consciousness fading as the wolf surged to the forefront. In that moment, I was neither Kate nor beast, but something in between, caught in the liminal space between two worlds.

And then, as suddenly as it began, it was over. The pain receded, leaving behind a thrumming energy, a wild vitality that coursed through my veins. I rose on shaky legs, marveling at the strength and power of this new form.

The jungle looked different through the eyes of the wolf, the colors more vivid, the shadows more alive. I could hear the whisper of leaves in the breeze, the distant call of a night bird, the scurry of small creatures in the underbrush. The world was a symphony, and I was finally attuned to its music.

It was exhilarating. Terrifying.

Everything I'd ignored from my parents and our pack, all the lectures and lessons I'd pushed away, flooded through me. *It's part of you.* Lukas' words filtered through my wolf back to me. *Did I want it to be?*

A faint rustling in the underbrush snapped me out of my reverie, my ears swiveling to catch the sound. The wolf in me tensed, ready to fight or flee, but then a familiar scent reached my nose, and my heart leaped with a mixture of relief and trepidation.

Through the shadows, I saw the glow of eyes—not the amber of a predator, but the luminous green and blue of my fellow contestants. Patrick emerged first, his sandy coat dappled with moonlight. KB and Willow followed, their dark and pale forms sleek and powerful as they moved through the foliage. Finally, Orion stepped into view, his black fur seeming to melt into the night.

I knew who they were by scent. They were all here, all shifted, and the realization hit me like a physical blow. It was one thing to know, intellectually, that we were all shifters, but it was another thing entirely to see it, to feel the primal connection thrumming between us.

I took a hesitant step forward, my paws silent on the soft earth. Patrick's gaze met mine, and even in this form, I could see the glimmer of his humor, the warmth of his spirit. He gave a little yip, a playful sound that eased some of the tension in my frame.

KB moved to my side, her presence solid and reassuring. There was an understanding in her eyes, a shared knowledge of the struggle and the wonder of this transformation. Willow, too, radiated empathy, her posture open and inviting.

But it was Orion who surprised me the most. The aloof, mysterious man I'd come to know seemed to melt away, replaced by a wolf whose gaze held a depth of emotion I never expected. He stepped forward, his muzzle brushing mine in a gesture of comfort and solidarity before he settled at KB's side.

At this moment, under the canopy of stars and surrounded by the understanding of my fellow shifters, I felt a sense of belonging, of rightness, that I'd never known before. The fears and doubts that plagued me seemed to recede, replaced by a growing acceptance of who and what I was.

Was this what it was like? Was this what I'd been trying to create with my roommates, my classmates, every single one of my connections?

I let out a soft whine, a sound of gratitude and connection, and I felt the others respond in kind. Our minds brushed against each other, not quite a full link, but a whisper of the bond that could be, that would be, if we let it.

KB leaped up and trotted past me, then jumped over a fallen log, her dark fur rippling in the moonlight. She glanced back at me, her golden eyes glinting with challenge and camaraderie. *Race you to the river!* Her thought slipped into my mind, a playful taunt.

I felt my own lips pull back in a wolfish grin as I accepted her challenge. The others fell in alongside us, our paws drumming the earth.

As we ran, I felt the last of my resistance fall away, the last of my human concerns and doubts dissolving in the purity of this moment. There would be time later for questions, for worries, for figuring out how to navigate this new reality. But for now, there was only the wind and the earth and the moon, only the song of the pack and the joy of the hunt.

We played in the water, then ran back through the jungle, heading for the highest point above the resort. My wolf peered through the trees, searching for something. For someone. I tried to ignore it, but the human me was worried about Lukas, too. Family emergency? After all my searching, I assumed it had to do with his father. That thought made me nauseous. The thought of my dad being sick, of losing him, made me want to curl up in the fetal position.

My spiraling thoughts were interrupted as we broke through the tree line, emerging onto a rocky outcrop high above the ocean. The four of us froze.

Mac and Trinity stood at the edge of the cliff, their faces illuminated by the glow of lanterns, their expressions a mix of excitement and solemnity. Another group of wolves gathered around them.

"Welcome, everyone," Mac said, his voice carrying over the sound of the waves. "With the full moon, we have a special challenge for you tonight. A treasure hunt to test your abilities as wolves and as a pack."

What? I sent to the others.

Willow snorted. *Of course they made a secret challenge.*

Trinity stepped forward, her eyes glinting with mischief in the lantern light. "Each pair will follow a series of scent-based clues hidden around the island. You'll need to use your wolf senses and your human cunning to find them all and reach the final location first." Her words lingered in the air, heavy with challenge.

A murmur of excitement rippled through the group, but I felt a sinking sensation in my stomach. *Each pair.* The words echoed in my mind, taunting me with the reminder of Lukas' absence. I pushed down the disappointment, willing myself to focus on the task ahead.

You're not alone, my wolf whispered, her presence a comforting warmth in my mind. I took a deep breath, steeling myself as Mac and Trinity handed out the first scent clues.

Stepping forward, I inhaled deeply from the piece of fabric the other wolves had sniffed before me. The scent was rich and earthy, with a hint of pine and something floral that tickled my senses. My wolf immediately recognized the notes—wild jasmine.

The grove near the twisted banyan, she suggested, the certainty thrumming through our bond. Had we passed a grove? I certainly hadn't noticed.

I glanced around, watching as the other wolves melted into the shadows, darting into the jungle with their partners. Sevina caught my eye, a smug smile playing on her lips as she leaned close to Max.

Turning, I let my paws carry me silently through the soft undergrowth, following the faint trail of wild jasmine that led deeper into the dense forest. The scents of the night enveloped me—damp earth, the sweet tang of ripe fruit, the musky undertone of nocturnal creatures stirring in the dark.

As I neared the ancient banyan tree, its sprawling roots curling like gnarled fingers into the soil, my wolf perked up, nostrils flaring. A new scent hit me—sharp and citrusy, mixed with a distinct mineral note. *Lemon balm and salt.* The smell led me beneath the tangled roots, where a patch of damp moss glowed faintly in the moonlight, saturated with the scent.

Mark it, my wolf urged, nudging me to leave a scratch on the earth as a sign of our discovery. I pressed my paw against the moss, the coolness seeping through my pads.

But even as I savored the small victory, I couldn't help but scan the shadows, searching for any sign of the others. Orion and KB were nowhere to be seen, their bond giving them an edge I couldn't hope to match. And Sevina . . . I caught a flash of her silver fur in the distance, Max at her side, and my stomach twisted with a mix of envy and frustration.

They're ahead of us, I thought bitterly.

I raised my nose to the strip of fabric tacked to a tree, searching for the next scent. The smell of seawater mingled with a faint, woodsy note—cedar. My wolf's instincts sharpened, guiding us toward the rocky coastline where the river met the ocean.

We bounded over roots and under low-hanging branches, my paws barely touching the ground. When we reached the river's edge, the scent grew stronger, pulling us toward a cluster of smooth stones that jutted from the water. I nosed around until I found it—a smooth pebble that carried the cedar scent, tucked beneath a fern.

There beside it was another strip of cloth. *Another clue,* I thought, a surge of pride running through me. But I couldn't savor it for long. I knew that somewhere out there, Sevina and the others were closing in on their own trails. We had to keep moving.

The last scent was faint but clear, but I couldn't name it. I recognized it from that day with Patrick on the kayaks. I bolted forward, racing through the moonlit trees, and for a moment, I let go, allowing my wolf to guide me.

The relief would've brought me to tears if I were in my human form. I couldn't remember the last time I wasn't clinging to the reins of my life. Being here in this place and now *not being alone* was overwhelming.

The emotions rolled over me in waves. The fear. The longing. The warmth. The grief. They swirled together into an overwhelming concoction, and all I wanted was to go back to my bed. To have Lukas there next to me, telling me it would all be okay.

My wolf bolted toward the scent, then pulled up short at the entrance to a cave. I steeled myself, swallowing the bitter taste of defeat as I approached Sevina and Max. They were basking in the glow of victory, their faces alight with smug satisfaction.

They'd already shifted back to their human forms and were wearing some kind of loungewear. Trinity stood holding out a set of clothes for me, motioning at a rock outcropping for privacy.

I went behind the rock, not at all sure how I was going to shift back into my human form. The wind rustled through the trees, and I dropped to my belly, trying to listen. My chest heaved, my heartbeat still working to slow. *Breathe,* I whispered, fighting the surge of emotions clawing at my insides—anger, fear, the wild exhilaration that still hummed beneath my skin.

My wolf whimpered, and I closed my eyes, focusing on the rhythm of the waves crashing against the rocks, letting their steady pulse ground me. Slowly, I let go of the frustration that burned hot in my veins, releasing it like steam into the cool night air. As the tension ebbed, my muscles began to loosen, the tight coil in my chest unfurling until only a quiet calm remained. My wolf stirred, reluctant to give up her hold, but I soothed her with a promise. *I won't bury you again. I promise.*

I meant it. I didn't know what my life would look like, but I wasn't naive enough to believe I could go back to who I was two days ago. I had felt her. I knew her now. I couldn't ignore that like I had before when I didn't understand.

When the calm settled deep in my bones, I began to change. My body tensed, then shivered as the magic of the shift rippled through me like an electric current dancing along my spine. My bones shrank and realigned with a series of sharp cracks, each one like a jolt of ice along my nerves, as my limbs shortened and reformed. The fur that coated my skin melted away, receding like dew in the morning light, leaving behind the cool kiss of the evening breeze against bare flesh.

Heat flashed through me, a searing wave that left me breathless before ebbing away as the contours of my human body returned. I gasped, my knees buckling as I knelt in the dirt, naked and shivering. But I was myself again—human, whole, and aware of the lingering wildness that still thrummed beneath my skin.

I took the clothes from Trinity and dressed. Slowly. Carefully. Trying to keep my stomach from revolting.

"Congratulations," I forced out after stepping back out onto the rocky outcropping, the words like ashes on my tongue.

Sevina's smile widened, showing a flash of white teeth. "Thanks, Kate. It was a close one."

My wolf bristled, a low growl rumbling in my chest, but I forced it down, refusing to give her the satisfaction of seeing me rattled. *We don't hate her*, I thought. Sevina wasn't a terrible person, she just knew what she wanted.

She can't have it, my wolf snapped, and I knew exactly what —who—she meant. In that moment, I was jealous of both of them. Sevina and my wolf were so confident, so sure. I was neither.

I turned to walk away, but Sevina's voice stopped me, sharp and mocking. "Kate? I hope you don't mind, but I've decided to choose Lukas. I know he's not here right now, but he should be back soon."

Her words hit me like a punch to the gut, stealing the breath from my lungs. I felt a wave of hurt, of betrayal, wash over me, so strong it made my knees weak.

I started to turn away again, but Max's voice stopped me, smooth and mocking. "Don't worry, Kate. You won't be lonely. I've decided to choose you as my partner for the next challenge. We haven't had much time together. Alone."

TWENTY-THREE

TALKBACKS

Patrick

Zara: So. You all shifted last night.

Patrick: Well, not all of us. Most.

Zara: . . .

Patrick: What is that look?

Zara: What look?

Patrick: You look a little smug.

Zara: Do I? Sorry, this is always my favorite part.

Patrick: What is?

Zara: The moment you all figure out who you truly are.

Patrick: Maybe I already knew.

Zara: You did. But there were others who didn't.

Patrick: Yeah. It was . . . I don't know. I haven't felt that emotional. Maybe ever.

Zara: This island. There's something about it.

Patrick: Did you slip something in our drinks?

Zara: Didn't even have to.

∾

Sevina

Zara: You won the challenge and chose a new partner.

Sevina: Of course. It's where Lukas belongs, with me. His family knows it, my family knows it. It's only a matter of time.

Zara: Hmm. And Lukas is back?

Sevina: Yes, he's resting.

Zara: Have the two of you . . . Well, I don't want to pry. But has there been a bond?

Sevina: Not yet. But we haven't had much time together.

Zara: So you think over the next couple of days—

Sevina: Oh definitely. Especially with his father. He needs to find a mate. I'm the obvious choice since I understand his responsibilities.

Zara: You grew up in Rheinhardt?

Sevina: Lukas and I first met when we were thirteen. You should've seen his face when he saw me here. Both of us have definitely grown up.

∾

KB and Orion

Zara: So.

KB: You don't even have to say it.

Zara: Okay, I won't. But I will say that you and Orion don't need to do talk backs anymore.

KB: But what if we want WiFi?

Zara: You are going to get this for the remainder of your trip.

Orion: Personal hot spot?

Zara: For your hut. And don't share.

KB: So, what does this look like for the next two weeks?

Zara: You two are home free. It looks however you want.

KB: No challenges?

Zara: No challenges.

Orion: Food?

Zara: Anything you want.

KB: So it's just a paid vacation.

Zara: Welcome to paradise.

Orion: Damn. If someone would've told me that, I would've done this day one.

KB: You tried to do this day one. Remember what you said to me at dinner?

Orion: Yeah. I remember.

KB: And then you kissed Willow.

Orion: To make you jealous!

KB: . . .

Zara: Seems like it worked?

~

Elise

Zara: You look upset. Is everything okay?

Elise: Maybe? I don't know. Everyone else shifted last night.

Zara: You didn't.

Elise: No.

Zara: It sounds like you wanted to.

Elise: No, I didn't want to, but I wasn't trying to *not* make it happen. So now I wonder if there's something wrong with me.

Zara: Sometimes this takes time.

Elise: Not for everyone else.

Zara: We can't control our magic, Elise. That's kind of the point of it. To teach us to let go. Have a little faith in something outside of ourselves.

Elise: Maybe that's it. Maybe I'm scared I shouldn't have believed it was possible for me.

CHAPTER

TWENTY-FOUR

Lukas sat next to Sevina across the room. I couldn't help but watch out of the corner of my eye as they talked, their heads close together. Every now and then, Sevina's laugh would ring out, a melodic sound that made the tiny hairs on the back of my neck stand on end.

Max leaned in, his breath hot against my ear. "Do you like seafood? They've got a fantastic selection here."

I nodded, my throat suddenly dry. "I do, yes."

His hand brushed against mine as he reached for his water glass, and I flinched. Max grinned, and a knot tightened in my stomach. "You seem a bit tense, Kate. Is it the competition? Or something else?"

Lukas' laugh drew my attention again, a deep, resonant sound that made my pulse quicken. He turned to Sevina, saying something I couldn't catch, and she responded by playfully swatting his arm. They looked good together if I was being honest. Too good.

Max's fingers drummed on the table next to my hand, drawing me back. "It's just interesting, isn't it? Being paired up like this. Forced proximity can do funny things to people." His eyes gleamed with amusement, and I felt a shiver run down my spine.

I forced a smile. "I suppose it can."

He leaned in closer, his lips almost brushing my ear. "I think it's already starting to work."

My heart started to pound. "Excuse me, I need to use the restroom." I pushed my chair back and stood, my legs unsteady.

Max's expression was a mix of confusion and amusement as I walked away. I didn't look back, didn't want to see if Lukas had noticed my abrupt exit.

The restaurant was beautiful, the food smelled incredible, but I couldn't escape the storm brewing inside me. The pull to Lukas, the discomfort with Max, and the gnawing fear that I was out of control.

I splashed water on my face in the restroom. When I finally returned to the table, Sevina was laughing again, and Lukas was leaning back in his chair, his eyes scanning the room.

I kept my head down and tried to focus on the salad in front of me, but the sounds of the room, the clinking of glasses, the hum of conversation, felt like they were pressing in on me.

Max leaned in, his shoulder brushing against mine. I could smell the musk of his cologne, and it made my stomach clench. "I don't understand why you're so standoffish."

I cleared my throat. "Really? That's your statement?"

Max's lips curved into a smile. "See, where I'm from, comments like that mean you're interested."

I scoffed. "Aren't you from out east?"

He nodded. "Manhattan."

I blew out a breath. That made sense, not that it was an excuse for his behavior. But I'd heard my parents talking about issues with packs out there. Any big city, really. Constant territory wars.

"Yeah. Doesn't mean the same thing in Minnesota," I said.

"Luckily we're not there, either." Max grinned, and I stared at my cherry tomatoes.

Somehow I survived through to dessert, then when Max made it clear he was ready to head back to our hut, I suggested we stay at the pool for after-dinner drinks. My voice sounded too bright, too forced, and Max seemed to enjoy my obvious discomfort. I didn't want to go back to the hut, not with the way my body was betraying me. What if Max tried something, and I lost it? Shifted right there and tore out his throat? Nothing was off the table as far as I was concerned.

I sat near the edge of the pool for over an hour, my arms wrapped around my middle. I watched the others from a distance, my heart pounding in my chest. Max was getting sloshed with David, Enzo, and Matteo, his laughter growing louder with each drink. Lovely. Just what I wanted for the night, Max with less of a filter.

"Kate!" he called, his voice slurred. "You should come over here!" I shook my head, trying to smile, but it felt like a mask. Max's eyes narrowed, and he started to push himself up from his lounge chair.

Just then, Lukas walked past, and the world seemed to hold its breath. Lukas' presence was like a black hole, pulling all the oxygen from the air.

He stopped next to Max's chair and leaned in. Max looked up, his face a mixture of surprise and confusion. Lukas murmured something, but I was too far away to make out any of it. He stepped back, then continued on toward the bar. Max's eyes were dark.

"Another round?" David asked.

Max shook his head. "No, I'm good. You guys enjoy." He

didn't look at me as he walked past, heading back to the path and our hut.

I stood there, frozen, as Lukas stopped for a drink, then turned and walked back to his side of the pool. He didn't stop, didn't look up, and didn't say another word.

It wasn't long before the rest of the group started to disperse, some heading back to their huts, others lingering by the pool. Lukas was still sitting with Sevina and a few other people. It looked like they were playing cards.

Nervous energy built in my middle, my mind spinning. *What had Lukas said to Max?* It was late, and I knew I should get to bed, but I couldn't force myself to walk toward the hut, knowing Max was in there.

So instead, I watched as couples started to peel off, heading back to their huts. When we were down to a skeleton crew, I looked up at the clear, calm sky and made a decision. I wasn't going to sleep anywhere near Max tonight.

I walked past the pool and started toward the beach, then made a beeline for the front desk. The woman at the counter gave me an odd look when I asked for toiletries, but she handed me a small canvas bag. I thanked her and walked past the lounge, where the last few stragglers were finishing their drinks.

I stopped at the showers and used the tiny soap to wash my face, then reached for the toothbrush and toothpaste. When I was finished, I turned off the water and dried off with one of the pool towels stacked inside the cupboard. I set that one in the dirty bin and grabbed two more.

The night air was warm, and the moon gave off enough light for me to easily find a hammock. I climbed in and wrapped the towels around myself, staring up at the stars. They were different here, brighter and more numerous than the ones I was used to back home.

This was crazy. I'd never slept outside as an adult, barely as a kid on a few camping trips as a family, but we'd still been inside a tent. But I was so tired. Bone-deep, soul-crushingly tired. I just didn't care anymore.

I wanted to relax, to let the events of the night melt away, but my mind kept circling back to Lukas. My wolf stirred inside me, and I felt that same magnetic pull toward him, even though he was nowhere in sight. It was like a rope wrapped around my middle, tugging me toward something I couldn't see. Or didn't want to. Everything about him was dangerous, and I was a moth to his flame.

I rolled onto my side, curling up in the hammock and pulling the towels tighter around me. The waves continued their lullaby, and my eyelids grew heavier with each pass. I let my mind drift, focusing on the gentle sway of the hammock and the cool breeze on my skin.

Eventually, exhaustion won out, and I slipped into sleep.

I didn't dream. Didn't surface.

Not until I woke to the first light of dawn painting the sky with hues of pink and orange. It took me a moment to orient myself, but once I was sure I was still intact and on land, I stretched out my stiff muscles.

Then I turned my head and froze.

There was something—no, someone—sleeping in the hammock next to mine.

TWENTY-FIVE

I blinked, trying to make sense of the scene in front of me. Lukas was in a hammock next to mine, and he was *moving*. I turned away from him, pretending I hadn't been watching him sleep, and tried to smooth my hair.

Lukas. Here. Not in his hut with Sevina.

I couldn't make sense of any of it. When I went to the beach last night, he was still at the pool with Sevina. Had he watched me go?

I swallowed against the lump in my throat. He'd left a two-word note in our hut when he'd left the island. I'd shifted alone. I'd had to do the surprise challenge alone.

And then the bombshell about him being a prince. Why the hell hadn't he told me? I'd had to hear it from Sevina. She'd known before me, they probably all had, and then here he was sleeping in the hammock?

Anger bubbled through me. I was a mess, and not just because of the night in a hammock. Lukas looked like he was on the most relaxing vacation of his life.

I wanted to punch him in the face.

Lukas let out a soft groan and stretched, the muscles in his arms and torso flexing under his light T-shirt. The golden light streaming through the palm fronds dappled intricate patterns on his skin, highlighting the contours of his face and the stubble on his jaw.

His eyes opened, and he blinked a few times before his gaze landed on me. For a moment, we just stared at each other, the silence between us filled with the sound of waves.

Lukas pushed himself up on one elbow. "Morning." His voice was gravelly. *Damn him.*

"What the hell, Lukas." I couldn't be cordial. Not this morning.

"You're mad?"

I scoffed. "You think?"

Lukas looked down at his hands, then back up at me. "I wanted to tell you, but I couldn't."

"Why not?"

He frowned. "It wasn't in the contract."

I stared at him, my mind struggling to catch up. "You're telling me that you signed a contract that said you couldn't tell the other guests who you were?"

He nodded. "Yes."

"Right. So, are we to conclude that Sevina's actions fall outside the scope of the contract's coverage?" My lawyer voice slipped out.

"Sevina knew me. Before we got here."

I blinked at him. "What?"

"Not as adults, but as kids."

I opened my mouth, then closed it again. What was I supposed to say to that?

Lukas continued. "Being a prince comes with a lot of baggage."

The sun rose higher in the sky, casting longer shadows on

the beach. The light was more direct now, less golden and more stark, making the pebbles and driftwood stand out in sharp relief. It felt fitting, like the world was shedding its soft, romantic glow to reveal the hard, cold truth beneath.

I nodded, not trusting myself to speak. He was finally opening up, and I didn't want to do anything to shut him down. I watched as he gathered his thoughts, his fingers drumming on the edge of the hammock.

Lukas took a deep breath and started talking. "Rheinhardt is a small country, nestled between Germany, Switzerland, and France. It's not on any maps you'll find in human history books, but it's been there for centuries. My family, the Nacht-wald dynasty, has ruled there for over a thousand years."

He paused, glancing at me to make sure I was following. I nodded again, and he continued. "The country is unique. It's a haven for shifters, a place where we can live openly without fear of persecution. The royal family, my family, has always been the bridge between shifters and humans there. We work with the Shifter Council to maintain balance and harmony."

I furrowed my brow. "Shifter Council? Like *the* Shifter Council?"

Lukas chuckled. "Yeah. The one and only. They work with packs around the world and handle the day-to-day governance to ensure our laws and traditions are upheld. The royal family, though, we're like . . . stewards. We oversee everything, make sure the council isn't overstepping, and handle diplomatic relations with other nations."

I took a moment to absorb all of that. "So, your father . . ."

"Is the High Alpha," Lukas finished for me. "And I will be once he's gone." He trailed off, his jaw clenching.

I blew out a breath. "I'm sorry about your father. I saw online he was ill."

"You looked online?"

"No, I—my mom is super into all that."

"All that?"

I fell back in my hammock. "Yeah. Your *royal* family."

Lukas nodded, his gaze fixed on the horizon. "He had a stroke. That's not something everybody knows, so if you could keep it to yourself."

I swallowed hard, warmth blooming in my chest. "Of course." I forced my lungs to expand, then gathered my courage to ask another question. "What does the High Alpha do, exactly?" I asked, trying to keep my voice steady.

Lukas exhaled slowly. "The High Alpha is responsible for maintaining peace and order among the shifters. That means enforcing laws, mediating disputes, and protecting our territory. It also means working with the human population to ensure our existence remains a secret and that we can coexist peacefully."

I raised an eyebrow. "And that's all done through the Shifter Council?"

"Mostly. The council members represent different regions and packs around the world. They bring their concerns and issues to the High Alpha, and we work together to find solutions. It's a system that's worked for centuries, but it's not without its challenges."

I nodded. "So that will be you someday."

Lukas' expression darkened. "Yes. And with that comes the expectation to find a mate. To continue the Nachtwald lineage." He looked at me, his gaze intense. "But I know how you feel about that."

My breath caught in my throat. "How I feel about what?"

Lukas shifted his weight, the hammock swaying. "About finding a mate. You've made it clear you want freedom, independence. You want to live your life without being tied down to anyone."

I opened my mouth, then closed it. He was right. I'd been adamant about that from the beginning, but now, sitting here with him, everything felt different. My wolf bristled, and I could feel her pacing just beneath my skin.

"I didn't think I wanted a mate either," Lukas continued, his voice barely above a whisper.

I pushed up on my elbows. "Then why are you here on this island?"

He looked at me, his blue eyes piercing. "For my mom."

I nodded. "She wants you to find a mate."

"She needs me to."

I took that in. I didn't need my tuition covered. It would be a nice perk, but Lukas . . . "You said you had responsibilities that didn't allow you to have a relationship."

He ran a hand through his hair. "Yeah. There aren't very many women who jump at the chance to take this on."

I snorted. "I can think of at least one who would."

Lukas shot me a look, and I sobered. He wet his lips. "I'm aware."

My pulse jumped. "Sevina makes sense, doesn't she?"

Lukas blew out a breath. "My family would be happy if I chose someone like Sevina. Her family has connections, money, influence. It's what's expected of me." He went silent, and when I glanced back at him, his face was turned toward the ocean. For a long moment, all I could hear was the soft rustle of palm leaves in the breeze, the gentle creak of our hammocks swaying. Then, finally, he spoke, his voice barely above a whisper. "Sevina does make sense."

I blinked, my heart twinging at the honesty of that statement. And the realization that somewhere, deep down, I'd wanted him to disagree with my assessment. But there it was.

I moved in the hammock, the ropes creaking beneath me,

and tried to steady my racing thoughts as pressure built behind my eyes. "Well, this has been a lovely chat—"

"Kate!" Max's voice cut through the air, and I whipped my head around. He and Sevina were jogging down the beach, their expressions a mix of relief and anger.

"Shit," I muttered under my breath. Of course they'd find us now. Assumptions were probably swirling in their heads when obviously they had no need to be worried where I was concerned.

Lukas was going to give Sevina exactly what she wanted.

TWENTY-SIX

Max loomed over us, his sharp jawline set like granite.

"What are you doing out here?" His voice was a low growl.

"Watch it," Lukas snapped.

My heart skipped a beat. I pushed myself up on my elbows, the hammock swaying beneath me. "I needed some alone time."

Max's eyes narrowed, and behind him, Sevina stood with her arms crossed. Her pale skin glowed in the early light, her long black hair cascading over her shoulders. But it was her eyes that held my attention—those striking violet eyes that were now fixed on Lukas.

"And what about you?" Sevina's voice was clipped.

Lukas didn't answer at first. He sat up slowly, his eyes avoiding both of them. "Must have dozed off."

"Hmm. Nice." Sevina's eyes flicked to Lukas and then back to me.

Max's nostrils flared, and I could sense his wolf pacing

inside him. It was so strange, this new source of information. It wasn't empirical, so I automatically didn't trust it, but I also couldn't deny that it existed. "You could've told me. I was worried about you."

Ha. I doubted that. More like it made him look bad. "I didn't think it was necessary."

"Necessary?" His voice was thick with sarcasm. "I think it was plenty necessary."

I clenched my jaw and met his gaze, my pulse quickening. "I needed to sort some things out, okay? I needed space."

"Not space from Lukas?" Max's jaw tightened, but before she could make a rebuttal, he exhaled sharply and turned on his heel. Sevina followed, her shoulders tense.

Lukas stood and stretched his arms over his head, exposing a strip of his stomach. I sucked in a breath.

"Cmon. They'll get over it." Lukas motioned toward the reception area and restaurant. "I'm starving."

I DIDN'T GO to breakfast. My chest felt like an over inflated tire, so I mumbled some excuse to Lukas and bolted back to my hut.

An hour later, I'd stuffed everything from that morning down deep and had a smile plastered to my face.

The air hung thick and humid as we lined up at the starting line of the challenge course. I could only see ropes and wooden barriers, and my stomach was already twisting. Upper body strength wasn't my strong suit.

Max didn't look at me as he stretched out his calves. My eyes flicked over to Lukas and Sevina. She was saying something to him in a low voice, her eyes narrowed. She wanted to win. Max wanted to win. I knew which one of their partners was better suited to make that happen. Give me puzzles, and

I was golden. But this? *One of these things was not like the others.*

A whistle blew, and we were off. The first obstacle loomed ahead of us—a deep pit of mud that looked like it had been churned up by a herd of wild boars. I hesitated for a split second, and that was all it took for Max to surge ahead. He didn't even try to help me, he just plowed through the mud like a bulldozer.

I stepped into the pit, immediately sinking up to my calves. The mud sucked at my Chaco's even though they were cinched tight. I flailed my arms, trying to keep my balance. Max was already halfway through, glancing back at me with a look that screamed impatience.

"Come on, Kate. It's just mud." His voice carried over the sloshing sounds of our teammates.

I nearly gagged at the feel of it squelching between my toes. Just mud. Barf. I gritted my teeth and pushed forward. It was cold and thick, making every movement a struggle. By the time I reached the other side, my legs felt like they were encased in cement.

Max was already at the next obstacle—a rope climb. He grabbed the rope and started hauling himself up with ease. I stumbled to the base of the structure, my fingers slipping on the wet rope.

"Need a hand?" Max called down, his voice dripping with sarcasm.

"So nice of you to offer." I shot him a glare and planted my muddy feet against the angled platform, trying to get a better grip. My fingers burned as I pulled myself up, inch by inch. The rope was slick, and my muscles protested with every movement.

David climbed next to me and shot me a smile. "You've got this."

I grimaced as he passed. Surprisingly, there weren't many others on the same track as us. Max had chosen a direction in the course, but there wasn't only one way through it. It was nice not feeling pressured. Also a little disconcerting since I had no idea how far everyone else was through the course.

Max reached the top and swung himself over, landing on the platform with a thud. He peered over the edge, watching me struggle. "You're going to get there eventually, right?"

I ignored him, focusing on my grip. My arms trembled as I reached for the next knot in the rope, my breath coming in short gasps. Finally, I made it to the top and hoisted myself over the edge.

Max was on a balance beam over a shallow stream. Despite his bulk, he walked across it with the confidence of a gymnast, barely even glancing at his feet. I took a deep breath and stepped onto the beam, my legs wobbling like a newborn fawn.

The stream below gurgled, the water crystal clear as it rushed over smooth stones. The greenery around us was lush, a stark contrast to the muddy chaos we were trudging through. Even growing up in Minnesota, I was awed by the vibrant color.

I took another step, then another, my heart pounding in my ears. I was halfway across when my foot slipped on a wet log. My arms pinwheeled, and I barely managed to catch myself before tumbling into the water. Max was already on the other side, looking back at me with a raised eyebrow.

He barked a laugh. "Careful, wouldn't want to get your hair wet."

Asshole. I had no doubt this was his punishment for leaving him alone in the hut the night before. I ignored him as best I could. My muscles ached, and sweat dripped down my temples, mixing with the mud on my skin. Finally, I made it to the other side and jumped off the beam.

Max was waiting for me at a fork in the path. "Which way do you want to go?"

I looked at the two options, panting. One path led up a steep hill, the other wound through a dense thicket of trees. Both looked equally unappealing. "You pick."

He didn't hesitate, choosing the hill. Of course, he did.

I kept up as best I could. We hit a series of hurdles and limbo bars—that was the best way to describe it—and I was halfway through them when I felt a sharp tug. The ground seemed to open up, and my right foot sank deeper. Then the mud sucked my shoe right off my foot.

I gasped and stumbled, slamming into the bar as I tried to process what had just happened. I bent down and started searching the murky depths for my missing shoe. My fingers plunged into the cold, slimy earth, and I shivered.

"Kate, come on!" Max let out a string of curses. "What are you doing?" He stood at the edge of the mud pit, his arms crossed over his chest.

"I lost my sandal!"

"Just go barefoot. We don't have time for this."

I gaped at him. "I can't leave it here."

"You're not going to find it."

I let out a hysterical laugh. "Well, I'm sure as hell not going barefoot!" Feeling mud on my feet was bad enough, but tromping over whatever was on the jungle floor? Sharp sticks? Snakes? *Bullet ants?*

To be fair, I had no idea if any of those things existed, but the fact that they *could* was enough for me to have a panic attack. It was irrational. I knew that. And yet I couldn't do it.

"Kate, seriously. This is ridiculous."

"I can't go barefoot!" I shouted. I was already on the verge of

a panic attack. All of my emotion stuffing hadn't been as successful as I'd hoped and was now bubbling to the surface.

Max scoffed. "You're being a princess. Just suck it up."

I gritted my teeth, tears pooling in my eyes as I prodded the mud with my other foot. "How about you just go. I'll catch up."

Max hesitated, then shook his head. "Fine. Whatever." He turned and started towards the next obstacle, leaving me alone in the mud.

I plunged my hand deeper into the mud, my frustration mounting. I'd been right there. How wasn't it more obvious?

I searched every inch of the muddy hole, starting to shiver from the cold. I was still wet from my fall, and since I wasn't running, the damp had turned into chill.

A clap of thunder made me jump, and I looked up to see the sky darkening. Damn it. I needed to get out of this mud pit, but I couldn't leave without my shoe.

My fingers brushed against something solid, and I pulled it up, only to find a rock. I threw it aside, my frustration boiling over. My vision blurred with unshed tears, and I blinked them back.

The first drops of rain started to fall, which didn't matter since I was already wet. But when another roll of thunder echoed across the mountain, my heart jumped into my throat. I was going to have to leave. I was going to have to brave the sole of my foot being torn apart on the trail and—

"Kate!"

I whipped my head around, squinting to see through the mist.

"Kate, what the f—"

"Lukas?" I gasped as he came into view. He was covered in mud, his hair already plastered to his forehead from the rain. And he was the last person I wanted to see right then. "Please don't—"

"Don't what? You're going to catch a chill out here—"

"Then let me catch a chill! I don't need your help. I'm just .. . taking a break."

"Max said you were looking for your damn shoe," he growled.

My lips pressed into a thin line. "Yeah, I lost it in the mud." He was here. *Why was he here?*

Lukas' gaze swept over me, and I felt a shiver run down my spine. He slogged closer, hoisting himself over the bars, his clothes clinging to him. "Where did you lose it?"

He didn't tell me I was stupid or that my search was ridiculous, and that shut me up. I pointed, and he dove forward with both hands.

I didn't want his help. I didn't want him there. But the ache that had burned into existence that morning flared until my lungs struggled to fill.

Tears spilled onto my cheeks, and I dropped my head, plunging my hands in the mud, struggling to swallow the lump in my throat.

We searched in silence, the rain pounding around us. My wolf stirred, and I tried to ignore it, but she was insistent. Watching him so intently, I could barely focus on searching the muck.

Lukas grunted, and a second later, he lifted my shoe. "Got it." He straightened, holding it up. I reached out to take it, but he shook his head. "Get on." He turned, crouching and splaying his arms.

"What? You want me to—"

"Get on my damn back, Kate."

I couldn't even bring myself to argue. I reached for him, throwing my muddy arms around his neck. He hinged forward, pulling me up until I could clamp my legs around his waist.

He smelled of something solid. Like wooden beams and

rain-covered concrete. The warmth from his back made me shiver as he caught me under my thighs, then carried me out of the pit. Lukas turned off the path and headed up the side of the mountain.

I tensed. "Where are you going?"

"To clean up and take cover. Wait out this storm."

I didn't question him. I was still shivering, and the mud covering my limbs was starting to make my skin itch. I lay my head against his back and tried to take as much weight of his arms as I could. Within minutes, the foliage opened up, and we stood in front of a small pool at the base of a waterfall.

"How did you know this was here?" I asked as he set me down on a rock at the edge of the water.

Lukas dropped to his knees, shoving my sandal under the surface. "The night I shifted. I went running and found it."

"And you remembered how to get here?"

He nodded once, then flinched as the wind picked up speed. "Hurry. Get rinsed off."

I sat, plunging my legs and arms into the water. I scrubbed at the mud, reveling in the sensation of it slipping from my skin.

Lukas set my now clean sandal next to me and moved closer. "Here." He pressed a hand on my back, then scooped water up and washed the backs of my shoulders. I closed my eyes, the sensation of his touch sending ripples of warmth through my body.

"You're a mess," he said, his voice low and rough.

My eyes flashed. "Thanks." I was grateful, but I knew if I cracked the door to my heart, even for a kind word, it was going to ooze out like a cracked egg.

Lukas grunted. "Just take this off." He tugged at my tank top. "It's soaking wet and you're freezing.

I did as he asked, then sucked in a breath as he washed the

dirt and grime from my back, his fingers playing my bikini string like a ukulele. My pulse hammered in my ears, and I forced myself to breathe.

When he was finished, he stepped back, his eyes meeting mine with a look that sent a shiver down my spine. "Better?"

I nodded, my throat too tight to speak. I quickly scrubbed my legs and washed my other sandal, then strapped both of them to my feet and stood.

Lukas wrung out my shirt and tossed it over his shoulder. There was another clap of thunder, and that time, lightning streaked across the sky.

He grunted. "We need to find shelter. The storm's getting worse."

I followed him, my skin tingling from the cold and the lingering sensation of his touch. We found a shallow cave a few yards away, and he motioned for me to go inside first.

The cave was small, barely big enough for the two of us, but it was dry. I sat down on the rock, and Lukas dropped beside me, stripping off his shirt and pulling me to his side. "Sorry. You need to get warm."

I exhaled, shivering at the feel of his skin against mine, then nearly sighing at the heat seeping into me. He was like a hot water bottle, and I couldn't help but sink into him, burrowing into his side.

Lukas blew out a breath as my cheek pressed against his chest.

Again I felt the urge to thank him. To say something. But I clamped my mouth shut. He was going to do what was best for him and his family.

And I was happy for him. Wasn't I?

The cave was dark, the only light coming from the flashes of lightning outside. The sound of the wind and thunder was muted, possibly because the only thing I was paying attention to was the steady beat of his heart. Lukas adjusted his position and lifted my legs over his.

I didn't move, didn't breathe as my wolf pressed against my consciousness. Her energy pulsed through me, urging me closer.

Lukas' heart picked up speed, and the sound of it made my pulse rush. Then his hand was moving, his fingers tracing a slow line down my arm. He dipped his head, his breath whispering over the crown of my head.

He reached my elbow and dropped his palm to my hip, his thumb moving in slow circles.

My insides rearranged themselves.

I tipped my head up, and as Lukas' lips brushed against my forehead, every rational thought flew out of my head.

"Kate," he whispered.

I pushed back just enough to angle myself so I could look at him. Our lips were inches apart, and the look in Lukas' eyes sent my stomach plummeting to my knees. I felt like I was standing on the edge of a cliff, teetering on the brink.

Lukas didn't move, didn't close the distance between us. He was waiting, giving me the chance to pull back, to stop this before it went any further.

Because I absolutely should've stopped it.

But as hard as I scrambled for control over my limbs, I couldn't force myself to pull away. I didn't want to. I wanted to feel his lips on mine, to lose myself in the heat and the storm and the wild energy that was crackling between us.

Lukas' hand lifted to cup my face, his touch achingly gentle. His thumb brushed over my cheekbone, and he dropped his head so close that the heat of his breath mingled with mine, the barest whisper of space between us. My heart thundered in my chest, and time seemed to stretch out like taffy. Then, before I could access rational thought, I exhaled and arched against him.

One brush of his lips, then a second.

My world exploded in bright light. He wasn't rushed or hurried. It was a slow, exploratory touch as if he was tasting something brand new. Then his lips finally pressed to mine, coaxing rather than demanding, a soft press that sent my pulse racing. He dropped his head, deepening the kiss, his lips parting slightly, teasing the seam of my mouth until I responded, letting him in.

His tongue brushed against mine, a gentle, coaxing slide that sent a shiver skittering through me. He kissed me like he had all the time in the world, each movement deliberate and unhurried, as though he wanted to map out every part of my lips, learn every way they fit against his.

My knees went weak, my lungs refusing to expand, and my fingers found their way into his hair, tangling in the soft strands as I pulled him closer, needing to anchor myself against the dizzying sensations.

The world around us faded, the entirety of my existence narrowing to his lips on mine, fingertips on my jaw. Lukas' hands slid down to my waist, tugging me closer.

"Kate," he murmured, his voice low and rough with want. "Tell me to stop. If you don't—"

I kissed him harder. I didn't want him to stop. The pull between us was magnetic, irresistible. My wolf clawed at my insides, desperate to reach further, to feel more of him.

Lukas twisted, rolling over me and gently laying me down against the smooth stone beneath us. I gasped at the delicious weight of him.

His tongue swept into my mouth as his hips rolled against mine, and I was lost in the headiness of his taste, his scent, the feel of his hard muscles under my fingers.

My wolf surged forward, straining against my skin, howling in exultation. Finally, *finally*. This was what I'd been craving without even realizing it, this bone-deep connection, this sense of rightness.

Lukas' hand slipped between us, his palm skimming over the sensitive skin of my stomach. I gasped into his mouth, arching into his touch, wanting more, wanting everything.

But even as I drowned in sensation, in the tidal wave of desire, a small, distant part of my brain recognized the danger. This was moving too fast, hurtling out of control. If we didn't stop now, I wasn't sure I'd be able to.

And he didn't want me. Or maybe some part of him did. I could admit that. But he wasn't going to choose me, and the fact that a piece of me wanted him to sent my heart palpitating.

I grasped at Lukas, my ankles winding around his calves, and as he slid his hand against the waistband of my shorts, the warning bell finally clanged to life.

I tore my mouth from his, panting harshly. "Lukas, wait. I can't—"

He stilled against me, his breath ragged in my ear. For a long, tense moment, neither of us moved. I could feel the rapid hammer of his heart against my chest, matching the frantic gallop of my own.

Slowly, as if it physically pained him, Lukas eased off of me. His blue eyes were nearly black, pupils blown wide with desire. "I'm sorry. I didn't mean to—I shouldn't have—"

I shook my head, trying to clear the haze of lust. My body screamed in protest at the loss of his touch, but I knew this was the right thing. *What was I about to do?* "No, it's not your fault. I —" *I what?* I wanted you? I needed you? The ache in my gut sliced through me, and I clutched my middle. "I'm sorry."

"Don't be sorry."

"I *am* sorry because I told you I didn't want this, and then I did that."

Lukas ran a hand through his hair. "Yeah, well. I think I did *that* first."

I huffed a laugh. "I think I'm terrible at this partner thing."

"Not even partners this time."

I exhaled, pressing my palms to my burning cheeks, and took in the world outside the cave. It was still raining, but it seemed to be lighter. I couldn't hear thunder. I scooted forward and scanned the sky. It was clearing, the dark clouds barely as they passed over us. "I think we're good."

I turned and reached for my shirt. Lukas handed it to me, then slipped his back on.

"Why did you sleep in that hammock, Lukas?" I asked.

His jaw ticked. "It didn't seem safe. For you to be out there by yourself."

I nodded. "You have to stop doing this. Coming after me. Don't get me wrong, I'm grateful, but—" I drew a deep breath. "We can't be partners anymore."

His brow twitched, and he glanced down at his hands. That ache in my center widened, yawning so wide, I thought it might swallow me whole. My wolf whimpered, and I squeezed my eyes shut, pressing my hand against the rock.

This was for the best. A little pain now was better than being shredded apart later. Lukas was making his choice, and it was for the best. We got caught up in the moment. I could still rein this back in.

One month. Hundreds of thousands of dollars. That meant no dating or kissing the wolf prince. Especially when he was all but betrothed to someone else.

If he wanted a distraction, it wasn't going to be me.

I drew a breath and pushed myself out of the cave.

TWENTY-SEVEN

Paul and I stood in our hut. My stomach was in knots, an iron band tightening around my chest. Paul watched me as I paced, then sat on the edge of the bed, then stood again.

He straightened the pillow on his cot. "You're upset."

I stopped pacing and faced him. "Mmhmm. Very astute, Paul." I grimaced. "Sorry."

Max and Sevina were pissed we lost the challenge. They didn't get to choose their partners, but luckily Paul and Elise were the champions, and he selected me. For one brief moment, I thought Elise was going to pick Lukas and Sevina was going to strangle her on the spot. She chose Patrick, and Lukas ended up with Lindsey.

Paul's brow furrowed. "Do you want to talk about it?"

I took a deep breath and exhaled, trying to get my thoughts in order. "Do you actually want to hear about it?"

Paul winced. "I'm not sure. I know it's the right thing to say."

That made me laugh out loud, and I flopped down on the bed. "Yeah. It is the right thing to say."

Paul walked over and touched the bed before slowly dropping down to sit next to me. "You have a thing for Lukas."

I groaned. If even Paul could see it, I was in serious trouble. I thought about denying it. Then realized Paul was probably the best person on the entire island to confide in.

I sighed. "I do. I have a thing for Lukas. But I don't *want* to have a thing for Lukas. I don't want to have a thing for anyone here. I was supposed to come, participate, then go home like nothing had happened."

"But something happened."

"Yeah."

He frowned, staring at his hands. "When I shifted in the restaurant, that was the first time that had happened in almost a year."

I dropped my hand from my eyes. "I didn't know that. You seemed like it didn't phase you."

"I'm good at that."

I moved so I could prop my head on the pillow, guilt settling in my middle. I'd been so wrapped up in my own drama, I hadn't been a good friend. "Are you okay?"

He glanced up. "Yes, fine. But I wanted you to know that something happened for me, too. My life isn't going to be the same. When I go back."

I blew out a breath. "Maybe it could be, though. Maybe with time—"

"You think this will go away, Kate?"

A lump formed in my throat. *No.* I knew it wouldn't. I'd shifted for the first time, and despite my best efforts, my wolf was not slinking back into the shadows.

"Why don't you want to have a thing for Lukas?" Paul asked.

I pursed my lips. "So many reasons. The first being I don't want a mate."

"Why?"

"Because then I'd have to depend on someone. I don't want that. And Lukas lives across the world. He's freaking royalty, and I'm a law student."

"So?"

"So I'm not going to give up my life for something that probably wouldn't even work."

Paul's eyes widened. "You don't think it would work?"

"Well, his family is ready to throw a wedding for him and Sevina."

"That isn't an answer to my question."

I pursed my lips. "I don't know! That's the problem. How can I know if it would work?" I threw up my hands and pressed my palms over my eyes.

Paul looked at me, his confusion evident. "But you want to be with him?"

I groaned. "A part of me does. Yes. The stupid, irrational part."

"But the logical part says you can't be with him."

"Right."

Paul grunted. "But the logical part of you has no information to go off of."

I huffed out a breath, then sat up and folded my legs underneath me. "Yeah. I'm aware. But that's how it is."

Paul nodded slowly, processing my words. "So you're saying there is someone you want, but you can't have them because you believe it would take away other things you want?"

I nodded. "Exactly." That was the best description I'd ever heard.

We sat in silence for a moment, the only sound the distant

lapping of water against the shore. Finally, Paul spoke again. "You've chosen to have faith."

I blinked. "What?"

Paul's expression was pensive. "You've chosen faith over experimentation. Because you're afraid the very act of testing your theory would require sacrifice."

My jaw tensed. "I can't just drop out of law school, Paul. I've worked too hard to get where I am. And if it didn't work out—"

"Wolves aren't like humans. They don't bond, then break up. They mate for life."

I rubbed my temples. "That's what I'm afraid of."

Paul's brow furrowed. "You don't want to be with him for life?"

I met his gaze. "That's not it. It's just . . . we don't always get to choose how long things last." Something right beneath my ribs pinched. "My oldest brother, Lee, had a mate. He lost her. In a car accident." I paused, swallowing hard. "She died, and he was never the same. It was like he lost a part of himself."

Paul's eyes softened. "I'm sorry."

I shook my head. "It's been years, but watching him go through that . . . I don't want something outside of my control to have that kind of power over me."

Paul was silent for a moment. Then he looked at me with a strange intensity. "Kate, there are already so many things outside your control. Your wolf, for one."

I frowned. "Yeah. Didn't want that either."

"Your wolf is a part of you. Just like your mate would be a part of you. You can't control either, but you can learn to live with them."

"Is that what you're doing?" I raised an eyebrow.

Paul swallowed. "Trying to. I understand it's easier said

than done." He studied me for a moment, then nodded. "But if you're choosing to have faith, what's the difference in choosing one story over the other?"

I sighed and flopped back onto my pillow. "I don't know, Paul. I don't know what's happening to me."

Paul put out a hand and set it on my shin. It was stiff and not comforting in the least. Somehow, that made me want to cry. "With what you know now and what you've felt with Lukas, do you think it's possible to return to the way things were? To pretend it never happened?"

I didn't want to answer. I didn't want to think about the fact that he was probably right. "It doesn't matter what I think. Lukas is going to choose Sevina."

"Hmm. Be careful about which story you choose to believe." He stood and crossed the room, switching off the lamp.

I WENT TO BREAKFAST LATE, hoping Lukas wouldn't be there. He wasn't. Paul and I ate together, and then I spent the rest of the day holed up in our hut. At four o'clock, Paul strode in and threw open the shutters.

The sunlight was too bright, too glaring for how I felt inside. "Why," I groaned.

He crossed his arms over his chest. "You know what tonight is."

I exhaled. "Yes. Your special reward."

"Our special reward. Since I chose you as my partner."

I scoffed. "Trust me, you'll have more fun at your fancy yacht dinner without me." I stood from the bed, my legs half numb from lying in the same position for an hour.

He was quiet for a moment. "I think you should come."

I shook my head. "Paul, I promise—"

"I don't want to go with anyone else, and if you don't go, then I'll have to sit with Elise and Patrick by myself."

I closed my mouth, immediately thinking of yesterday when Max left me in the mud. I'd asked him to, but still.

"It's just dinner. And a boat ride."

I drew a breath. "Do I have to look nice?"

"Yes. Absolutely."

I QUICKLY SHOWERED and dressed in a white eyelet dress that hit just above my knees, then pulled on my sandals and walked down the dock to the boat. The yacht was sleek and modern, its white hull gleaming in the morning sun. I took a deep breath, the scent of salt and seaweed filling my lungs.

Paul was already on board, standing at the railing. Elise and Patrick were nowhere to be found, which was a small blessing. The crew helped me onto the deck, and I felt the gentle sway of the boat beneath my feet.

The breeze had picked up since I was out that morning, the wind whipping my hair around my face. I pulled it back into a ponytail, then looked up at the sky. It was a brilliant blue, not a cloud in sight.

I should've been excited about this. A private yacht party? It was something straight out of a movie and should've been the perfect distraction. Yet all I could think about was how much I wanted to be anywhere but here. I wanted to be back in the hut, wrapped in my blanket, pretending that the last few days hadn't happened.

But they had. And Paul wanted me to be here.

I walked over to the railing and looked down at the water.

It was so clear I could see the fish darting between the rocks and coral.

Paul walked over, standing next to me. He nudged my elbow. "You made it."

I nodded, not trusting myself to speak. The waves lapped against the hull of the yacht, a rhythmic sound that should've been soothing but instead felt like a countdown.

Paul looked out at the horizon. "You know, I've never been on a boat before."

I raised an eyebrow. "Really? Never?"

He shook his head. "I'm more of a computer chair kind of guy."

I grinned. "You don't seem like a computer chair guy." I motioned to his tanned skin. "Not anymore."

The corner of Paul's mouth lifted. "How are you with surprises?"

I frowned. "Not great. Why?"

Paul grinned. "I wanted to tell you that I understand. About the control thing." He leaned against the railing. "My whole life, I've been out of control in social situations. I don't see things the way most people do. I don't read cues the same way. It's been a constant struggle." He paused, his eyes distant. "But then I found a friend who helped me. She gave me advice. Simple rules to follow." He adjusted his glasses. "Like make kisses last longer."

I grinned. "Pretty sure Willow is still thinking about that night at the bonfire."

A blush crept up his neck. "That gave me confidence. Made me feel like I could be myself, and it wouldn't always be the worst." He turned to face me, his expression serious. "So now I want to be that friend for you. And I want to give you some advice."

I swallowed hard. "Okay."

He took a deep breath. "Hear him out."

I blinked, confusion washing over me. "What? Who?"

Paul smiled, and his eyes flicked to the right. I followed his gaze and froze.

Lukas. He stood on the dock, his hand wrapped around a blue glass bottle. "Mind if I join you?"

CHAPTER

TWENTY-EIGHT

The yacht glided through the water, leaving a shimmering wake in its path as it moved away from the dock. The resort and its lights shrank in the distance as we circled the island. The ocean was as smooth as glass, reflecting the barely waning moonlight. It was a perfect night, the sky peppered with stars.

The yacht itself was a masterpiece of modern design—sleek, with a minimalist aesthetic that screamed luxury. Polished wood, chrome accents, and leather seating created an atmosphere of sophistication. The table in front of us was set with pristine white linens, crystal glasses, and silver cutlery that gleamed under the soft ambient lighting.

The resort staff catered our gourmet dinner, and it was nothing short of a culinary work of art. Delicate seafood dishes were paired with perfectly cooked vegetables and artfully arranged accompaniments. Each plate looked like it belonged in the pages of a high-end food magazine.

Every bite was perfect, but I barely tasted the food. Lukas wore a black button-up shirt with the sleeves rolled up to his elbows, and his hair was a tousled mess of waves that made me want to run my hands through them.

I stole glances at him, my pulse quickening every time he touched his fork to his plate. The way his blue eyes caught the light, the way his jaw tensed as he chewed, the way his fingers drummed against the table in time with the music playing softly in the background. It was all too much.

I sipped my cocktail, hoping the alcohol would calm my racing heart. It didn't. Instead, it only heightened my awareness of the scent of his cologne mixed with the fresh ocean air.

"So how did this happen?" I motioned at him, trying to find something to talk about that didn't make my cheeks burn.

Lukas leaned back in his chair, his gaze settling on me. "Patrick switched me."

"What do you mean Patrick switched you?"

"Patrick was Elise's date. He switched me. Then Elise and Paul opted out."

I parsed through that information. Why would Patrick and Elise give up a night on a yacht? Paul, I understood. He was a sweetheart, and for some reason, he believed that I was capable of not being me. "Did you bribe them?"

Lukas grinned. "I plead the fifth."

"Ha. Nice. You did a little constitution research?"

"Unlike Americans, we learn about the rest of the world in our history classes."

I laughed out loud. *Damn it, he was charming.* I tried to come up with something witty or insightful to say, but my mind was filled with one question. What was Lukas doing here? Why was he spending the night with me instead of Sevina after how he'd left things in the cave?

"Lukas, what are we doing here? I'm not going to pretend I don't feel something, but we both know—"

The servers came to clear our dinner plates, and I stopped

mid sentence. After they left, Lukas picked up the blue bottle he'd set on the deck before we started eating. He placed it at the center of the table. "Spin the bottle?"

I raised an eyebrow. "I was in the middle of something."

His eyes flickered. "Can we play? Please?"

Again the servers appeared, this time bringing out our dessert along with small cups of gourmet coffee. I picked one up, watching the dark liquid swirl in the white china.

"Fine," I murmured. I didn't know what he was hoping it would accomplish, but it probably couldn't hurt anything. I was already mashed on the inside.

Lukas took a sip of his coffee, then set it aside and gave the bottle a spin. It whirled and wobbled, then came to a stop, the lip finally pointing directly at me.

I swallowed hard, my throat suddenly dry. "I guess I'm up."

He leaned in, his eyes locked on mine. "Truth or dare?"

My pulse quickened, and I took a deep breath, trying to settle my nerves. "Truth."

Lukas raised an eyebrow. "What do you think of me, Kate?"

I blinked, my hand tightening on my cup. I took a sip of my coffee, hoping it would buy me a few more seconds to gather my thoughts.

"I think," I began slowly, "that you're . . . complicated." I glanced up at him, and he nodded for me to continue. "I think you're loyal to your family and your pack, which I admire. You don't want a mate, but you're willing to do it for your parents."

"That's it?"

My lips flushed. *You're so sexy, it hurts. You're funny and strong, and I feel safe when I'm with you. You have freckles on your shoulders, and I love how your hair curls at the nape of your neck.*

My wolf surged within me, forcing the words to the surface. I fought them, but couldn't keep her from forcing out, "You're very attractive."

Lukas' lip twitched. "You find me attractive?"

"I think that's more than one question." I was sweating.

"Just clarification."

I set my cup down, my hands trembling. "It's not a good thing."

He frowned. "Why not?"

"Because attraction muddies things. Makes you explore things you don't want to explore. I've never been a fan of emotional investment." I hesitated, then decided to take a page out of his book and be honest. "I've always been the one to keep my distance, to protect myself. So, no. Not a huge fan of attraction."

"Mmm. Protect yourself from what?"

I took a deep breath. "From getting hurt. From losing someone I care about."

"So your family. You're not close?"

I picked up my fork and speared the tip of a decadent chocolate torte. "We're close. Kind of. I don't know." I pondered that question, my chest tightening.

We talked a lot. Texted. But did I ever share anything beyond a travel log of my life? The whats and whens. The idea of saying something real . . .

"I don't think I know how to be close." I blew out a breath and took another bite of chocolate. "How's that for truth?"

"It's perfect."

I didn't meet his eyes as I reached out and spun the bottle. It spun, slowed, then stopped, pointing directly at me again.

Lukas laughed, the sound low and rich. "Looks like you have to ask yourself a question."

I scoffed. "Not fair."

His eyes gleamed with mischief, and my heart did a little flip. "Or you could take a dare."

"Hmm. Okay. I dare myself to take another bite of—"

"Uh, no, that doesn't count."

I scoffed. "You're making the rules?"

"Definitely."

"Then what counts?"

He observed me, then motioned at the space next to him. "How about I dare you to sit here? Instead of way over there."

I was suddenly breathing through a crazy straw. "Hmm. Okay." As dares went, he was letting me off the hook. I moved my chair next to his, then reached across the table and retrieved my coffee.

Lukas didn't say a word, but his eyes tracked my every movement. When I was settled, he spun the bottle. It stopped with the lip pointing directly at him.

His jaw tensed. "Truth," he said, then didn't hesitate. Before I could ask him a question, he turned his head, and the words were already pouring out.

"I came here with dread in my heart. My parents had set this whole thing up, trying to force me into a mate. I told you the truth. I didn't want that. I didn't want to be forced into anything, especially not something as important as a mate bond."

Lukas paused, his gaze still fixed on the dark water past the railing. "I was fighting against my family, against what they thought was best for me. They knew Sevina was coming, and they thought that would be the perfect solution. She's a good person, and it would've made sense for us to be together. It would've made my family happy."

There was a heaviness in his voice, a visceral weight of expectation. I couldn't imagine what it would be like to carry that kind of responsibility, to have so many people depending on me for their future.

Lukas exhaled. "But I knew it wasn't right. Nothing about

it felt right." He turned back to face me, his eyes searching mine. "And then I met you."

Every cell in my body went quiet. Like they were iron filings all pointed at the end of a magnet.

Lukas' chest rose and fell in quick succession. "I wasn't supposed to find anyone else. That wasn't part of my plan. But you. You were different." His voice softened. "I love that you have your own goals, your own dreams. That you're willing to fight for what you want. I admire your ambition, Kate."

"Lukas—"

"I felt something the first time I saw you in the WiFi lounge."

My eyes widened. "You didn't give me the time of day in the WiFi lounge."

"Uh, yeah. Because I didn't know what the hell to do with myself."

I thought back to that moment. How I'd tried to read my emails four times before giving up.

Lukas took a deep breath, then plucked my hand from the table, his thumb brushing over my knuckles. "Sevina isn't a bad person. She deserves to find someone who wants to be with her as much as she wants to be with them. But that person isn't me. She's not what I want."

Lukas looked down at our joined hands, then set mine back on the tabletop. "I guess it's your turn to spin."

I reached for the bottle, my fingers trembling slightly as I gave it a spin. It pointed off into the water, so I spun it again. When it stopped, the neck of the bottle pointed at Lukas again.

His eyes were locked on mine. "Truth."

I nodded, clearing my throat. The question bubbled to the surface before I could stop it. "What did you paint on my neck? When we were on the beach with the mirrors."

Lukas' tongue flicked over his lips. "Edelweiss."

I furrowed my brow. "Edelweiss?"

He nodded, his gaze intense. "It's a flower that grows in the mountains near my home. It's been a part of our family crest for generations. It's a symbol of bravery, of love, of enduring hardship." His voice was low, almost reverent. "It's a flower that only grows in the harshest conditions, at the highest altitudes. To see it bloom is a rare and beautiful thing."

A smile crept onto his face as he reached for his coffee. "When my father was a young man, he climbed to the top of the highest peak in our region to find one. He brought it back and gave it to my mother as a symbol of his love and devotion. Since then, it's been a tradition in our family for each generation to find an Edelweiss and—" His voice caught. He took another sip of his coffee, then set his cup on the table. "They find one and give it to their mate."

Lukas didn't look up. He stared at his cup, his brow pulled together. I stared at him, my thoughts spinning like tops. I wasn't even close to forming a response to that revelation before Lukas turned his chair, facing me head-on. "Kate, if you don't say something—"

"I don't know what to say." My breath hitched. It was the truth. I felt like someone had just cracked me over the head with a frying pan.

Lukas was telling me that everything I'd felt, every moment where I'd been aching, singed from the inside out, he'd felt, too.

Lukas took my hand again, and electricity zinged up my spine. "I talked with my mother and father this morning. My father is out of the woods. His stroke was severe, but he's recovering. His body is strong, and our doctors believe he'll make a full recovery."

"That's amazing."

He slid his other hand over mine. "I've been wanting to

travel to America and spend time with the packs there. To understand what they need, how we can support them. I want to know what's going on in the shifter world, not just in Rheinhardt but everywhere. I want to feel connected to them."

My shoulders slumped forward. "That all sounds perfect, but—you don't—" I sucked in a breath.

Fear clawed at my insides. I couldn't just decide to try this. I couldn't rip out the pages in my book, crumple them up and start fresh, could I?

Paul's words came back to me. *Be careful which story you choose to believe.*

Where had that story come from? My desire to prove my parents wrong? Watching my brother suffer?

I closed my eyes and tried to parse through the emotions swirling in my chest. I mentally picked up the book I'd been living by, my own personal life manual, and set it aside. Then picked up the story my parents had been telling me from the time I was little.

The one that said my wolf would take me places I could never go on my own. Or that finding a fated mate would be the pinnacle of my magic. It would give me wings, not anchor me like I'd decided to believe.

Peace washed over me, and my wolf pushed a surge of warmth through my center.

But what if it wasn't true? What if I stopped paddling up stream and the flow dashed me on the cliffs?

"Kate—"

"I want this," I whispered. "I didn't want to want this, and that's really difficult for me to admit." I opened my eyes and looked at him. "I don't know how to do this. How to let someone in."

Lukas leaned forward, his eyes searching mine. "And you

think I do? I've spent my whole life putting on a face for other people. You saw it the second you met me."

I shook my head, the knot of fear tightening in my chest. "No, you don't understand. I don't just mean that. I think there's actually something wrong with me." I pulled my hand back, curling it into a fist and placing it against my heart. "I saw what happened to my brother. I saw what it did to him when he lost his mate. It destroyed him. And I can't—" My voice broke, and I swallowed hard. "I can't go through that."

Lukas stayed quiet for a moment. "So you just don't love?"

Again. The best explanation I'd heard in just five words. I nodded, tears pricking my eyes. "Exactly."

He nodded once. "How is it working for you?"

My lips twitched. *So good.* I had everything I wanted, didn't I? The cracks in my defenses widened, threatening to split me open. Lukas was right there, offering me something I didn't know how to take. But again it was Paul's words that haunted me, that echoed in my mind. *You can't go back.*

And I knew, deep down, that he was right. I couldn't go back to the way things were before. Not after everything that had happened. I pictured myself returning to my apartment, settling back into my life with my roommate, attending my law classes like nothing had changed. But the image felt hollow, like it wasn't my life anymore. *One month. Hundreds of thousands of dollars.*

It was too late. I already cared. I already felt something so deep that it scared the hell out of me. And going back to the way things were, pretending this hadn't happened, pretending I hadn't met him . . . it wasn't an option anymore.

I tried to push the thought away, but it clung to me, seeping into every corner of my mind. And then, as if a dam had broken, I felt it—the grief, the fear, the realization that I was already in too deep. I couldn't stop the tears from welling up in my eyes, couldn't stop the tremble in my voice when I spoke. "I can't stop it. I feel it, but I don't know what to do with it."

Lukas stood. He pulled me up from my chair and wrapped me in his arms. "Let me show you." He brushed his lips over my temple. "Please, Kate. Let me show you."

Let go.

I sucked in a breath at the words from my wolf, and the moments in the jungle flashed into my head. The second I'd decided to release my hold on her and let her truly run.

I'd built walls around myself, and for good reason. But those walls had kept me isolated. Separate. They'd kept me from feeling the full force of my own life. The full force of myself.

I exhaled, and as Lukas rubbed his hand over my back, I squeezed my eyes shut and let the walls crumble. I let the thread between us yank tighter, and a peace I'd never felt before coated me like a thick blanket.

I didn't know what this meant for me. But in that moment, I knew I was done fighting it. I was done trying to rationalize it away. I was done trying to control the force raging inside me.

I tipped my head and looked at Lukas, really looked at him. "I never saw you for your title."

He watched me. "Because I never told you?"

"I don't think it would've mattered. I just—" I shook my head, reaching up a hand to trace his cheekbone. "I've only ever seen *you.*"

Seen wasn't the right word. It didn't do justice to what I understood about Lukas. It was more than what I could absorb with my physical senses. I felt him. I knew him. And maybe that was why all of this was so terrifying. Because it wasn't a question. I was good at ignoring questions I didn't know the answer to or searching hard enough until I figured them out. But a certainty? A certainty, I couldn't explain away.

Lukas brushed his lips over my brow. "I know it doesn't make any sense. I know our lives are wildly different. But I want you as my mate. I need you, Kate. I—"

"Will you hate me if I'm terrible at this?" I pressed my lips to his jaw.

"You won't be."

"But if I am—"

"It's not possible." Lukas tugged against my waist, pulling me flush against his body. He smoothed the tendrils of hair that escaped my ponytail behind my ear.

I closed my eyes, absorbing his touch. "What comes next?"

Lukas' intake of breath was audible. He dropped his head, his mouth brushing my ear. "I take you to the lower deck. And pick up where we started in that gods-forsaken cave."

CHAPTER

TWENTY-NINE

Lukas led me down the stairs. He opened a door to a private bedroom on the lower deck, and we stepped inside. A queen-sized bed with crisp white sheets sat in the center, flanked by nightstands with small, glowing lamps. A window overlooked the water, and the moonlight danced on the waves.

Lukas turned to me, his eyes darkening. He reached out and ran his fingers over the buttons of my dress. "You're always so proper."

I scoffed. "I've been in shorts and tank tops most days."

Lukas chuckled, then started to unfasten them, one by one, until the white, eyelet fabric parted down the middle. I exhaled, my breath trembling as his hands brushed against my skin.

I reached for his shirt, tugging at the hem until he lifted his arms and allowed me to pull it over his head. *I would never get sick of that view.* I ran my hands down his chest, feeling the warmth of his skin and the steady thrum of his heartbeat.

Lukas' hands traced the curve of my hips, then down my

245

thighs until he found the hem of my dress. He lifted it slowly, and I raised my arms, allowing him to pull it over my head. And then I stood before him in my lace bra and panties, my breath hitching as his gaze roved over my body.

He made quick work of his own pants, and my eyes widened at the sight of him in his boxer briefs. Lukas stepped closer, his hands skimming up my sides to the clasp of my bra. He gave me a questioning look, and I nodded, my throat too dry to speak. He unhooked the clasp and slid the straps down my arms. I bit my lip, watching his reaction as he took in the sight of me. His pupils dilated, and his breath quickened.

"You're stunning, Kate," he murmured, his voice rough. Heat pooled low in my belly, and I reached for the waistband of his briefs, but Lukas stopped my hand then turned, pulling me to the bed. "Get comfortable."

I moved further onto the bed, resting my head on the pillows, then gasped as Lukas dropped his head and pressed his lips against the inside of my ankle.

My breath caught as his mouth traveled in slow motion up the inside of my leg. I shivered, the anticipation building as he kissed the curve of my calf, then my knee, and I reached out, bracing myself against his shoulders. Lukas exhaled a hot breath against my inner thigh, and I struggled to keep my balance.

Then he stopped. Lukas' head whipped up, and his eyes locked on mine. I opened my mouth to ask, but the question died on my lips as his hands clenched around my thighs. He growled, low and feral, and then abruptly stood.

I frowned as Lukas strode to the door. "Where are you going?" I called after him, my voice breathless. He didn't answer, and I was too stunned to follow him. I waited, my skin still tingling from his touch. Then, after what felt like an eternity, the door swung open, and Lukas walked back into the room, his expression dark. My eyes caught on the Sharpie clutched in his hand.

"Lukas, what—"

He grabbed a washcloth from the bathroom, ran it under water from the sink, and in seconds, he was back hovering over me. He pressed against my knee, nudging my leg wide, and that's when I saw it. The arrow. The words Barnes had written at the bonfire. I'd completely forgotten they were there.

I laughed as Lukas brought the cloth to my skin and started to scrub. "Lukas, this is ridiculous. It's already fading."

"Not fast enough." Lukas rubbed until he was satisfied, then blew on my skin, sending ripples of pleasure coursing through my body.

I bit my lip to keep from laughing as he tore the cap from the marker off with his teeth.

"Hold still." His voice was a low growl, and I shivered. I watched as he drew over the faint lines of Barnes' arrow, tracing it with precision, then added his own words next to it.

For Lukas and only Lukas.

"There." He re-capped the marker and tossed it on the floor, then threw the washcloth in the general direction of the bathroom sink.

I ran my fingers through his hair. "You've officially claimed me."

"No." Lukas lifted, then repositioned himself directly over my chest. "That comes now."

I moaned, arching my back and gripping his shoulders as he dropped over me, teasing me with his tongue. His teeth grazed my skin, and I gasped. Then he was kissing up my skin, nipping at my collarbone, and tasting my neck.

Lukas found my mouth with his, then slid his hands down to my hips. He hooked his thumbs into the waistband of my underwear, then dragged them down my legs. I wriggled and used my feet to pull them off completely, then tugged at his briefs.

Lukas pushed up long enough to help me take them off, and then he was everywhere. My skin flushed and tingled as he kissed his way over every inch of my body. He teased with his tongue, and I arched my back, my hands gripping the sheets. Lukas' hands held my hips in place, his thumbs brushing against my skin. I was on fire, every nerve ending alive.

"Lukas, I'm—"

He didn't stop, moving as if my words drove him wild. He doubled down, his hands wrapping around my waist, his lips more insistent. I scrabbled for purchase, my body writhing as he discovered every sensitive spot.

And then I reached for him, forcing him to look up. To meet my eyes.

He panted, his pupils dilated and black. "Is something wrong?"

I shook my head, laughing and gasping for breath. "No, I just . . . I want this to be together." I ran my hands over his shoulders, his upper arms, watching his face as I pulled him higher, then wrapped my arms and legs around him.

Lukas dropped his head to the hollow of my neck and whispered, "I can do that."

I couldn't speak, couldn't think as our bodies melded. My heart seemed to shift rhythms, matching his as he dropped his chest against mine. We moved together, our bodies in perfect sync, and that warmth, that peace I'd felt in his arms on the deck, seemed to magnify a thousandfold.

The force within me, my wolf and her magic, flowed like warm honey out of my body and into his. New, raw power filled me to the brim, stretching against my skin and bursting out like rays of sunlight.

As our physical pleasure climbed layer by layer, my soul

seemed to expand, breaking free of all the limits I'd set for my body and my heart. I cried out, grasping onto Lukas as I tumbled, the world shattering around me.

"Kate. You're mine. Do you hear me?" Lukas gasped, his voice raw, his breath ragged. And then we collapsed against the mattress together, our bodies slick with sweat.

I lay there, my chest heaving. Lukas buried his face in my neck, his breath hot against my skin. I felt like I was floating, like every part of me was tethered to him. Stitched in, more permanent than Sharpie.

I didn't want to move. I wanted to stay there, wrapped up in the warmth of him, pinned under his weight. I stroked my fingers over his shoulder blades, the knuckles of his spine.

And the heat in my core didn't fade. Lukas' hand slid over my skin, and it was like striking a match.

"What is happening?" I gasped, my body reigniting as Lukas moved over me, his mouth trailing kisses along my collarbone.

Lukas groaned, then rolled off the bed. I reached for him, but he only chuckled and grabbed my hand, pulling me with him. "Have you ever heard the stories of taking a mate?"

I searched my memories. My parents had talked about it being intense, but never once had I considered they were talking about *this*. About the physicality of it. The spirituality of it.

Lukas led me to the bathroom and turned on the shower. Steam filled the room, and I shivered as the cool air mixed with the heat from our bodies. Lukas stepped under the spray, then reached out a hand for me. I stepped in, exhaling as the hot water cascaded over my skin.

Lukas' hands were everywhere, sliding over my shoulders, down my back, and I couldn't get enough. I tilted my head back, letting the water soak my hair, and Lukas took the opportunity to press his lips to my neck. I moaned, my fingers digging into his arms as he sucked gently on my skin.

The water made everything slick, and I slid my hands down his chest, feeling the hard planes of muscle beneath my fingertips. My body was insatiable. Inhuman. The energy and fire, I'd never felt anything like it.

Lukas' breath hitched, and he pulled back, his eyes dark with need. He turned me around, pressing my back to his chest, and I gasped as his hands splayed across my stomach. He curved around me and molded our bodies together. "We're not leaving this boat, Kate. This room. Not until well past breakfast."

I reached my hand behind my head, curling it around his neck. "Yes, please."

THIRTY

TALKBACKS

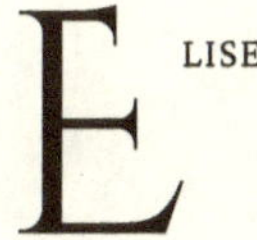

Zara: So tell me why I didn't see you getting on the yacht last night?

Elise: I'm not really a boat person.

Zara: Hmm. I'm sorry. I'm sure we could've come up with a different reward.

Elise: No, it's okay. There were others who . . . well, it seems like they're definitely into yachts. Like, really into them.

Zara: . . . That was very kind of you. You know that, right?

Elise: Well. If I wasn't going to enjoy it, someone should.

~

Paul

. . .

ZARA: I noticed you were in the restaurant for dinner along with Elise.

Paul: The lobster was excellent. I'm generally not a lobster person.

Zara: Is Kate a lobster person?

Paul: . . . I think she's more interested in schnitzel.

Zara: And you? Besides lobster, what are you interested in?

Paul: . . . I might be a West Coast kind of guy.

LUKAS

ZARA: So—

Lukas: Don't even say it.

Zara: I wasn't going to say it.

Lukas: Yes, you were. And I don't want to hear it.

Zara: . . . Katemostdefinitelyhadathingforyou

Lukas: Ha. Okay. I guess I did want to hear that.

Zara: AndIwasrightabouteverything.

Lukas: Not that.

THIRTY-ONE

A few days later, Lukas and I walked hand in hand along the stretch of beach in front of the Luna Bay Resort. The waves whispered against the sand, the sun casting its final golden rays on the horizon, making the water shimmer like a sea of liquid gold.

"There's KB and Orion." Lukas nodded toward the trees that held our hammocks. KB and Orion were sitting on a pair of cushioned lounges, each holding a glass of something fruity.

"Hey, lovebirds!" KB called, motioning for us to join them. "Grab a drink and come sit."

We walked up to the beach bar. Lukas got a beer, and I asked for a sparkling water. We joined our friends, sitting on the lounges conveniently placed across from them. The same ones we'd sat on for evening cocktails three days straight.

"The rest of the crew is still on their little romantic dinner spree." KB glanced over at Orion as she took a sip of her drink.

It was so nice. Not having to participate in the challenges. Just relaxing, eating good food, spending as much time as possible in bed with Lukas. An absolutely proper vacation.

"I think Paul's close." KB winked at me.

My eyes widened. "Really? Did you talk to Willow?"

Orion grinned. "I'm guessing they join us by Sunday."

I SAT in the WiFI lounge, waiting for Lukas to finish his call with his parents. He'd insisted that I jump on the video call with them, and I reluctantly agreed. It wasn't that I didn't want to meet them, I just didn't want to make a bad first impression. He assured me they'd love me. I wasn't convinced, considering they had other plans for Lukas on the island.

I tugged at the hem of my blouse, smoothing it over my jeans. I'd changed out of my swimsuit and into something more presentable.

"Kate, it's ready." Lukas' voice pulled me from my thoughts.

I took a deep breath, then walked over to the small table where his laptop was propped up. His parents' faces filled the screen, and I couldn't help but smile. They looked exactly like their pictures. His dad had the same piercing blue eyes as Lukas, and his mom had the same strong jawline.

"Hello, Kate!" His mom's voice was warm and inviting. "It's so wonderful to meet you finally!"

"Hi!" I waved, realizing I had no idea what to call them. Mr. and Mrs? Your highnesses? "I've heard so much about you." I sat in the chair next to Lukas, trying not to fidget.

Lukas' dad nodded. "Yes, we've heard so much about you, too. Lukas has been keeping us updated."

Lukas took my hand, and I instantly felt more relaxed. We talked about his father's health, what was happening with Lukas' younger brother and his university applications. I launched into a brief summary of my life, explaining my classes in law school and my love for hiking and cooking. They asked questions and seemed genuinely interested, which put me at ease.

As I talked, I noticed the background of their video. They were sitting in a cozy living room with a large stone fireplace behind them. Family photos lined the mantel, and a large painting of the Rheinhardt mountains hung on the wall.

When Lukas' dad launched into recent reports of problems with packs on the East Coast in America and how he wondered if Lukas would be better off bringing me back to Rheinhardt, I couldn't help but smile. It turned out even royalty fussed over their children.

Lukas was compassionate but assertive as he allayed their concerns, assuring them he'd be fine in Minneapolis. I didn't bother explaining how far Minnesota was from the East Coast before we said our goodbyes.

Lukas closed the laptop and turned to me, his eyes searching mine. "Well? What did you think?"

I smiled up at him. "I think they're wonderful."

We walked out of the lounge to find Paul and Willow standing at the door of the restaurant. Her cheeks were flushed, and she stared up at him like he'd just invented fire.

"Hellooo, Willow." I walked up and glanced between the two of them. "Paul."

He gave me a quick glance. "Kate, if you could keep walking, I'd like to keep kissing Willow, now."

"Hmm. Yep. Absolutely." I turned and took Lukas' arm.

"He's ballsy," Lukas whispered.

"Yeah. He is."

～

MY HEART WAS full as we gathered on the beach for our last cocktail party. Torches flickered and the muted thump of bass from the speakers mixed with the murmur of conversation and laughter as we mingled.

I stood with Lukas, our shoulders brushing as we listened to Patrick recount how he and Lindsey got stuck in their shower when one of the hinges broke off of the glass door. I laughed, glancing up at Lukas to see his eyes crinkling at the corners.

He wrapped his arm around my waist, and as soon as Patrick was finished, leaned in and whispered, "Come with me."

I nodded as he took my hand and gave an apologetic wave, leading me away from the group. We walked down the beach until the music and laughter became a distant hum. The waves lapped at the shore, and the moonlight painted a silver path across the water.

Lukas stopped and turned to face me, his eyes dark and intense. "I've been wanting to do this all night."

"Do what?" I asked, my pulse quickening.

"This." He took a step closer, his hand cupping my cheek as he lowered his lips to mine. The world fell away as we kissed, the only sound the rush of blood in my ears and the hush of the waves.

When we finally pulled apart, I was breathless, my skin tingling with the memory of his touch. Lukas grinned, his eyes sparkling with mischief. "I think we need to cool off."

Before I could protest, he scooped me up and waded into the water. I squealed, wrapping my arms around his neck. "Lukas, I'm not in my suit!"

He laughed, his chest vibrating against mine. "I've got you." He walked until the water was up to his waist, then set me down. The shock of the water against my skin made me gasp, and I held onto his arms for balance.

Lukas looked down at me. "Kate, I—" He was interrupted by a wave that splashed over our hips.

"You were saying?" I teased, pushing my hair out of my face.

He grinned, then pulled me closer, his hands sliding down my back to rest on my hips. I knew what he was getting at. It was our last night on the island. Our last few hours in paradise before the real world and our old lives came crashing back in.

"Lukas—"

He pressed a finger to my lips. "Shh. Just be here with me."

We stood there, our arms looped around each other like lassos, swaying with each lift of the waves.

"I've been waiting for you, Kate. My whole life, I've been waiting for this," Lukas murmured.

I closed my eyes and let myself sink into the sensation of his warmth, the cool water, the night air on my skin. Tomorrow, we'd part ways. Only for three days as Lukas returned to Rheinhardt to retrieve his things and fly back to the States to meet me.

But it was going to be three days too many.

I exhaled, my breath hitching in the back of my throat as all my fears tumbled through me at once. What if we couldn't navigate the transition back to our regular lives? What if the magic we'd found here on this island was nothing more than an illusion, dissolving the moment we stepped off that plane? *What if we weren't right for each other?*

I'd seen enough reality TV to know that couples who seemed smitten in their bubble of perfection rarely survived real life.

Lukas must've sensed my unease because he reached over and took my hand, threading his fingers through mine. "You know what I love about this?" he asked, his voice low and steady.

"What?" I barely recognized my own voice.

"That neither of us knows how this is going to turn out. That's what makes it beautiful."

I shook my head, my hair brushing against my shoulders. "I don't understand how you can find comfort in that. I want a guarantee."

Lukas chuckled, the sound deep and rich. "Guarantees are boring, Kate. Life is supposed to be unpredictable. Exciting."

"Terrifying?" I countered.

Lukas turned to face me, his eyes glistening in the moonlight. "What if this is the point? What if the best things in life are the ones we can't control?"

I frowned. "What if I like control."

He grinned, and I saw the decision in his eyes a second too late. Lukas scooped me up and waded out into the water, then tossed me into the waves.

I gasped, pushing to the surface, sputtering. "What the hell, Lukas?" I swiped at my hair, which was now plastered to my face.

"You needed to let go." He stepped closer, the water lapping at his waist.

"Let go?" I shoved a wall of water toward him. "You're the only one who let go."

"Only so I could pick you up again." Lukas barreled toward me, scooping me up into his arms even as I tried to wriggle free.

He shook his head, droplets of water flying. "I'll always be here, Kate. For the things we can control and the things we can't."

I glared at him, but then he kissed me and said, "Sorry, I thought it would be funny."

I grinned against his lips, then laughed as he attacked my neck. When he was finished, I slipped down his body and held him, closing my eyes and resting my head against his chest. The water licked at my legs, but I didn't feel the cold. Not when my body was pressed against his.

"I don't care if we have a day, a week, a month, or years. I want it, Kate." Lukas' voice rumbled against my cheek.

I swallowed. "That's a lot more poetic than throwing me into the water."

He chuckled, and the sound vibrated through his chest. "There's a belief in Rheinhardt. A story my mother used to tell me when I was young."

I looked up at him, wanting to watch his face as he said whatever was coming next.

Lukas pushed the hair from my forehead. "We believe that when a shifter finds their mate, it's not just a bond in this life. It's a spiritual connection that transcends time and space. We're not just bound in life but also in death. Our souls are intertwined, forever."

I blinked at him, my heart pounding. "Forever?"

He nodded again. "Even after we leave this world, we'll find each other again. That belief has been passed down through the generations of my family. We're the protectors of Rheinhardt, and our connection to the mystical has always been strong."

I let his words sink in, then tipped my head back to look at the sky. The stars were barely winking into view. Could it be true? If it was, then Lee would be able to see Sarah again. That thought sent a rush of warmth through me, and for the first time, I felt a sliver of hope. "I want to believe that."

He pressed his forehead against mine. "Then do. Because I'm yours, Kate. Body and soul."

I closed my eyes, letting my heart slow and my breath steady. "I'll take it."

EPILOGUE
SIX MONTHS LATER

The air was crisp and heady, filled with the scent of pine and earth as Lukas showed me down the steps of the plane to the tarmac. In the distance, the dense Black Forest loomed, its shadows teasing the edges of my imagination. It was like stepping into a fairy tale.

I pulled my coat tighter around me, the cold seeping through the fabric as I looked around. Snow dusted the ground, and the sky was a pale grey, hinting at more to come.

"Welcome to Rheinhardt." Lukas' voice broke through my reverie.

"It's beautiful." I looked up at him. "And not at all intimidating."

He grinned, his eyes twinkling. "Just wait."

A sleek car waited for us, and as we drove through the winding roads, the landscape transitioned from quaint villages to stretches of untouched forest. The trees were tall and ancient, their needled branches full and green.

When we finally pulled up to Lukas' estate, my breath

hitched. *Estate?* It was more like a castle. The structure was a blend of medieval architecture with modern accents, stone towers juxtaposed with sleek glass windows. Dormant ivy crawled up the stone walls, and the grounds were immaculately kept, with sculptures and fountains dotting the expanse.

"It's a bit much, isn't it?" Lukas' tone was casual, but I could hear the undercurrent of pride. Maybe a little nervousness.

"Just a tad." I stepped out of the car, my boots crunching on the gravel. "I don't even know where to start looking for the moat and drawbridge."

He laughed. "We had those removed a few centuries ago. Not very practical."

I turned to him. "Hold on, I need to show my parents."

Lukas let out a groan. "Not more parents . . ."

I gave him a look and pulled out my phone, already dialing. "They've been begging me for a tour of the estate, and this is the best I can do."

He held up his hands. "I didn't say I wouldn't do it. I just—"

My dad's face appeared on the screen. "Hey, Katie."

I smiled. "Hi, Dad. Where's Mom?"

"Probably in the kitchen." He started moving, the screen bouncing up and down. "What time is it there?"

"Umm, about eleven?"

My mom's face came on screen, and her eyes lit up. "Oh my gosh, you're there? You're standing on the grounds? Did you feel the energy? I heard that the castle was built on a ley line, and that's why—"

"Mom, I just got here." I held the phone up, giving them a view of the grounds in front of the car.

"Oh, that's beautiful." My dad sounded appreciative, but my mom was practically hyperventilating.

"Where's the castle? Show me the castle!"

I laughed, turning the phone around and giving them a panoramic view of the estate.

My dad whistled. "That's quite the place, Lukas."

"Thank you. You'll have to come visit in person one day."

The audio was silent, and I turned the screen around to make sure my mom hadn't fainted.

When I saw her face, her eyes glistened with tears. "I've been reading about the Nachtwalds for decades. I just never imagined I'd have a daughter dating one."

"I'm not *dating* him, Mom."

Lukas laughed, then peered over my shoulder. "Where's Lee?"

"He was supposed to be here." My mom frowned. "I'll text—"

"Hey, guys. Sorry I'm late." Lee's face popped up on the screen, and my heart melted.

"Lee!" I waved at the phone. "How's the job? Are you settling in okay?"

He nodded. "Yeah, it's good. Busy, but that's to be expected."

"I miss you." I bit my lip, trying to keep my emotions in check.

He grinned. "I miss you too, Sis. But hey, I'm glad you're getting to experience this. Looks amazing."

"It's surreal." I glanced at Lukas, who was watching me with an unreadable expression. "Alright, I should go. We need to get inside before we freeze."

"Alright, dear. Take lots of pictures!" My mom waved, and my dad nodded in agreement.

"Will do. Love you guys."

"Love you, Katie."

I ended the call and slipped my phone back into my pocket. "And now that's done."

Lukas held out his arm, and I took it. He led me through the gardens, then through the back entrance to the house so the rest of his family wouldn't stop us. He snuck me up the back stairwell, and once we climbed to the third floor, slipped me into his room.

It was like stepping into a world where old-world charm met modern luxury. The room was expansive, with high ceilings and large windows that let in the soft, diffused light of the winter afternoon. Rich, dark wood paneling covered the walls, giving the space a warm, inviting feel. Heavy drapes in a deep maroon flanked the windows, contrasting beautifully with the sleek, modern furniture.

A massive four-poster bed with intricately carved posts dominated the room. The bedspread was a plush, deep charcoal, and the pillows looked like they were made of the softest down. There was a sitting area near the window with two leather armchairs and a low table, perfect for reading or enjoying a quiet moment.

Lukas slipped my purse from my shoulder, setting it on a chair near the door, then turned and lifted a brow. "What do you think?"

I swallowed, my throat dry. "It's . . . incredible." I ran a hand over the smooth wood of the bedpost. "I don't think I've ever been in a room this luxurious." It was like something out of a magazine. And it was so Lukas.

He grinned as he walked over to me. "I'm glad you like it." He reached for my hand, pulling me toward the bed. "I'm ready to collapse."

I nodded, my legs feeling like jelly. We both fell onto the bed, sinking into the mattress. It was like being enveloped in a cloud. "This is amazing," I murmured, my eyes closing.

Lukas chuckled, his voice rumbling through the mattress. "I can call for food if you'd like." He leaned over, his lips brushing against my ear. "Or we can just stay here and enjoy the peace and quiet."

I shivered at his touch, warmth spreading through me. "Food sounds good," I teased.

"Mmm." He nuzzled my neck, his breath hot against my skin. "But not as good as this."

I laughed, my heart pounding in my chest. "True."

Lukas pulled back, his eyes dark with desire. "Or this." His lips moved with mine, and warmth spread like a fire from my core to the tips of my fingers and toes. His hands slid up to cradle my neck. I groaned, my fingers sliding into his hair.

We'd spent a month in our bubble, then months in the US with me in classes and needing hours to study every night. Now, for two weeks, we were here with nothing to do but celebrate the holidays. I'd never been more grateful that I didn't have to be anywhere.

I'd already sent emails to my professors to see if I could transfer to a school in Rheinhardt next fall. Some of them had ties with universities there, and since I was only going into my third year, I could potentially get into a program that would allow me to practice in the EU.

I didn't know what it would look like, but I was doing everything I could to make it happen. It was as if some unseen force was drawing me there, just as it had drawn me to Lukas, and I couldn't help but follow.

Lukas' hands slid down my neck, and I shivered as he brushed over my collarbone. My mind was buzzing with a thousand thoughts. *What if I couldn't transfer? What if I hated it there? What if—*

I shut down my thoughts and tuned in to my body. I was getting better at that. Refusing to pick up the reins.

As Lukas' fingers dipped below my shirt and brushed against the curve of my bra. I sucked in a breath, and he pulled back, a smirk playing on his lips. "Do you want me to stop?"

I shook my head, my cheeks burning. "Please don't."

"Good." He traced circles over my ribs, and I arched into him. "I think we need to christen this bedroom properly, don't you?"

I laughed, the sound breathy. "I think that's a good idea."

"Then we can move on to the rest of the estate. The garden, the kitchen, the library . . ."

"Library?"

Lukas grinned. "Oh, there's plenty of furniture to get creative with." He pulled my shirt up, and I lifted my arms to help him slide it over my head. He tossed it to the side, then leaned in to kiss me again. I lost myself in the sensation of his lips, his hands, his body pressing against mine.

Control had always been my answer to life. Control and predictability. I thought that was the way to make the most out of what I had. The irony was that the tighter I held on, the more my life shrank. Instead of my world expanding, it became smaller and smaller until I was living inside a tiny box of my own making.

I'd been wrong about finding a mate. Wrong about my magic. Wrong about everything, really.

Letting someone in didn't mean giving anything up. I wasn't sacrificing my life. I was expanding it.

That was what happened when I let go. Instead of a single path, there were endless possibilities. Instead of a single destination, there were infinite places to explore.

And I wanted every single one of them to be with him.

"I love you, Kate," Lukas whispered.

Damn you, Wolf Island and Luna Bay. I trailed kisses over his jaw. "Body and soul."

. . .

Preorder Season 2...

About the Author

 Luna masquerades as a well-adjusted, functioning adult, but she secretly still believes in magic and wild things hidden just beyond the veil of our world. She has a fairy garden (with lights!) and lives with her husband and children near the Rocky Mountains in Colorado. She adores shiny objects.

www.ingramcontent.com/pod-product-compliance
Lightning Source LLC
Chambersburg PA
CBHW061756190726
48289CB00007B/1976